SHAPERS

Robert R. Chase

A Del Rey Book

BALLANTINE BOOKS • NEW YORK

A Del Rey Book
Published by Ballantine Books

Library of Congress Catalog Card Number: 88-92215

ISBN 0-345-35945-3

Manufactured in the United States of America

First Edition: April 1989

Cover art by David B. Mattingly

DREAMS OF GORY

The roaring drew him back from unconsciousness. His arm hung straight in front of him, painfully swollen with blood. His lips felt fat and bruised. The roaring was the air, he realized, rasped into incandescence as the hull rammed through it at supersonic speeds.

With immense effort, he turned his head. Where Virginia should have been was a monstrosity of shattered bone, bloody hair straining forward as if caught in a strong current. Part of the shoulder harness had torn away, allowing the upper part of the body to batter itself against the instrument panel.

He raised his head to the instrument panel, and the sense of nightmare became complete. It was totally unfamiliar.

By Robert R. Chase
Published by Ballantine Books:

THE GAME OF FOX AND LION

SHAPERS

I. THE SPINDRIFT MAN

i

EACH STRIDE ACROSS THE MULTICOLORED SANDS BROUGHT A rhythmic surge of pain to Hickock's left hip and thigh. That, Dr. Mackern assured him, was to be expected. The constant stress on the remaining pieces of living bone would encourage them to assimilate the synthicalc rod that served to anchor quadriceps and hamstrings. It should be healed in less than a year.

Yellow-orange sunlight flooded through the ranks of clouds, washing over his face. It felt different depending on which patch of skin was warmed. Hickock yawned open his jaw just to feel the clone grafts stretch along cheeks and forehead. He looked piebald in a mirror. Yet even in the past few days he had been able to notice the changes as the skin tone of the grafts approached that of the rest of his skin, and tufts of fuzz appeared, promising to restore his hairline.

The wind off the ocean blew salt and other less nameable odors into his nostrils. It whipped into motion the thin wires connecting the powerpack on his shoulder to the waferphone in his ear, tickling his cheek.

If he was very still, he could hear the voice whispering in the waferphone, almost indistinguishable from the wind.

"Shapers," the voice said. "Innovator, Explorer, Starswallower, Seaking, Skybreaker . . ." The litany of names droned on, colorful, meaningless, yet vaguely comforting. It was Dr. Vaheri's voice. Hickock looked behind him. Vaheri stood a hundred fifty meters away, staring out to sea to give him the illusion of privacy. The doctor's stated reason for being there at all was to prevent Hickock from overexerting himself. They both knew that was the least important reason for his presence.

"Home: crowded, underwater, hot, humid, dry—" The image exploded across his consciousness. Forests of broken, blackened wood standing straight and leafless as megaliths. A dry, choking dust that made his eyes water. In the distance, painfully bright, sunlight rippled off quicksilver.

I used to think that the city had melted.

He stood back from the memory, frightened by its intensity. Vaheri's needles must have swung off the scale with that one, he thought.

He felt no urge to follow the memory to its source. It was safer being terra incognita to himself.

He scanned the beach for Reeve. She sat high on a ledge, cross-legged, hiding behind cornrows of braided hair— probably communing with some Cosmic All. Good luck to her. If she could read his mind, she was one up on him.

There was an indefinable sense of strangeness. He blocked out Vaheri's whispers and concentrated on the beach. Large, dark boulders rounded with wave action, patterned with maroon ripples. Metamorphic. The word seemed right. He felt a tiny thrill of victory at reclaiming that patch of reality.

Next, the grains of sand: red and golden, some translucent, refracting as brilliantly as tiny novae. He cupped their wet coarseness in his palm and lifted them to his face. Thin shreds, green and brown. Organic. He sniffed. Dampness, a hint of decay—and there, hovering at the edge of sensitivity, a spicy pungency, totally unfamiliar.

Tentatively he extended his tongue. Even the taste of salt was somehow new. He spat and let the clump fall. I know sand, he recognized. Again, he remembered dust and ash. But not this sand.

Black walls of water, crowns shredded into whiteness, surged in from the horizon, crashing nearly at his feet. Wind textured the shifting surfaces, making them striated. At certain angles, Hickock found that he could see deep into the water, down to the sea bottom. For the merest of instants, he could discern dark, branching lines snaking their ways across the sands.

Veins in the sea . . .

Something lived in those depths, something he should be afraid of. He bit his lip, searching for a clue as to what it could be. Nearly on the horizon, an oblong shape skipped across the water like a stone.

Something else had skipped across the water that way. He tensed involuntarily, hearing the roar of air across the hull, gasping with the serial impacts as the craft touched the wave tops, the sudden spin that forced him deep into the acceleration couch, and the searing heat blazing from floor and control panels.

"Hickock? Are you all right?" Vaheri was panting with exertion, peering up at him in concern. Hickock opened his eyes and took several slow, deep breaths.

"I . . . was remembering," he said. The look of expectation on Vaheri's face was almost comical. "The accident, I think. It was out there, wasn't it?"

Vaheri tried to conceal his disappointment. "Well, yes, if 'out there' extends five hundred kilometers. We were lucky to be there to pick you up.

"Let's start back. You're still not up to strength."

The guards on the cliffs stepped back until they were almost out of sight.

Halfway back, Hickock spotted movement near a spume pool on the rocks. A fish crouched there, regarding him warily as it gnawed on an anonymous morsel.

"Aquavian," Vaheri said, following his glance. "They are fairly common in these latitudes."

Aquavian. He had never heard the term before. Should flying fish have binocular vision? Or should their wings be usable as crude hands?

Abruptly the wings flashed into a reddish-orange blur and the creature darted into the waves.

"You get to see a lot of nature around here," Vaheri volunteered. "Or you can just enjoy the solitude. That is why I am so grateful to have this position with Innovator. I was raised in Wavelasher's breeding pens. There was one Shaper who knew absolutely nothing about human beings. It treated us like its own spawn, and then grew furious when half of us died."

Vaheri's eyes were remote beneath his gray-tinted glasses. Hickock looked at him as if for the first time, imprinting on his memory the short-clipped, receding hair, the small chin, and the graying stubble.

"I suppose that in the natural course of things, I would have become one of those statistics," Vaheri continued soberly. "Luckily, when I was only eight, Innovator and Skybreaker formed a temporary alliance and devoured Wavelasher's domains. Along with Wavelasher itself, of course. Innovator was already receiving a substantial return on its own human herd, so it received most of us as its part of the alliance settlement, while Skybreaker got the mineral resources.

"So I am now a research assistant working for the most dynamic, if the not yet the largest, lineage group on the planet. Supposing I had survived Wavelasher's pens, I could have aspired no higher than eggman." His voice was expressionless.

"You like it here," Hickock suggested.

Vaheri shrugged. "It beats nearly every conceivable alternative."

They had reached the electric car. Its scallop-fringed blue-pink-and-white-striped awning billowed in the breeze. Hickock swung himself into the passenger seat. The leg throbbed with the release of tension. Vaheri unclipped a microphone, gave their destination, and switched on the motor.

It occurred to Hickock that he could overpower Vaheri, throw him out of the car, and escape. Except that he had no idea where to escape to. Ignorance was his true jailer. The guards were superfluous.

The car surged up a standing wave of sand. Balloon tires ran along a roadway made of the vines that held the dunes together. The beach expanded before them, and the cliffs towered higher as they fell back to the left. On the flats to the right, crèche-nurses and their charges scoured the sand for delicately tinted exoskels and other treasures cast up by the waves.

Macadam surfaced through the sand. The car picked up speed. At the usual place, Vaheri turned left into a tunnel in the cliff face. They stopped three times for uniformed guards to check Vaheri's papers. Hickock had none. At each station, after the guard sergeant examined Vaheri's clearances, he would place a phone call, then raise the steel gates into the stone ceiling.

Vaheri parked in a small, neon-lit garage just beyond the third gate. Hickock followed him into an elevator. It ascended a short distance before opening on a richly carpeted hallway. Vaheri knocked, then motioned Hickock in.

"My boy! How good to see you. Dr. Vaheri tells me that you are making excellent progress." Mackern's rough voice filled the room. The nose, which jutted out above a curly black beard, started at the nostrils broad like a duck's bill but quickly narrowed to pencil thickness. His pear-shaped body shook with enthusiasm. Cyrano, Hickock thought, in need of a diet. The eyes were very alert.

"We have guests today. Jason you already know." Mackern nodded at the man Hickock had already come to think of as his keeper. "These gentlemen are Colonel Garrison and his aide, Major Hollings. Their specialty is—hah!—data retrieval. They intend to solve your mystery."

Garrison was seated, a thin man with close-cropped white hair. He gave a perfunctory nod. Standing behind him, Hollings projected affable alertness. Jason Yader stood to the side and one step back from Hollings, feet spread, hands clasped behind his back.

So Yader was military as well, and subordinate to Hollings. That might be a useful datum.

"I'm afraid I can't be much help," Hickock said apologetically.

"Nonsense, my boy. It is we who are to help you. Every day a new piece of the puzzle falls into place. Soon we shall have the whole picture." Mackern gave a quick half-furtive, half-defiant glance at Garrison.

"For instance," he went on, placing his forearm next to Hickock's, "compare our hands. As you can see, the coloring of your clone grafts is as light, perhaps even lighter than, my skin. Yet your original, undamaged skin is considerably darker. Does that suggest anything to you?"

Hickock shook his head.

Mackern assumed a professorial bearing. "Sol, the star under which we evolved, was, to say the least, a more violent star than our present benign sun. Being more massive, it produced large amounts of ultraviolet radiation. Most was absorbed high in Earth's atmosphere. However, substantial amounts did get through to the surface, causing mutations, skin cancers, and other disagreeable complications. Our skin cells evolved pigmentation systems to protect themselves. In tropical races, the pigmentation became permanent and hereditary.

"In higher latitudes, where the need for protection was intermittent, the protection could be temporary as well. The lighter-skinned races would 'tan,' as they called it, on ex-posure to ultraviolet.

"Nowadays a considerable portion of our race never sees the surface. Even those of us lucky enough to live in the ever-beneficent and liberal service of Innovator—"

Garrison shot him a warning look, which, as far as Hick-ock could tell, was ignored.

"—and are allowed, at least to some extent, the freedom of the surface world, still we never tan because we are never exposed to enough ultraviolet radiation to trigger the reac-tion. Yet you have obviously been so exposed, and in the not-too-distant past."

"You've made your point," Garrison said impatiently. "What does it mean?"

"There are two locations where I imagine an unprotected human might receive a sufficient amount of ultraviolet." He stepped over to a map that covered all of one wall. "One is the high plateau region of the equatorial landmass—the larg-est landmass on the planet, and so the least interesting to our patrons. Even the seas are deserts that close to the equator. A marvelous place for activities requiring, shall we say, pri-vacy. At the extreme elevations, protection from short wave-lengths would be minimal.

"The other possibility, of course, is Salamander."

"That's preposterous!" Garrison interrupted. "Humans would need pressure suits to survive in either place, and those suits would certainly prevent your tanning. And if any place is less interesting to the Shapers than the plateaus, it is Salamander, a planet that can never be made habitable for them."

"Just so," Mackern agreed. "But our task is not to ac-count for amnesiac Shapers. Humans could find both areas very useful. We know Explorer was liquidated. Do we know, positively *know*, that all its human herd was assimilated into Starswallower's?"

Garrison looked thoughtful. "An interesting question. Where does it lead you?"

"At the moment, nowhere. It is merely another piece of our puzzle."

"Carry on, then. I have only a little more time before I have to make my report."

"Thank you, Sir." Mackern turned back to Hickock. "Let us review the problem. Here you are, a basically healthy, intelligent young man. Your knowledge of various academic subjects, the sciences, history up until the time of the arrival, is in the upper one percentile of our population. Your knowledge of yourself, however, is nonexistent. You can tell us nothing of your friends, your crèche-mates, your family, not even what lineage group you belong to."

His eyebrows came together portentously. "Such selective amnesia is clearly unnatural. It must have been imposed to protect information someone considers very important. It follows that you must be a very special young man."

"If that is true," Hickock said hesitantly, "then it may be my duty to be uncooperative."

"Your loyalty does you credit," Mackern said, nodding, "especially since it can have no object. But we want no group secrets from you. Just the most basic information. Where do you come from? Who is your owner? Once we know these things, we can send you home. We will have the solution to our mystery, and your masters will have you back. Everyone will be pleased. Herd leaders always find it mutually advantageous to counsel cooperation."

There was a quick, almost unnoticeable pause, as if Mackern expected some sort of reaction.

"Well, perhaps we can work around the problem. Your skin gives us one clue. Your knowledge patterns may give us another. Using our files, we may be able to correlate your areas of specialization with the known propensities of given human herds.

"Let us begin with, say, radio astronomy."

Hickock felt blank. "What about it?"

"Define it," Mackern said brusquely. "Tell me everything you know about it."

"Well, stars, planets, even interstellar gas, all emit radio waves in various frequencies. These can be analyzed so that one can deduce the temperature, electrical activity, even the chemical composition of the emitter."

"Analyzed how?"

"I . . . really don't know."

"What would you say is the main advantage of radio astronomy over optical astronomy?"

"You can see into places otherwise hidden," Hickock said confidently. "Like inside dust clouds."

"What apparatus is used?"

A quick succession of images rose from Hickock's memory. Large black dishes silhouetted against a crimson and yellow sky, like ears that seemed to twitch in the heat shimmer. An even larger structure swinging silently in orbit, eclipsing a half sun as it hurtled into the darkness beyond the terminator.

"Just more powerful radio antennas, I guess. Made directional somehow."

"Change of subject: nuclear fusion."

Hickock frowned. "Like power supplies? Laser implosion units?"

Mackern steepled his hands thoughtfully. "I was thinking of natural fusion. The sort that occurs in stellar interiors."

Hickock's eyes focused on middle distance. "It's hard to know where to start. The process begins whenever the gravity in a star's interior becomes so great that it overpowers the electrical repulsion of the hydrogen atoms' electron shells. The nuclei are forced together, releasing energy, which prevents further gravitational collapse.

"Of course, nothing is ever that simple. There are two

basic processes: the carbon cycle and the proton-proton cycle . . .''

The office receded from Hickock's consciousness. He was pulling up facts learned long ago and, he suspected, with considerable effort. He could smell the dust in the classroom air. Neutrino fluxes, photon emission, absorption, reemission, reabsorption . . . Fact fit into fact, like atoms in a crystal lattice, building slowly into a complex structure of prismatic beauty.

''. . . the hydrogen being almost completely used up, the gravitational collapse resumes until the kindling temperature of helium—'' Hickock broke off. The silence was too complete. Hollings appeared frightened.

''Did I say something wrong?'' Hickock asked. ''I'm afraid I learned all of this long ago.''

''I have no idea,'' Mackern said in a hoarse voice. ''Knowledge of nuclear fusion theory has been designated a capital offense by Innovator—and by every other Shaper of which I have knowledge. If I knew enough to criticize what you just said, it would be Colonel Garrison's duty to ensure that my death would be excruciating, prolonged, and public.''

''I see.'' Hickock tried to force a wry grin. ''I take it you make no provisions against self-incrimination.''

''What?'' Mackern roused himself. ''Oh, have no fear for yourself. Since you are not a member of Innovator's herd, its knowledge laws technically do not apply to you. In fact, if you could tell us how you come by your knowledge, I am sure you would be well rewarded.''

Hickock licked his lips. ''I'm afraid I don't remember. Why is this particular knowledge forbidden?''

It was Garrison who replied. ''I was hoping you could tell us.''

Hickock laughed nervously. ''Sorry.'' He glanced quickly

around the room, feeling trapped. He had to gain the offensive somehow.

He walked over to the map. The few landforms were mostly brown, featureless outlines. The ocean areas were structured into irregularly sized ovals bordered by pale yellow fringe. Hickock looked down at the legend. Pale yellow: buffer.

Each of the ovals contained a name: Quickturner, Seaking, Innovator . . . Within Innovator's territory lay an island with a settlement marked on the west coast: Freair. That must be where he was now.

Locating the legend again, he pressed his thumbs together so that the little fingers spanned five hundred kilometers. He rested the right-hand finger on Freair and swung an arc to the west. The left-hand finger came to rest on a pencil mark. Next to it was a note: 5/7/53. It was well within the oval marked "Seaking."

"Is . . . Innovator on good terms with Seaking?"

Garrison's laughter was harsh. "Hardly."

"But you picked me up—in hostile territory? Then you must have known ahead of time that I would be landing there."

He turned away from the map, confronting both Garrison and Mackern. "You must know more about me than you admit."

"Very neat," Garrison said approvingly. "Logical. Completely wrong."

"You knew where to pick me up," Hickock insisted.

"Ah, we knew," Mackern conceded, rolling his eyes. "But what did we know? Prophecies, sibylline utterances spoken in arcane and suitably obscure terms. Fire from the skies, terror in the depths, the coming of one destined to cause the rise and fall of many. You can imagine just how surprised we were to discover there actually was something in all that nonsense. Especially since you came burning out of the west and nearly impacted on our own pitifully under-armored observation craft.''

Something was clamoring for Hickock's attention. 5/7/53. He looked down at the digital watch he had been given. 5/29/53. He counted back to the first day he could clearly remember. Four days.

Had all that time been spent receiving bone implants and clone grafts?

''Are you all right?'' Vaheri asked anxiously.

''Shut *up!*'' Hickock squeezed his eyes shut, knuckles at his temples, straining after an elusive memory that darted away into the disordered dimness of his mind.

There had been two awakenings.

Color-coded wires coiled away from ankles, wrists, and the helmet that enclosed most of his head. Vaheri sat in the background, intently studying a bank of instruments just out of the range of vision. Mackern stood over him, sweating nervously.

''Let us try again. Your name is Patrick M. Hickock.''

''Yes.''

''Why was your ship engaging one of Skybreaker's?''

''I don't know. What is Skybreaker?''

''Vaheri. Level two.''

A tension grew where the electrodes touched his skin. It invaded his bones, making them rigid and unresponsive as wood.

''What Shaper do you belong to? What is your lineage chain?'' Mackern demanded.

''Shaper . . . lineage . . . I don't . . .''

''Tell me your mission,'' Mackern demanded. ''I must know all about your mission.''

Giant hands seemed to press down on Hickock's chest. He could not answer. He had to answer. He shook his head, gasping.

''Vaheri. Level three.''

"Christ, Leo, look at these readings! The procedure isn't meant for this sort of resistance. Any more power and I may well damage the nerve tissue."

"Dr. Vaheri." Mackern gestured with his head. For the first time, Hickock noticed a camera hanging from the ceiling, its fish-eye lens surveying the whole room. Vaheri seemed to wilt. He pressed a series of buttons.

The pressure became absolute. Hickock was unable to breathe.

"We need information," Mackern said, enunciating carefully. *"Who is the head of your lineage group? What is your mission?"*

Hickock strained, trying to reply and not reply. The rigidity moved in from his rib cage and penetrated to the center of his chest. His heart labored against it, each beat coming more slowly and painfully than the last.

". . . formation. Tell us. Now."

His chest imploded, sucking him down into darkness.

"Hickock, what's the matter?" Vaheri and Yader were supporting him on either side. Hickock wrenched away from them.

"You!" he said, pointing at Mackern. His finger shook so much that he had to grab the wrist with his left hand to steady it. "You tried to kill me."

"What? Nonsense." Mackern's eyes slid away. "We saved your life."

"You kept pushing," Hickock insisted. "You asked questions you knew I couldn't, *couldn't*, answer! I was strapped down. There were wires—"

"Your craft was sinking. The metal itself was on fire. Two good men were terribly burned cutting through to you."

"—like an electric chair. You kept increasing the power. Vaheri warned you of the consequences. You didn't stop because you didn't care."

"There was hardly enough of you left to put in the regeneration tanks. For three days, we thought we might lose you at any moment. We have quite an investment in you! We had no intention of throwing it away.''

''You thought I was a spy.''

''That was—is—a possibility.''

''So I was a threat. You raised the power to kill—''

''We did kill you,'' Mackern said, his voice almost inaudible. The confession seemed to deflate him.

''Ah?'' Hickock cocked his head to one side, like a man who feared he may have missed a punch line.

''Oh, it was nothing personal. Or intentional. We had to find out how strong your conditioning was. We found out.''

—imploded. He fell up a deep well toward a circle of light, which grew—

Current surged through the paddles on his chest. His body arced upward, every cell trying to scream.

''. . . sider our position.'' In his gruff way, Mackern was almost pleading. ''You fall out of the sky, pursued by Skybreaker's fighters, announced by prophecies even a Babylonian would consider lurid. Your craft, your very gene patterns are unidentifiable. Your memories are shielded by a type of hypnotic blocking we have never seen.

''Innovator considers mysteries of this sort personally dangerous. I'm kept around to deal with them. You must know how it is, wherever you come from. If I am less than effective in protecting Innovator's lineage group, it will have my gonads for fish fertilizer.''

''You look fatigued,'' Vaheri said. Although he spoke to Hickock, he was casting worried glances at Mackern. Hickock nodded, heart pounding.

''We've made a lot of progress today, more than we had looked for,'' Vaheri said, speaking rapidly. ''I think that we can end this session.''

Mackern, pale and shaking, agreed.

ii

"I DIDN'T THINK YOU WOULD BE FREE SO SOON," YADER said.

"Right."

"I have some errands I was going to run. Want to tag along?"

"I have a choice?"

"You may have the freedom of your room."

Thirty-six square feet and a locked door.

"I'll tag."

"Thought you'd be reasonable."

This time, there were only two checkpoints: one just before they entered the elevator, and one when they exited at cliff-top level. Yader had to show both his own papers and the pass he had for Hickock.

"You should try a chain-and-nose-ring combination," Hickock muttered. "It would make the relationship immediately apparent and save everyone time."

"Tsk, tsk. Bitterness ill becomes you."

They emerged at the bottom level of a covered mall. Small shops alternated randomly with anonymous office fronts. Yader took an escalator to the mid-level. Almost directly across from the head of the escalator stood a storefront stand under the sign LEISURE HORTICULTURALS. Yader waited while the manager explained to another customer the air-freshening qualities of a certain luminescent reddish-brown moss.

"May I help you, sir?"

"I'm here to pick up an order of neRoses."

The manager looked doubtful. "Those are still in the experimental stage, and the price—"

"Is outrageous, but was paid five days ago by Janet Yader."

"Ah, Miss Yader's order. Let me see if it is in."

Hickock looked about the mall. A group of midgets clambered in and out of ceiling ventilation shafts, apparently working on the lighting. The crowd on the top concourse parted to let a hulk well over two meters tall lumber through, very careful not to brush the enforcer's club hanging on his hip.

Two . . . individuals walked out of an adjacent office. Hickock stared, sure that something was wrong but unable to say immediately what it was. Both had long hair and were trying to grow beards, though the patches of whiskers on their cheeks were hardly thicker than the hair on their long, bare arms.

Then Hickock saw that the breasts beneath the form-fitting tank tops were definitely feminine.

One of them, noticing his attention, turned and smirked.

Yader came away with his parcel. "You prejudiced against maphs or something?"

Not recognizing the word, or even sure of what he had just seen, Hickock said, "Yeah."

Yader grinned. "Me, too." He held out his purchase. "Take a look at these. They cost an arm and a leg, but Nanny Kit is worth it."

Hickock peered into the box. Feathery greenish-yellow stems darkened toward one end and split apart into half a dozen layers of petal-like shreds. There was a slight, sweetish scent.

"For centuries, roses were the most highly regarded flower of at least half the human race," Yader informed him. "Sweethearts and family members sent them to show their love. Religious mystics and alchemists considered them symbols of transcendent cosmic unity."

Hickock frowned. "These are roses?"

"Of course not." Yader sounded offended. "None of those survived Earth. These were part of a Botanicals Group demo project to show the genetic variability of land fauna. It did help convince Innovator to concentrate more heavily on dry agriculture. As a side benefit, we produced a type of beauty otherwise unobtainable on a planet that has never known pollinating insects."

They ascended to the third level and crossed a corridor to a mover station. Flat-bottomed cars about three meters long stood on a siding. The "track" was a motionless series of jet-black bearings arranged in beaded rows. Hickock seated himself on a side bench, bracing himself as the rollers directly beneath the car propelled it forward into the sunlight.

One line change and several stops later, he and Yader stepped off at an almost deserted station. A long gravel path led to a two-meter-high whitewashed wall.

"We're not that far from the cliffs," Yader explained. "The nurses have always had nightmares about the kids getting out to play and falling over the edge."

A sign announced the GOLDEN DAYS CRECHE in rainbow colors. Yader identified himself to the porter. The gate swung open.

"I'll check with the day supervisor," Yader said. "She should have a good idea where Nanny Kit is."

Hickock remained outside the administration building. The inside of the wall was decorated with paintings. In one, stick figures watered a garden. In another, children capered around a large animal with an indefinite number of legs. In the third,

people leaned out the window of a spaceship, waving a tear-
ful farewell to a planet already engulfed in flames behind
them.

"She's in the Maze," Yader said, coming down the steps.

They walked around the administration building and
through a play area, then came to a wall of bushes clipped
as smooth as the outside wall. The path led into a narrow
gap. Seen close up, the rich brown of the foliage dissolved
into a mosaic of hair-thin leaves: black, yellow, red, and
blue.

"This was my favorite place when I was a kid," Yader
said. "I thought I could get lost forever and no one could
ever find me."

He paced surefootedly through a series of turns and
doublebacks that quickly left Hickock totally disoriented.
The living walls towered above them, shrouding the path
in dimness. Small shadowed forms brushed past them
twice. From time to time, breathless giggles penetrated
from either side.

Without warning, they were at the center. Hickock blinked
against the sudden sunlight.

Children were playing in small groups. At their center,
seated on a rock under one huge, arched shade leaf, sat a
small, incredibly old woman. Except for age blotches, her
skin was as white as her netted hair. Tight fists worked on
needlework with jerky precision.

Yader cleared his throat. "Nanny Kit," he called, raising
his voice. "I'm sorry we weren't able to make your jubilee
last week. Janet made me promise to bring you these neRoses
as soon as I could get free."

Blue eyes peered up uncertainly through thick glasses.
"Which—which one are you?" she asked, her voice quavering.

"Jason," Yader said patiently. "This is my, uh, colleague,
Patrick Hickock."

She took the bundle of neRoses and fingered them wistfully. "My grandmother used to say that she could remember roses. From when she was very little."

They took seats on adjoining rocks. Yader and Nanny Kit caught up on gossip: which of the older teachers and nurses were still with the crèche, who had died or retired, who had been forced to leave in disgrace. Nanny Kit had very definite ideas about the new staff members. Her opinions were no less pronounced concerning those outside the crèche.

"Are you still working for that Garrison?" she asked sharply.

"Yes, Nanny. Colonel Garrison. Special Projects."

"Don't trust him," she declared, her pursed lips moving in a circle as she sucked her gums. "Never did."

"No, Nanny," Yader said agreeably, "but Innovator has a great deal of confidence in him. And the colonel did give me this time off to see you. Even if it is too late for your jubilee."

As intended, that switched the conversation to the jubilee party. How many of her former charges had been able to come! Even several of those who had been sold or traded to alien herds had been able to send their greetings.

Nanny Kit's eyes grew misty. "When I think how many years ago I failed at the genetics an' they snipped my womb for the baby poppers. I cried for days, sure I would never have any little ones."

"Instead, you have had hundreds," Jason said. "And lucky for us that they made you a crèche-nurse instead of letting you have your own get."

"Then when I got too old to hold my own," she continued, as if she had not heard him, "there seemed nothing ahead for me but the fertilizer vats. I never have got over learning that all of you established a fund for my upkeep.''

"Only the worst criminals should ever go to the vats," Yader said, his voice hard. "Soon they may be a thing of the past.

"Anyway, the only thing the fund is used for now is your medicines. The crèche knows very well that your mere presence here earns your keep just in making these kids feel secure.''

Hickock recognized Yader's words as the sort of thing anyone might say to a beloved older relative. Yet as he sat there, it did seem as if Nanny Kit were somehow the pivot point of the entire crèche. The children playing on the ground about her would glance up from time to time to see if she was still there, then go back to their activities reassured.

"But it's not fair," Nanny Kit said, shaking her head.

"What's not, Nanny? If they're—"

"All the times I hurt you! You would run in here trying to hide, and when I found you, you would bury yourself in my skirts and beg me to protect you.''

She was silent a moment, her face slack. "Every time, I gave you back to them. Then they would hurt you some more.''

Hickock bit his lip, wanting to be away from what had become an intensely private conversation, yet afraid that any movement would draw embarrassing attention to himself.

"That was Jimmy," Yader said gently. "You never hurt me, Nanny.''

"That was all of you," she said, giving him a piercing glance.

"Well, then, if not for you, I wouldn't be here at all." His tone became serious. "Nanny, we have all had to do things we wish we hadn't. You, me, Garrison, all of us. We hope that each generation will have to make fewer such choices.

In the meantime, we seize the chances as they come by, and try not to lose strength. Nobody did that better than you. Nobody taught it better, either.

"So don't waste yourself on regretting things you could do nothing about. I wanted to join, belatedly, in celebrating your jubilee today. If I'm going to upset you, I just won't come anymore."

"Hmpff! And have you been learning blackmail from Garrison, as well?"

Yader flashed a boyish grin. "You bet!" He stood up. "I have to be going now. If you're a good girl, and if I'm lucky, I may be able to see you before I'm off on assignment again."

Hickock rose with Yader. Nanny Kit seemed to take note of him for the first time.

"Young man, do you work for this Garrison?"

"No, ma'am," Hickock said. "Though I guess you'd have to say that I am working with him at present."

"Don't trust him."

Hickock hesitated, unsure if she was restating her previously expressed opinion or giving a command. "I don't intend to," he said, deciding on the latter.

"Good." For a few seconds, she seemed lost in thought. Then, in a stage whisper loud enough to be heard across the clearing, she said, "Take care of my boy."

"Ma'am?"

She leaned forward, continuing in the same thunderous whisper. "I always worry about Jimmy. The Shapers talk of improvements, but too many of them looked like mutilations to me. They can find it hard to cope. Afterward."

Hickock stood, smile frozen on his face, waiting for her to continue. When it became obvious she would not, he said, "I'll try."

"Mmmm." She sat back, looked around in mild distress, found her needlework, and bent her attention to it.

* * *

"You are very pensive," Yader said.

They had departed the moveways and entered, after the inevitable identity checks, the part of the island controlled by Special Projects.

"Nobody has ever defined your position for me," Hickock said slowly, "but as far as I have been able to tell, you are some sort of intelligence officer, or special agent."

Yader pursed his lips. "Close enough. Garrison would say too close. So what?"

Hickock shrugged. "I just never thought of ruthless secret agents as the types who brought flowers to their old nurses."

The afternoon wind had freshened off the ocean. Yader's face was half averted. The words were whipped away, almost unheard, from his mouth. "I don't know how it is where you come from," he said, "but here we help each other, when we can. We have to. Vaheri's told you how it was in Wave-lasher's pens. I've seen reports of other places where it was worse. Much worse. Everyone turned against each other. Survival of the fittest, they called it. The joke was, nobody survived.

"Innovator isn't that bad. We are allowed to retrieve and live as much of old human culture as helps make us more productive. The more extreme forms of genetic experimentation have been curtailed as ineffective. Each year we bargain a little more freedom. These days, if you accumulate enough productivity points for the lineage group, you are allowed to choose your own mate and plan your own family. Within limits, of course.

"This is good. It is also precarious. Innovator could change its mind. Or it could be devoured by rival Shapers. Even if neither occurs, it will someday 'grow to engulf the sky,' as they put it. Then the lineage group will dissolve. There will be civil war for as much of a year between, at last count, some twenty-odd members of the first generation. The winners will establish their own patriarchies. We—those of us who survive—will have to learn how to deal with their whims.

"So we appear soft to you?" Yader seemed to consider the point. "I guess some things do mean a lot to us."

He turned to Hickock, his eyes shadowed and unreadable. "They are why we are ruthless."

iii

HICKOCK PAUSED AS HE STEPPED THROUGH THE DOOR, WAIT-
ing for his eyes to adjust to the dusk. "You're on your own,"
Yader had said. That meant that it was the covert team's turn
to monitor his movements. It didn't matter. Hickock was
grateful for the illusion of privacy.

An orange-red line edged the horizon. Rainwater pools
reflected a sky only just perceptibly brighter than the surrounding rock. Unfamiliar stars salted the advancing darkness. Patches of light detached themselves from the starry
background: aquavians feeding on the flitters and sectoids
that inhabited the cliff edge. The buzzing of their wings dopp-
lered in and out of the crashing of the waves far below.

Hickock walked carefully across the terrace to an empty
table at its far edge. He could light the lamp to signal if he
wanted service. For the moment, it was enough to sit in the
cool, cleansing breeze and listen to the surf shattering on
faraway rocks.

He pulled a cigar from his shirt pocket and puffed it into
life. He contemplated the orange coal, wondering whether
he had smoked before. It felt natural.

According to Mackern, smoking was not only psycholog-
ically soothing but medically beneficial, as well. This particular cigar contained, besides the stock supply of vitamins

and anticarcinogens, tissue regeneratives especially prescribed by Vaheri. And God knew what else.

He heard a quick rhythm of leather striking stone. A shadow approached from one side to loom over him.

"Mind if I join you?"

"Yes."

The shadow settled into a chair on the other side of the table. "You're a hard man, Hickock."

"Maybe. If that is really my name."

"Do you have problems 'bout that?" The alto voice was suddenly concerned.

"I'm told that all your people found was a name tag on a badly charred uniform. Such was the carnage that the proximity of the name tag to my body may have been only coincidental."

"No, you're Hickock, all right." The voice sounded relieved.

"You, of course, have access to supranormal channels of communication." Hickock jerked free a hair from his head and offered it to his companion. "Perhaps you should work on this. I dread to think what specimens Mackern may have supplied to you."

The hair was taken from his fingers. Milk-white teeth split the ebony face. There was laughter, and a soft wooden rattling.

"Shit, man," Reeve said. "For a dummy, you know the oddest things. Not a hundred people on this planet understand what I can do with a . . . specimen. Not one of them would ever give me one voluntarily."

"Mackern might," Hickock suggested. He puffed, exhaling the bittersweet vapors thoughtfully. "His references to lurid prophecies and arcane utterances make him sound just the least bit skeptical."

"That's just pretend. Dr. Mackern can't be skeptical of a

program he has encouraged Innovator to invest two human generations in.''

Hickock considered this. ''I thought it was the seventh son of a seventh son who was supposed to be psychic.''

Again there was surprised laughter. ''You do know it all! Maybe you have just a bit of the sight?''

Hickock shook his head.

''Well, you're right, though. I was supposed to be male. But things get screwed up even in the best-run pens. When they found out the mistake, the first thought was to flush me down the drain and get a new egg for the popper. Only Poppa had gone on to the next world in the meantime.

''Mackern had just taken over the project. He was *scared*! So he goes to Innovator and he says, 'Don't cancel the project. We've put in this much effort, let's see how it turns out. Women are supposed to be more psychically sensitive than men anyway. And this girl's people hadn't been that long out of the jungle at the Departure. They had bred for magic longer than any other race on Earth.'

''What a line! But Innovator bought it, for a while.''

''So you are psychic?'' Hickock asked.

''Yeah. Some of the time.''

''What do your powers tell you about Shapers?''

Reeve went absolutely still. ''More than you'd ever like to know, hon,'' she said finally. She looked down at the waves. Dots of light darted over—and sometimes through—the wave tops as aquavians searched for prey.

''That was my test,'' she said. ''I'd just had my first period. Mackern came to me, his eyes all red, his breath smelling funny. He said that Innovator had commanded the test for that evening. Mackern had tried to put it off with test data he had gathered on me. No way. Either I succeeded immediately, or 'the project' would be terminated.

''After all, he said, I'd had twelve good years. That was

more than many got. That's when I realized he thought I would fail.

"Mackern felt much more upset about this than I did. I guess the cramps hurt so much I had trouble taking fear seriously. He seemed to take it personally. He always had treated me kinda like a daughter. Then again, maybe he was just a dirty old man regretting he'd never had the nerve to make it with me.

"They took me down to the Nares. Most of the time you just float there and the Speakers-to-God interpret. This time I was suited up and the Speaker had me swim out of the Nares, as if I was a goddamn mer.

"It was so dark that, except for my suit lights, I could hardly see my own hands. I couldn't tell up from down. Currents shifted erratically on every side. Something huge was stirring.

"Then it was all around me. Wherever my lights fell, there was a pulsing, mottled gray. It was as if I'd been swallowed. Maybe I had been.

"I put out my hand—I don't know if to protect myself or because I realized that I had to make contact. The flesh was rough and warm, almost hot. Something went through me like a shock. I began babbling into my breathing mike."

"What did you say?" Hickock asked after a pause that threatened to lengthen indefinitely.

Reeve shook her head, rattling the cornrows. "I don't remember. Just dream fragments. Coldness. A loneliness so old and so complete that it couldn't even name itself."

She stopped and licked her lips. "Mackern, Vaheri, they've studied Shapers all their lives. They'll drone on for hours about how they're unisexual marine quasi-vertebrates, how they can bud genetically tailored offspring to do everything from hunting food to excreting the shells for their starships. They know how each Shaper genetically indoctrinates each offspring for complete obedience. They'll draw charts about how this creates lineage groups. But they don't know shit about what goes on inside.''

She faced Hickock. ''You and me, we don't know much about each other, but we do know we're kinda alike just because we're both human. We know that we get hungry, that we need shelter, we like sex, stuff like that. Maybe I do something that seems a little weird, so you ask yourself, 'What could make *me* behave that way?' That question makes sense because you see me as a variation on yourself. You can't help it.

''Shapers can't understand that sort of thinking. While their patriarch is alive, they don't have free will. Maybe they aren't even fully conscious. Their offspring are so thoroughly indoctrinated that they don't even have the feeling for them that we have for pets. More like machines. When they become patriarch, they know how to command. They remember, dimly, what it means to obey. Ideas like cooperation, negotiation, compromise are more bizarre than quantum mechanics to them. Shapers in other lineage groups aren't just competitors—they're regarded as fuckin' different *species*.

''It's even more than that. Way deep down, at a level Shapers themselves are hardly aware of, they don't even believe in the universe.''

Hickock shook his head in incomprehension.

''They're so used to indoctrinating their offspring, they don't really believe that other creatures exist apart from them. If other Shapers or humans don't obey instantly and perfectly, they must be malformed offspring whose budding has somehow been forgotten. They see rock formations on the ocean floor and wonder when they excreted them, and why.

''Innovator doesn't sleep, exactly, but it does dream. When it dreams, it drifts on the currents, thinking that it has somehow shrunk down inside its own bloodstream and is exploring its body, the world.''

''That,'' Hickock said distinctly, ''is crazy.''

Reeve responded with a short shriek of laughter, edged with hysteria and sadness. "Man, you got that right. My training—drugs and trances and playing games with old cards—is supposed to liberate me from the confines of the here and now. Too liberated, and I never get back to reality.

"But at least what I babbled back then was interesting enough that Innovator decided to keep me around. There must have been some truth to it."

"That was some time ago," Hickock observed. "What have you done for Innovator lately?"

He could see her face more clearly now, in the light spilling over from nearby tables. Her smile was almost feral.

"You, honey. You're what I've done for it lately."

"Sibylline prophecies," Hickock mused. "That makes no sense, though. I mean, if you can just read my mind, you can shortcut all of Garrison's and Mackern's little games, make your report, and I—can be disposed of as will then appear appropriate."

Reeve sighed. "Occupational hazard, hon. I don't really have a power. *It* has *me*—when it wants me. In between times, I have to fake it: stay ambiguous enough that no matter what happens, I can point to something I said as predicting it."

"And when the power actually comes?"

"Then I have to be obscure just to be consistent."

Hickock turned on the table lamp. While ordering a sandwich and something to drink, he might think of a way to learn just how much Reeve knew. Or thought she knew.

"There's another occupational hazard," Reeve said after the server had taken their orders. "Sometimes, if you have the sight too clearly and speak it too plainly, people don't like what you say. I hinted a few things at Mackern. He shut me down but fast!"

"Why?" Hickock asked uneasily. "If he does believe in your power, he should be extremely attentive."

"Because you are a walking time bomb," Reeve answered softly. "I know that. Mackern suspects it. You go off at the right time and place, a lot of walls could come down.

"Wrong time and place—" She shrugged. "Maybe we all get killed. I go one way. I think Mackern does, too. Garrison, though . . . That man's idea of security is a nice, clean, safe cell. He might be inclined to cut his losses with you.

"That's why I can't tell even you what I know. That mindblock of yours may be the only thing keeping you alive."

"What about Yader?"

"Which Yader?" Reeve asked bitterly. "Oh, he's okay. But he works for Garrison. Don't you forget that."

Their food came. When he was finished, Hickock rose to leave. Reeve placed her hand on his forearm.

"When your time comes," she said urgently, "remember me. Remember all of us."

Hickock gently disengaged her hand. "I don't have that much say in what I remember."

Yader was watching a flatscreen video in his adjoining room. Hickock sat himself down uninvited and tried to pick up the thread of the story.

It was a continuing serial entitled, Yader told him, *The Sea Beneath the Sea*. The setting was Snowball, a satellite of the gas giant that was the next planet out from the sun. An ice crust three kilometers thick covered an ocean ten kilometers deep. For reasons unexplained, the crust was melting.

A team of humans under a Shaper in Starswallower's lineage group had been sent to assess if the newly formed seas could be made habitable for Shapers. In a previous episode, the exploration vessel had been caught in a whirlpool and sucked down into the subcrustal ocean. Now the team was trying to find its way back to the surface before its life-support systems failed.

After watching for nearly thirty minutes, Hickock asked, "Is this Shaper supposed to be a bit dense?"

"Delicate question," Yader admitted. "Shapers under a Patriarch's indoctrination appear, at least by comparison, slow and inflexible. All humans, of course, are to give unswerving loyalty and obedience to all Shapers in their lineage groups. On the other hand, primary loyalty is reserved for the Patriarch.

"As you probably guessed, this show was produced under Starswallower's auspices for trading points with the other lineage groups. Specifically, it was produced by humans in the herd of Explorer, one of Starswallower's first-generation offspring. As far as we can tell, Explorer was budded for the express purpose of countering Innovator's threat. Once Explorer matured and started building its own lineage group, it showed itself to be frighteningly effective. It's not giving away any group secrets to let you know that the combination of Starswallower's resources with Explorer's flexibility and pragmatic opportunism had everyone from Innovator on down worried.

"Luckily for us, it started behaving erratically. Starswallower summoned it to a confrontation, probably to reinforce and/or revise its indoctrination. Something went wrong. Explorer was devoured. A general purge followed. We lost all of our intelligence sources. Starswallower's entire lineage group went incommunicado. We hope that we'll be able to get a line on what really happened at the trade talks that have just opened."

On the screen, the episode came to a double climax: at the same time that ruins were found drifting beneath the ice, implying that Snowball had been colonized by Shapers a million years before, the adventurers realized that their attempts to return to the surface were being sabotaged by a spy working for Innovator!

Hickock stood, stretched, and turned to his room.

"No beddy-bye without your nightcap, specially brewed by the kind Dr. Mackern."

Hickock stopped. "He didn't mention anything about it to me."

"You rattled him so much this morning that he forgot it," Yader said, holding out a cup. For the first time, Hickock noticed the raised white scar that curved down the right side of Yader's jaw. "He's worried about your continued hip pain. This is to reduce the inflammation around your synthicalc rod."

Hickock took the cup and sniffed. The odor had a chalky complexity.

"I understand your concern," Yader said. "You've figured out my job. If you were perceived to be a threat to Innovator's lineage group, you would be instantly eliminated. Your death would be left to nothing so awkward or unsure as poison."

"You can't imagine how reassured I am."

"It *is* perfectly harmless."

Hickock nodded and drained the cup. He staggered into his room, unlatched the sleeping plate from the wall, and fell on top of it.

They were such smug bastards, so sure that they could squeeze everything out of him, he thought as he floated down through grayness. But they had missed one very important point in their questions about fusion and radio astronomy. They had not asked how he felt about those subjects.

It was important that he knew—and that they did not—the anger, searing as the surface of the sun, that those subjects kindled within him.

iv

THE ROARING DREW HIM BACK FROM UNCONSCIOUSNESS. His
arms hung straight in front of him, painfully swollen with
blood. His lips felt fat and bruised. The roaring was the air,
he realized, rasped into incandescence as the hull rammed
through it at supersonic speeds.

With immense effort, he turned his head. Where Virginia
should have been was a monstrosity of shattered bone, bloody
hair straining forward as if caught in a strong current. Part
of the shoulder harness had torn away, allowing the upper
part of the body to batter itself against the instrument panel.

He inhaled, trying to ignore the pain that lanced through
his ribs. The inside of his mouth was thick with sticky sweetness. The air burned.

*". . . to unidentified craft . . . Respond . . . into pattern
with escorts . . . land . . . or be destroyed . . ."*

Static crackled across the communicator. Coded traffic
between other vessels was being picked up as well: *"Tango,
tango, delta, fox-trot, bravo . . ."*

The hell with the fighters. Their itchy trigger fingers were
the least of his problems.

He raised his head to the instrument panel, and the sense
of nightmare became complete. It was totally unfamiliar.

Red lights flashed across half the board. More alarming were the banks of dead telltales.

Hickock glared at the readouts as if he could force them to make sense. Numbers flashed across them too quickly to be understood. A parabola glowed from a small screen, changing color from green at the top through yellow, orange, and finally red. A dot blinked rapidly near the end of the orange curve.

Near the right armrest of his acceleration couch stood a joystick surmounted with a squeeze grip and three buttons. It looked like something in a museum exhibit. He pushed the red button. Nothing seemed to happen.

He squeezed the grip. The cabin shuddered. Air-drag deceleration almost vanished. One set of readout numbers rose quickly, then began to decrease. The parabola flattened as the red part of the curve lengthened and almost touched the blinking light.

Hickock nodded. He pulled the stick back, squeezing hard.

As the nose rose, the craft went into an end-over-end tumble. Centrifugal force slammed him back into his acceleration couch. Instinctively he clenched the joystick and tried to pull himself forward.

The tumbling increased. Couch straps bit into his shoulders. Virginia's corpse tore loose from the remaining harness and smashed against the ceiling. Hickock's mouth opened in a soundless scream as he tried to relieve the sudden increase in pressure in his neck and head.

Cursing his stupidity, he shoved the stick diagonally forward, opposite the direction of tumbling. The shuddering intensified, simultaneously becoming sub- and supersonic. With a loud crack, the bulkhead ripped apart, disclosing for the briefest instant the blue-and-white-splotched planet below.

Then a wall of flaming air tore him away from his couch, tossing him—

* * *

—onto the floor. He came up in a crouch, arms in guard position. His eyes darted left and right after evanescent dream images. The only sound was the white noise of the air-circulation ducts.

Light blazed from the ceiling. He raised a hand to shield his eyes.

"You all right?" Yader asked, stepping through the doorway. "I heard a scream."

"The lifeship," Hickock said stupidly. "It broke up."

He rose slowly from his crouch. "The drink!" he said accusingly.

"Give you nightmares?" Yader asked. "Mackern said it might."

"No!" Hickock shook his head. "It wasn't a nightmare."

He felt himself over. His ribs were unbroken. There were no bruises on his shoulders from the harness. His mouth was dry—not bleeding, so far as he could tell.

Then his fingers discovered circular welts on his jaw, under each ear, and on each temple. There were three similar marks across his forehead.

"Nasty bites," Yader commented. "Sectoids probably got you on the terrace without your noticing it. We'll have cleaning crews coming in tomorrow to make sure they didn't come in on your clothes."

"Liar," Hickock muttered. It didn't matter anyway. Drowsiness drowned his anger, leaving barely enough strength to control his fall back to the sleeping plate.

". . . complete and absolute failure!" Garrison declared, pacing the room.

Mackern barely noticed him. His eyes were red with exhaustion. Curly strands of hair were pasted flat with sweat across his bald spot. His desk screen replayed the scene yet again. Hickock, Medusa-headed with wires, writhed spasmodically in a rebuilt acceleration couch. The violence of the thrashing disturbed Mackern. He could break his neck that way, he thought. It has been known to happen.

"How can you say that?" he asked absently. Physiological data crowded so thickly into five lines at the bottom of the screen that he had to slow the replay considerably to take it all in. "The presumptions of the test—"

"I know very well the presumptions of the test," Garrison snapped. "You theorized that Hickock's memory block acted only on the conscious level. Ask him if he is a pilot, and he will reply, truthfully, that he doesn't remember. But put him in a life-threatening situation, and his reflexes will tell their own story.

"We had to make the simulation as realistic as possible. Since the instrumentation on his own craft is still largely a mystery, we substituted a standard aerospace control panel, one on which he would have to have trained, since it is one of the very few things that are standard among the herds.

"If we were right, he would take control of the craft. The course he would lay, the distress messages he would send— all might serve to disclose his base, the size of his task force, perhaps even the lineage group he belongs to.

"Instead, he destroyed the simulated vessel, proving that he isn't a pilot, after all. We are back to square one. Worse than that because, drugged as he was, he was smart enough to realize immediately that we had staged the whole event. He will be just that much more intractable from now on."

Mackern looked up in bleary wonder that a man with so little imagination could have the power of life and death over so many. Himself included.

He cleared his throat. "I'm afraid you've, ah, misinterpreted our results. It is true that our experiment did not terminate the way we had planned. That is because we learned something totally unexpected."

He rewound the tape and set the machine on slow motion.

"He awakes. Quickly he perceives the danger of his situation. He looks to the instrument panel and, *there*, you see the rapid increase in heartbeat, most probably because he finds it unreadable."

"Confirming my analysis exactly," Garrison interjected.

"That spike of panic you see most likely results from the fact that he felt he *should* have been able to read the panel," Mackern said in exasperation. "Nonetheless, he quickly regains control of himself. He finds the joystick, experiments with it, figures out the basic parameters—see the grin?—and pulls back to get the craft out of its dive."

He slowed the replay even further. "Two misfortunes now occur in rapid succession. The craft is not streamlined for supersonic atmospheric flight. The change in altitude destabilizes the simulation. Hickock and the joystick are thrown backward, exacerbating the tumble past the point of no return.

"But—watch this very carefully—even though the physiological readings show that he is very close to blacking out, he still takes the proper action to bring his ship back into control.

"It is too late. Carrying out its programming literally, the simulation computer destroys the craft as, presumably, it would have been destroyed if it had actually been subjected to such buffeting."

Garrison had stopped pacing and was watching Mackern closely. "All of which leads to what?"

Mackern leaned back, enumerating points on his fingers. "Hickock is indeed a pilot, one so well trained that he can figure out a strange control system in less than a minute and execute difficult maneuvers while being battered into unconsciousness.

"We have learned that his masters have spatial capabilities so vast and seemingly exclusive that their pilots receive minimal atmospheric training. We have further learned that their entire fleet, including training craft, has a command and control system like nothing seen on this planet since the Arrival.''

"That is impossible," Garrison objected. "There is no such lineage group."

"None," Mackern corrected, "that we know of."

V

HANGING IN THE VOID WAS AN ORANGE-YELLOW SUN. A sand-colored pebble floated closest to it. Thirty degrees away and a bit farther out was a blue-and-white-mottled marble: Shapers' world. Still farther out and more than ninety degrees away was a ball striped white and purple. A satellite small and white as a snowflake was barely visible against the bulk of its gaseous companion.

"We have had to compress both temporal and spatial scales," Major Hollings said apologetically. "Those blue dots are the regular inner system traffic: freighters carrying raw materials from Salamander; mining crews going out to the planetoid belts; exploring teams and planetary engineers on their way to Snowball.

"About two weeks before Event, one of Starswallower's convoys encountered an unidentified intruder. We don't know what happened because all the message traffic is in code. We do know that one ship was either destroyed or captured." A dot winked out. "The other members of the convoy suffered varying degrees of damage.

"Raids and skirmishing are the order of the day, of course. The odd thing was that the lineage group behind this action could not be immediately identified. It is suggestive that first Starswallower, and then Skybreaker, launched reconnaissance patrols into space above and below the orbital plane. As far as we know, all that they should have been able to find there are the husks of a few burnt-out comets.

"At E minus one, a small, lightly protected convoy was launched from Skybreaker's waters on a one-G acceleration curve to Snowball. It appears that it was a decoy. We did not realize it was under attack until its escort broke cover—" A globe of red sparks blazed into visibility around the convoy. "—to repel the intruder."

Hickock watched in fascination as the globe of battle craft deformed and lengthened into a cone drifting with apparent languor—although the crews must have been experiencing murderous accelerations—in the direction of the Shaper world. The intruder still did not register on the display. Its position had to be inferred from the maneuvers of Skybreaker's vessels.

The cone thickened, then inverted. It splashed outward, returning to its globe shape.

"The intruder must have taken damage to its thrusters," Hollings said. "It is still making half-G acceleration but is easily being overtaken. As you see, englobement is now complete. Skybreaker's ships move in for the kill."

The red sparks shimmered more and more quickly. Shadow memories rose before Hickock: superheated air rushing through the companionways; bursting pipes spraying scalding steam, almost drowning out the alarm klaxons; Fleet Go'el Captain Judith Helfand calmly surveying the damage, then quietly giving the order to abandon ship.

The last seconds of countdown before the launching of the life-ship. An acceleration that squeezed the air from his lungs and pushed back the loose flesh from his cheeks as if to peel it away from his skull.

A brilliant, soundless flash stunned his retina. Hickock fell back into his seat, vaguely aware of the wetness on his cheeks. All the red sparks had disappeared with the explosion.

Mackern leaned forward eagerly, his face thrust into the field of the hologram so that it loomed, monstrous, above Shaper's world. "The name of the ship," he demanded.

The memories, the images, the feelings, worst of all, the faces of those who had once meant so much to him were evaporating. Hickock strained after the fading ghosts.

"Vengeance," he gasped.

Mackern smiled with satisfaction. "Its mission?"

A door slamming shut. Echoes dying on the air.

"I don't remember."

After a pause, Hollings resumed his narration. "The entire Skybreaker attack force was destroyed in the explosion. We don't know what, if anything, the reinforcements were able to learn from the wreckage. The next item of significance that we pick up—" Shapers' world grew as he spoke, swelling until it could barely be contained within the hologram "—is the ionization path you see now."

A white line extended itself and twice bounced shallowly off the thicker lower atmosphere before beginning its long, curving descent to a patch of ocean three-quarters of a world away.

"Luckily, or I suppose I should say, through the foresight and excellent planning of our other Special Operations groups, there was a task force at the splashdown point."

The hologram vanished. Mackern regarded Hickock pensively. "We are making progress," he said slowly. "Perhaps if you see our latest restoration work, it will dissolve your memory block completely."

He motioned Hickock to follow him. Hollings and Yader crowded into the elevator after them. The doors closed and the floor fell away. Hickock counted ten pulsebeats before full—for a few seconds more than full—weight returned and the doors slid open.

They were in a huge, clearly artificial cavern. Banks of ceiling lights made the concrete floor dazzling. White-suited figures, singly or in small groups, worked on benches littered with randomly wired-together machinery.

Beyond them lay the saucer. Its lower half was seared black. Technicians clambered in through a ragged hole in the bottom. Mackern indicated a set of metal stairs that had been rolled against the side of the craft.

From the platform on top, Hickock gazed down into the interior, through a gap in the hull roughly a meter wide.

"Go on down," Mackern boomed. "make yourself at home."

Cautiously Hickock swung down to the deck. Light cylinders stuck to the walls threw irregular pools of illumination. The carpeting crackled faintly beneath his feet. He knelt to examine it.

Melted Velcro, now brittle. The cloth fiber beneath it was scorched. Both carpeting and walls were stained with irregular dark-brown patches. He tried not to think of what had caused them.

He moved forward to the pilot's station. Covered with soot as they were, every light and dial on the console was filled with meaning. On a hunch, he dropped to his knees, running his fingers along the right side of his couch. There was an indentation in the carpet where the Velcro had been pressed into powder. Within it, three holes sunk into the carpet defined a triangle.

Mackern wheezed as he climbed down behind him. A technician lying on his back under the console put down his tools to watch Hickock.

"You do quick work," Hickock said, loudly enough for Mackern to hear. "Last night the instrumentation was completely different."

The technician frowned and went back to his work.

"The control panel has been a puzzlement to us," Mackern said, ignoring Hickock's comment. "The control surfaces are awkwardly arranged. Some are almost unreachable from the pilot's position."

Hickock seated himself in the acceleration couch. His fingers sought for—and found—the familiar ridges at the end of the armrests. They resisted his pressure. Then the plastic crumbled, disclosing the curved control buttons beneath.

"It minimizes reaction time to have them here," Hickock explained. "The pilot is also saved from having to strain against acceleration."

"Is that the reason for this?" Mackern asked, inspecting a helmet with a transparent visor that covered the entire facial area. "Crew members need protection from loose debris in the cabin?"

Hickock shook his head. "The visor is a screen for the fiber optics in the helmet. Ship's computer prioritizes data and flashes it directly in front of the pilot's eyes."

"Fascinating."

Hickock found the storage compartments and began unlatching them. They were empty, but he found grim satisfaction in being able to remember what they should have contained. Small arms. It made sense that those had been sequestered. But emergency rations?

"You find food threatening?" he asked Mackern.

"Everything can be dangerous," Mackern said impassively. "Your supplies are being examined for clues to your origin. Eating habits can be quite herd-specific."

Feeling frustrated, Hickock climbed out of the cabin. Unimportant memories floated on the surface of his mind. The important ones, so close that he could almost feel them, stayed resolutely hidden.

The work on the base of the saucer caught his attention. There was something wrong about the searing.

Mackern followed his gaze. "It burned from the inside out," he said.

"An overheated engine," Hickock said uneasily. "Or a power surge that jumped the superconductors—"

"A malfunctioning destruct device," Mackern countered. "Had it performed as designed, your entire craft would have been incinerated within a few seconds of splashdown.

"If I were you, I would seriously consider my loyalties. Effective as it is, your mind block appears to be only a fail-safe, to be activated in the unfortunate event that you survived capture. Your greatest present danger is not from us, or even from Skybreaker's agents, but from your own—"

There were furtive, rapid sounds behind him, and Hickock saw Mackern's eyes widening in alarm. He pivoted and ducked automatically. The metal muzzle was less than a meter away, still rising toward his eyes.

He sprang from his crouch, his left hand knocking aside the barrel as his right fist drove into the sternum of his attacker.

The welding laser clattered to the floor. The technician rolled with the punch, into the side of the saucer. Hickock's hand hurt, but not as much as it should have. Looking closely, he recognized that the technician's torso bulged with body-armor padding.

Unnecessary hands grabbed hold of him.

"You must forgive our guest," Mackern said to the technical supervisor. "He has been under intense strain for two weeks and tends to overreact."

There was no hint of apology or distress in Mackern's voice. Only quiet satisfaction.

vi

THE WIND BLEW OFF THE LAND, FLATTENING THE SWELL
that rolled in from the horizon. That was about as much
variation as one could expect on a planet whose axis of ro-
tation was inclined only two degrees to its orbit, and which
had no satellites and only negligible landmasses. "We have
much more variety in weather than almost any other place
on the planet," Yader had informed him with a straight face.
"Sometimes it rains, and sometimes it doesn't."

Hickock strode along the beach for his daily exercise. As
before, Vaheri paced him from behind. The waferphone in
his ear played a new set of word-association games: *"Au-
thorities: nurse, proctor, dorm reps, Mother, Father . . ."*

They were a welcome distraction. He could forget how
angry he was with his captors for tricking out of him information he did not know he possessed, and how angry he was
with himself for being angry. Self-control was crucial. Without it he had literally nothing at all.

Reeve's words of the night before came back to him,
seeming bitterly ironic in retrospect. One thing was absolutely certain: he was neither superman nor messiah. If
Reeve thought otherwise, it proved that any talent she possessed had burned itself out when she predicted his arrival
point.

Oddly enough, he felt relieved. It was bad enough not to know who his own people were, or if they were determined to have him dead rather than captive; bad enough to be in the custody of people who had already killed him once by mistake and would do so permanently if he were, for whatever inscrutable reason, perceived to be a threat. To add to those uncertainties the responsibilities of a messiah would be insupportable.

He listed what he had learned. Curious patterns were becoming evident in the scores of apparently unrelated facts about Innovator and its human herd. He had learned that he had been trained to defend himself and to pilot spacecraft. More interesting was his acquaintance with two fields of knowledge entirely forbidden to his captors—and the almost uncontrollable anger both sparked within him.

And he had known about the Go'el. His memory block was still at work, leaching the knowledge from his consciousness. Only traces were left. The Go'el was dead. So, as far as he knew, was everyone else in line. Therefore, he was Go'el. There was no content to that thought, other than of a duty unfulfilled.

Perhaps he was stranger than Mackern suspected.

He stopped, listening. A high, pulsating wail wafted above the cliffs from inland. It was almost lost in the sotto voce word games from the waferphone and the susurration of the wind.

"Hickock! Get to—" Static, like a high-pitched power saw, erupted from the waferphone. Wincing, Hickock pulled it from his ear.

Vaheri was running toward him, shouting incomprehensibly. Guards appeared on the cliff top, gesturing to him. As Hickock stared, trying to interpret their signals, they and the rock on which they were standing exploded, sending powdery landslides down to the beach.

Hickock trotted forward to the debris to see if anyone had

survived the fall. A manta-shaped shadow passed overhead. Two dark-suited figures dropped from the craft, hit the beach, and rolled to sitting positions. Each held large-barreled weapons pointed up at forty-five-degree angles. One weapon coughed with recoil. A second later, sand and a kind of fog burst around Vaheri. He fell forward. Even at the distance, Hickock could hear bone hitting rock.

Looking back at the attackers, he saw the second barrel shudder. He threw himself down, forcing his face into the cool, wet sand. The ground heaved. Sand stung the back of his hands, followed by a numbing coldness spreading over every square centimeter of exposed skin.

Hickock held his breath as long as he could, then slowly exhaled. The air he drew in was only slightly bitter.

He felt, rather than heard, footsteps approaching on either side. Hands grabbed him under each arm and dragged him quickly across the sand. Then he was lifted and thrown roughly onto metal flooring.

"Tie this meat up, Krane, and let's get the hell out of here."

That, Hickock decided, was not the way he would refer to a just-rescued colleague.

Engine noises crescendoed. The deck tilted beneath his back. He tensed, trying to discover if his muscles would still respond.

A metal binder snapped shut on his left wrist. Hickock opened his eyes. A man, presumably Krane, was leaning over him, reaching for his right hand. Hickock grabbed the forearm, planted his foot on the chest, and rocked backward. Krane grunted softly and hurtled over Hickock's head.

Hickock staggered to his feet. A strong wind rushed through the still-open doorway. The beach was receding into hazy distance. Choppy rows of waves fell away as the manta surged upward.

Krane's partner turned from the control panel by the cargo door. Seeing Hickock, he reached for the holster strapped to his thigh. Hickock whipped the free end of the binders in a short, flat arc. Coiled steel wrapped around the other's right arm. Hickock leaned away, pulling the man off balance, and pivoted, slamming his abductor's head against a metal strut.

There was movement behind him. Hickock swung the body around, ducking his head behind the chest. A groan that seemed torn from the lungs was accompanied by the sickening smell of burning flesh.

Holding his living shield before him, Hickock threw himself on Krane, cramming him into the wall. Krane's hand, grasping the laser, writhed around the body of his partner like a searching serpent.

Hickock grabbed the wrist as the manta banked. Krane's partner sagged, slid away from Hickock, and rolled across the deck and through the doorway. Krane levered himself off the wall, toppling both of them. Hickock twisted in the air, landing on top, but the slope of the floor had increased more than he had realized, and they rolled over and over until the wind roared brutally across his face. He stared up at clouds so close he could almost touch them while Krane's hands forced his chin back and back because there was nothing but air behind his head.

Hickock had instinctively been pressing every square centimeter of body he could against the deck to slow his slide. Suddenly he relaxed. Krane flailed out to save himself as Hickock slid beneath him. Suddenly released, Hickock grasped Krane with both arms and thrust him over his head.

Boots flutter-kicked his chest and were gone.

Hickock twisted convulsively and stretched himself flat on the deck. Centimeter by centimeter he crawled up the deck, away from the ravening open doorway.

He reached the companionway and pulled himself upright. Another jumpsuited figure was coming down the ladder. Looking up from the rungs, the newcomer let go of the railing and fumbled for his holster. Hickock swung the binders around his neck and yanked. As they stumbled together, Hickock pressed the laser against the attacker's side and fired. He held on to the laser as its owner tumbled the rest of the way down to the cargo bay.

Pointing the laser high in front of him, he advanced the rest of the way up the ladder. His head rose into the cockpit which was domed with clear plastic. The chair to the right was empty. A hand extending from the left-hand chair clenched a joystick. Hickock touched the laser to the back of the chair and pulled the trigger.

The hand jerked back. The manta lurched and began a long, downward turn.

Hickock unsnapped the harness and shoved the pilot down the companionway. Seating himself in the pilot's chair, he steadied the joystick, trying to bring the manta level.

"Grab Bag Leader to Grab Bag One. Bring your heading around to one-seven-four. Hostile craft are three minutes from intercept on your current course."

He had worked with a similar control board in his "dream" of the night before. A yellow dot blinked in the center of a green display. A landform, outlined in red, receded to the right side of the screen. That would be Freair. Four other yellow dots defined a square around the central dot, which was, he realized, his own craft. Ten red dots appeared from the screen's edge, closing rapidly.

He looked through the canopy. The manta was skimming above a nearly flat layer of gray clouds. Black wedges far off to either side were half the Grab Bag escort force. There was no sign of his pursuers.

"Grab Bag One, your cargo door is still open. Report your status."

Hickock snapped on the dangling headset.

"Grab Bag Leader," he said, rubbing a metal button on his watch across the microphone in what he prayed would be a convincing imitation of static. "Our grab . . . booby-trapped . . . exploded in the cargo bay. Can't close the bay door . . . won't respond to controls . . ."

That should explain why his path was slowly curving around. If he could ditch the manta reasonably close to shore, he might be able to swim the rest of the way in. In the meantime, Innovator's fighters should chase off his unwelcome escort.

"Grab Bag Force, this is Grab Bag Leader. Grab Bag One has been converted by prey. Delete, repeat, delete."

So much for that idea. On the display, the escort fighters began converging on the central dot.

Hickock pushed the joystick as far left and forward as it would go. The manta turned sharply and abruptly fell into a sickening slide. He jerked the joystick back and forth with growing expertise, fighting a wobble that threatened to degenerate into an uncontrollable spin. Clouds boiled around the canopy.

He pulled out of the turn and set his heading for the mainland. The fighters that had been his rear guard dropped quickly to meet him. Hickock bit his lip, knowing that the manta could never outmaneuver fighters, even without the drag of the open cargo door. Since he had no idea of the manta's weaponry, if any, fighting them would be just as futile.

Three seconds to unity. Two seconds. One second.

Hickock forced the joystick hard left, clenching its head for maximum thrust. The manta flipped up on its side, presenting for that instant the thinnest possible silhouette to the attackers. Streaks of heat seared across the fuselage. Swathes of black, radar-absorbent coating vaporized, disclosing gleaming metal beneath.

Then the attackers were kilometers behind him. High relative velocities and Hickock's last-minute evasive action had kept the lasers from focusing long on any one spot. That tactic would not work a second time. The second group of fighters was rapidly overtaking him. In just a few seconds, they would be directly above, matching speed and firing at their leisure.

The manta dropped through the bottom layer of clouds. He had to get down on the deck and ditch as quickly as possible. Clouds had shortened the range of the lasers to the point that the attackers had had to be right on top of him before firing. Below the clouds, their range was limited only by the curve of the horizon.

He put the manta into the steepest dive he could control. The ocean below was gunmetal gray, lined with crest after crest of waves. A dark, uneven line joined sea to sky.

On the display, the nearest yellow dot touched his. Hickock involuntarily tensed his neck in anticipation of the blast, raging at the unfairness of being killed within sight of safety.

The explosion was like a sudden flash of heat lightning. A second later, the shock wave caught the manta, flinging it into an uncontrolled spin.

Fighting the joystick, he saw from the corner of his eye the remaining yellow dot shear away from the approaching red line. Then it, too, flared and disappeared.

Ocean and sky slowed their insane cartwheeling, rocked vertically left and right, and steadied in their accustomed positions. Hickock pulled straight back on the joystick, squeezing as much power from the engines as either he or the shuddering manta could stand.

The manta leveled out not two meters above the water. Rows of waves blurred past beneath like miniature mountain ranges.

Now if I can gain just a bit of altitude and turn inland . . .

Dipping slightly into the turn, the manta's left edge decapitated a row of waves. It whirled like a top, sending up a long line of spray as it cut itself deep under the surface.

Salt on knuckle cuts stung him back to wakefulness. Hickock opened his eyes and watched without interest as waves swirled up the sides of the canopy and subsided. Smaller waves, inside the cockpit, broke across his arms.

One slapped his face. He coughed and snorted the sharp saltiness out of his air tubes. Fully awake, he punched the harness release and floated free of the seat. He took three deep breaths and dived down the companionway.

The uprush of the water and his own natural buoyancy hindered him. He grabbed the railing and pulled himself down, hand over hand. His lungs ached. He would have floated back to the cockpit for another breath had he believed any air remained.

Swirling darkness met him at the base of the companionway. A gray rectangle tilted halfway up to vertical marked the open doorway. Hickock kicked himself over to it, grabbed the upper lip, and propelled himself upward.

His breath exploded from his lips as he broke surface. For a few minutes he floated, pulling in deep gulps of air, expending only that minimal effort necessary to keep his mouth above water.

All around him, trough to crest to trough again, was rhythmically heaving grayness. His eyes searched the horizon with a growing sense of panic. He saw nothing but line after line of ever-diminishing waves, churning white on black into the distance.

Then, from the crest of one wave, he saw a dark, irregular line whose very stability marked it alien to the ever-changing choppiness. He dropped into a trough and paddled swiftly to maintain his orientation.

It might be just a bank of clouds, he thought anxiously.

At the crest of the next wave, he craned his neck as high

as he could out of the water. There was no doubt. Ahead, pink beaches underlined long, low cliffs.

His left arm ached. The binder still clasped his left wrist, steadily pulling him down. He wondered how long it would be before the weight drained away his stamina.

Taking his bearings once more, he began swimming with strong, slow strokes to shore.

vii

MACKERN ENTERED THE WAITING ROOM, SURVEYING IT with one quick unobtrusive glance. Small groups of two and three stood about in earnest, low-voiced discussions. Several tried to catch his eye. He ignored them, wrapping himself in inviolable privacy.

"Well, at least we now know what to do with your mystery boy," Hollings had said earlier. "Give him a commission! In one action, he's given those Skybreaker bastards a lesson they've needed for more than a year."

The problem was that both knew administration of the lesson had been mainly a matter of luck, that the manta and its fighters should never have been able to penetrate within fifty kilometers of Freair. The base of Mackern's stomach clenched as he realized who would undoubtedly bear a good deal of the blame.

Across the room, Rasloe, of Population Resources, put up a finger to get his attention. Mackern turned away, pretending to study a part of the mural that girdled all four walls of the room. In fact, the entire room was worthy of consideration. The black-and-white-tiled floor, for instance—was there anything to the story that it had been designed to remind herd leaders that they were about to step onto a game board, one on which every play was not only for their individual lives but also for the survival of their race?

Then there was the mural itself. On its face, it conformed in every particular to the explanation given every touring class of schoolchildren. In the top corner, flares like flaming scythes erupted from a ravening sun. Below, fire storms swept over grasslands and forests. The upper stories of city buildings blazed like giants' torches.

In a clearing that might have been a city park, colored in cool blues and greens and taking up nearly all of one wall, hovered one of the Shapers' huge, saucer-shaped starships. A line of families carefully chosen to represent every race and ethnic group wound through the clearing, dwindling to ant size below the interstellar ark. Most of the men and women stood with eyes and hands upraised, as if giving thanks to their celestial saviors. A member of the Church of the Deliverance could have made the message no plainer.

Yet here and there the discerning eye noted jarring details. Was that man shielding his face in horror from a burning building or from something he saw inside the starship? For that matter, was it only Mackern's own perverse temperament that saw, in the lowered entry to the starship, a striking resemblance to a carnivore's open mouth?

Mackern had never prided himself on artistic insight, but the small golden plaque on the far wall, so apparently unrelated to the subject matter of the painting, was all the confirmation he needed of such arguably treasonous thoughts.

Those who have eyes, let them see.

Yes. Yes, indeed.

A doorway clicked open. Chamberlain Jose Rivera stood in the doorway of the Leaders' Hall.

"All are now assembled," he announced in his dry, quiet voice. There was no need to emphasize the fact that all humans had been assembled for twenty minutes. "Deliberations may now commence."

Well then, Mackern thought, striding purposefully across the black and white tiles. Once more onto the game board.

Since he was not himself a herd leader, Mackern sat on a back bench. He glanced up involuntarily at the minicam with the fisheye lens hanging from the ceiling. A small red light warned him that the camera was on.

War Minister Dalkan stood without preliminaries.

"Yesterday at thirteen-twenty hours, five aerial warcraft, since identified as emanating from Skybreaker's lineage group, penetrated our airspace. During this time, ground radar was inoperative for a crucial twenty minutes.

"Two of our coastal patrol craft were lost to the attackers. One of the attackers, a cargo carrier, landed on the beach roughly three kilometers south of this room. It took off after abducting one of the assets of the Special Projects Office. That asset, a young man of unknown origin who had been undergoing intensive interrogation, was able to take control of the cargo carrier and divert it back to our waters. The asset was recovered. All participating Skybreaker craft were destroyed."

There was an appreciative muttering. Like Hollings, they had not appreciated the full extent of the disaster. Dalkan did. Mackern had been surprised when the low-keyed, almost scholarly man had been chosen for what was arguably the most important herd leadership post, the more so since many of his counterparts in other herds would charitably have been called berserkers.

Dalkan, however, had talents that were too easily underestimated. The first was a loyalty to Innovator that was completely natural and so had not been purchased with the impairment of intelligence and initiative that was the price of genetic indoctrination.

That intelligence was, perhaps, even more highly prized by Innovator than the loyalty. Dalkan knew the exact tactical weight of every battle unit from the spur-shelled warrior spawn—which had been produced by Shapers in basically unchanging pattern for the past three million years—to the latest deep-space cruisers. He also had a nearly intuitive feel for the total battle strength of each of the twenty most powerful Patriarchs. In the five years that Dalkan had been war minister, Innovator had grown in influence from a second-rate lineage group needing to swing from alliance to alliance to keep from being devoured, to one of the dozen most powerful.

Dalkan did not look especially proud of that at the moment.

Mackern regarded him sympathetically. What the war minister would say next, if his integrity was sufficient to overcome well-founded fears, would be treason per se in most lineage groups. The fact that Mackern would be the main course would be little consolation to Dalkan if his own head were the appetizer.

"The ground radar situation has been corrected. Skybreaker's agent has been apprehended, questioned, and deleted. Security measures have been tightened to prevent a recurrence.

"Much more disturbing has been the failure of the orbital pickets. They should have signaled a yellow alert as soon as Skybreaker's task force left its own territory. In fact, no input was received from them until a somewhat confused message reported the explosions of the last two fighters.

"Inquiries concerning this breakdown have been hampered by the bifurcated command chain—" Dalkan's voice broke. He rubbed a knuckle across his upper lip to cover it. "But it appears that the I-spawn in the orbital stations have been receiving only sporadic and sometimes contradictory instructions.

"Furthermore, their efficiency has been compromised by lack of necessary supplies, particularly for the water regeneration facilities. Oxygen content had fallen to critical levels.

Had this continued as much as a week more, the stations would have become totally inoperative.

"I-spawn prime on each station were aware of the situation, but did not complain because their indoctrination led them to believe that such action would be disloyal."

Dalkan grimaced. "Remedial measures—"

"I am in pain."

Dalkan stopped short, his face suddenly white. Every other person in the room had become rigidly attentive.

The voice itself was not extraordinary, although the consonants were especially soft and fluid. This was the result of implanting a small microphone in a throat that, however modified, was still basically human.

That for which the Speaker interpreted most emphatically was not.

"Why have you done this to me, Mackern?" the Speaker continued. The voice came equally from walls and ceiling. *"Do you wish my death, the shattering of my lineage group? Do you wish to lead a rogue herd?"*

Palms slapped impact-resistant plastic. Raising his head, Mackern looked down a laser barrel, its tip a small o of perpetual astonishment. By mistake, he met the eyes of the guard holding it. The determination, corrupted by pity, that he saw unnerved him. No young man should have to feel either sorrow or guilt in carrying out what would clearly be his duty—if it came to that.

After all, you have had dozens of good years. More than most ever get.

"I desire nothing but your continued life and the increase of your lineage group," Mackern said, distantly pleased with the steadiness of his voice.

"I diminish." Somehow that soft, emotionless voice conveyed the essence of agony. *"I devour myself. My thoughts . . . fragment. Dream shards invade my consciousness."*

"As sovereign, you may discard my regimen and resume

your former eating habits," Mackern said evenly. It's testing me, he thought. It is in real distress, but all it wants is reassurance.

Kept firmly in the back of his mind was the possibility that he had made a basic miscalculation. He was all too aware that his work with Innovator was both unprecedented and profoundly unnatural.

"Is that your advice?"

"No," Mackern said. "It is not. All our research on Shapers and related species—" Of whom there were damned few. Like *Homo sapiens*, Shapers had consolidated their position at the top of their evolutionary tree with the extermination of all their nearest rivals. "—shows conclusively that the feeding-growth feedback cycle is the principle cause of aging and death among Shapers. You have already grown close to critical size. Much larger, and your neural network will be desynchronized. As the biochemical signals within your body fall out of phase, your thoughts will become confused and your reflexes spastic. This biological noise will establish its own fatal resonance. You will have 'grown to engulf the stars.' "

"Already there is confusion. I cannot control my spawn. I cannot defend the group. Soon the other lineage groups will discern this."

The herd leaders were staring at Mackern with tight-lipped fear. Rasloe's bald head glistened with sweat. Even if Innovator did not give the order for Mackern's execution, some of his peers might take matters into their own hands if they became frightened enough. Despite their surface sophistication, several were more than slightly influenced by the Church of the Deliverance. They might laugh at the notion that Shapers were direct manifestations of God, deny that Innovator was their personal savior, but in their heart of hearts . . .

What would be considered an appropriate punishment for attempted deicide?

"I understand your distress," Mackern said. "I warned you to expect it. Death has been evolution's handmaiden for a billion years on this planet. It is unreasonable to expect to cheat it without difficulty.

"We scheduled your regeneration attempt for a period of relative political calm. It is as unfortunate as it is unexpected that our seizure of Hickock has catalyzed the situation.

"However, you should not underestimate the extent of your success. You have shed nearly two tonnes. All the reports I receive from mers, speakers, and my own research staff indicate that your health is basically sound. You will not have as good an opportunity in the foreseeable future.

"My advice is that you continue my regimen at least one more budding period. By the end of that time, the worst will be over. New strength, new clarity will flood through you."

Having run out of things to say, Mackern fell silent, feeling like a salesman who has been accused of puffing. If the reaction of his peers could be any guide, he should make a quick peace with the Almighty. Silence stretched into an encapsulated eternity.

"*Hickock.*" It was as if Innovator had lost the train of thought midway through Mackern's speech. "*Bring the creature before me . . . for evaluation.*"

viii

Inside the tube, Hickock had no way of knowing when the magna-car slid beneath the waves. It was nearly impossible to tell that they were even moving. An almost imperceptible downward slope, occasional nudges to the left or right as the car's inertia fought the irresistible restraint of a curve, were the only hints that the car was going well over 150 kilometers per hour.

A row of buttons was set into the wall above Hickock's armrest. Curious, he pushed one at random. Part of the wall seemed to fall away, revealing the tube wall blurring by so quickly that it appeared paradoxically motionless. He was about to shut it off when they shot into a six-level-high switching ganglion. Cars like their own shuttled in with no appreciable deceleration, shifted up or down to their proper tracks, and sped out in less than five seconds.

He tested the other buttons. The car's routing computer revealed itself, spreading a white net on a field of blue. A rectangular legend disclosed which nexuses were switching ganglions and which were submarine cities. At Hickock's insistence, Mackern grudgingly supplemented that data.

Nearest the land were the shallow sea farms. Traditionally ignored by the Shapers, those nutrient-rich waters were now intensively exploited in cultivating aquatons, the single-celled base of the food chain.

In deeper waters, turbulence tractors plowed across the ocean floor, masticating thousands of years' worth of sedimentary goo and sending it up in hot-water plumes to the lighted layers, where it made a sort of broth for the nourishment of aquatons. Where the ground was too rocky for that, bladder weed anchored itself to boulders and spiraled into complex floating jungles.

"Agriculture is an alien concept to Shapers," Mackern said, "one which has taken root, so to speak, only within their last generation—that is, within the last two hundred years.

"Before that, adult Shapers established their own hunting domains, marine equivalents of the kings' forests on medieval Earth. There they would pursue and devour whatever pleased them, particularly the sharphin, which were their only real competitors at the top of the food chain. Their hunting spawn would encircle the sharphin herds with sonic nets hundreds of kilometers wide and tighten the nets until the sharphin were so close together they could hardly move. Then the Shapers of the lineage group would rise, led by their Patriarch, and glut themselves.

"From the air, the sea looked like a raw, open wound.

"The story comes down to us from the time of Starfinder, Patriarch before Innovator. In those days, sharphin had become scarce from overhunting, and those that remained had become increasingly clever in avoiding hunting parties.

"Jacques Bouvier, a herd leader among the humans, proposed capturing sharphin and breeding them. A minimal number of hunting spawn could keep them in bays rich with aquavians which are their dietary mainstay. With one stroke, Starfinder could assure its own supply of sharphin and deny it to all competing lineage groups."

Hickock remembered the night on the terrace, the wings of aquavians cutting almost silently through the darkness.

The bay beneath them had been a breeding pen. Probably everyone on the terrace, everyone in Freair, except himself, had known that.

How much else, he wondered with a twinge of desperation, had he seen and, in total incomprehension, completely ignored?

"You would think nothing could have been more obvious to Starfinder, especially once it had been pointed out to it. After all, Starfinder was one of the most sophisticated of its generation. It was one of forty-odd Patriarchs to develop interstellar drive roughly simultaneously. It was one of the fifteen to participate in the rescue of humanity from Earth; one of the half-dozen with enough insight into our race to keep from inadvertently destroying its herd.

"Yet for the longest time, Starfinder found the concept of self-interestedly aiding one's prey totally incomprehensible. At one point it argued that the entire concept violated the second law of thermodynamics, maintaining that the energy spent providing for the prey had to be less than that obtained when they were slaughtered.

"Bouvier's logic was compelling enough that eventually Starfinder allowed a pilot project. But even when that proved itself successful, Starfinder would still converse with him for hours on end concerning the paradoxes inherent in animal husbandry and agriculture.

"Many of the Shapers were unwilling to make the experiment. Their lines are all but extinct."

The magna-car raced beyond the seas devoted to aquaculture. The tube assumed a steeper slant, from the subcoastal plains to the muddy bottom lands. Above them, the ocean was a warm desert, traversed at seasonal intervals by horizon-spanning clouds of jumpersquid, skipping themselves in low arcs across the surface. Aquavians would follow, darting in and out of the living clouds to feed. Those that came too low too long would be grabbed out of the air by schools of leaping sharphin. And following the sharphin would come the Shapers' hunting spawn.

Two hours more and they would cross the Rift, where the planet gave birth to itself at the rate of one centimeter a year, pushing out new seafloor, spewing out sulfur and metallic oxides through cobalt and ocher cones. The Rift was home to Innovator's morphions, which filter-fed on the dissolved metals and metabolized them into the ceramic alloys of everything from superconducting cable to starship hulls.

An hour beyond the Rift was their destination: the Abyss.

Mackern checked with Hollings in the adjoining guard car over the intercom. There were no further messages from Dalkan nor from Innovator.

"Don't you think you are taking this too seriously?" Hickock asked, noting Mackern's fretfulness. "Vaheri insists that Innovator is the most humane of Shapers. I understand that you had fears when Reeve was called for a similar audience. They turned out to be groundless."

Mackern showed no surprise at Hickock's knowledge of Reeve's experience. "The ground rules were simple for Reeve. There was to be a test. I knew its general content. I feared she would fail, and in that, I admit, I was wrong.

"Your case is entirely different. Even after all we have learned, you are still a complete mystery. I have no idea what Innovator wants with you. I wish I were sure Innovator knew."

Hickock cocked his head, waiting for an explanation.

"Its self-diagnosis may just possibly be accurate. It may be insane."

"How do you judge insanity in a genus in which each individual considers itself a separate species?" Hickock asked.

"It is not easy," Mackern said morosely. "I hope you don't consider that concept itself crazy, however. It is probably the most important insight Reeve has given us into our masters.

"Never forget that Shapers reproduce unisexually. There is never any lateral mixing of genes. Environmental adaptations and mutations transfer vertically only, from Shaper to spawn. Theoretically, there is no reason why any two Shapers should not be separated by more than a million years of evolutionary divergence."

Hickock considered that fact in silence. He swayed slightly as the magna-car rushed through another switching ganglion. The routing computer displayed the population and industrial data of the nearest submarine city.

"Have you then been taken in by your own semantics?" he asked. "Are we dealing with half a hundred intelligent races instead of one? Unless divergence has been limited by a played out genetic structure—no, damn it, the whole point about Shapers is the directability of the genetic coding . . ."

Mackern grunted, somehow pleased with the question. "Theory is constrained by reality. It appears that every ten to twenty generations, Shapers suffer a population collapse. Often in the past, they have been caused by a population excess that has overstressed the food chain. The most recent occurred after the Deliverance with the introduction of human herds to supplement and in some cases take the place of Shaper spawn."

"We are deleterious to Shapers?" Hickock asked. "Then why—"

"We are the biological equivalent of thermonuclear weapons," Mackern said wryly. "Fifteen Patriarchs participated in the Deliverance. At that time, there were some three hundred Patriarchs on the planet. One Shaper generation later, half the surviving lineage groups had human herds. Two generations later, all Shapers were descendants of those first fifteen. At crucial tasks, we were so much more effective than Shaper spawn that all Shapers without human herds were exterminated. Our very success caused the collapse.

"Judeo-Christian mythology records two population bottlenecks for our race. The first was with our original parents; the second with Noah's family. This seems to be the normal evolutionary mechanism with Shapers."

The magna-car doors slid open three uneventful hours later. Surrounded by a cordon of guards, Hickock and Mackern stepped into a nearly silent station. Red-garbed hulks faced them, holding rifles at port arms. In front of them, Hollings conferred with his counterpart.

"This is the human component of Innovator's bodyguard," Mackern murmured. "We are about to be turned over to them. Obey any commands instantly."

Hickock nodded.

Their own guards stepped backward, pivoted, and reentered their car. The red guard commander glanced quickly over Hickock and Mackern and barked a one-word order. "Strip."

Following Mackern's example, Hickock shed his clothes, careful to move slowly enough not to startle the guards, yet not so slowly as to appear to be malingering.

The nude Mackern was something of a surprise. There was less flab and more muscle than Hickock would have guessed. His well-trimmed beard gave his face the appearance of still being formally dressed. He looked incongruously top heavy.

"In there." The red commander pointed to a brightly lighted tunnel. "You first," he said to Hickock.

Cameras swiveled to greet him as Hickock entered the tunnel. The floor jerked into motion, carrying him forward at its own measured pace. The glowing walls flared into painful incandescence. At the same time, a prickling raced through him, separating each hair from its neighbor. It was like being forced through an invisible sieve.

The floor stopped. Hickock found he could open his eyes. Black briefs, rebreathing harness, and face mask hung on the wall. A hulk—guard? guide? attendant?—indistinguishable from those on the other side of the wall said, "Yours."

Hickock slipped on the briefs. Mackern helped him adjust harness and face mask. A rubbery substance suck-sealed the mask along forehead, temples, mastoids, and under the line of his jaw. He adjusted a chest knob. Air smelling of plastic and metal, hissed into the mask.

"Communications check." Mackern's voice was stereophonically crisp. "Confirm operational status."

"Confirmed." Hickock replied.

Part of the wall slid back, disclosing a vaguely humanoid form in an elevator.

"Your Speaker will guide you from here," the hulk informed them.

Hickock approached it slowly, fascinated with each detail that proximity brought to his attention.

"Just a modified mer." Mackern's voice in the earphones sounded impatient. "It needs to breathe oxygen-enriched water to support a normal-sized braincase. That is the only important difference."

The creature stood midway in stature between the hulks and normal humans. It was pear-shaped with blubber. The almost hairless skin was a mottled blue-black.

The head commanded the most attention. From the top of the skull to the eyes, the oddness was controlled: no more than baldness, smudge on smudge coloring, and a nearly submerged tracery of veins.

Then the nostrils split and widened. Two spongy bags spilled from them, attaching themselves to the cheeks before falling to chest level. There was more three-dimensional complexity to them than Hickock could take in at once. He wondered what the function of those organs could be.

He felt himself lighten as the elevator descended.

"Hickock." The Speaker's lips were motionless. Looking closely, Hickock thought he saw the flutter of an Adam's apple.

"Innovator desires your immediate presence," the voice in his ears continued. "You will follow us to the Nares. Replenishment of food and air will be provided as needed."

"How long will this audience last?" Hickock asked.

The Speaker looked mildly surprised. "As long as it may please Innovator," it said in a tone of gentle reproof.

Mackern's voice was low in his ears. "It is said that fifty years ago Rupert Kaiser spent three days and nights expounding the Kemp-annotated version of Smith's *Wealth of Nations* to Innovator. That time period has a legendary air to it, but it may be accurate. The larger brains of Shapers lead to longer attention spans. Marathon sessions are not uncommon."

The elevator doors slid aside. Hickock followed the Speaker into a pale, translucent tunnel. Floor, walls, and ceiling curved indistinguishably into each other. The Speaker walked slowly, as if pained by its abnormally long feet and webbed toes. Large dimples in the floor, smooth dips and rises of no apparent pattern, forced Hickock and Mackern into an awkward, mincing step. The whiteness was tinted with yellows and browns. Ripples played across the surfaces, like sand just beneath the waves, or the ribs of a huge beast as seen from within.

"Morphion extrusions," Mackern explained. "We have left human territory."

The tunnel swelled into a hemispherical node and dead-ended. The Speaker directed Hickock to the center. It pulled a tether from the center of the floor and snapped it onto Hickock's belt.

"What is this for?" Hickock asked as the Speaker repeated the procedure with Mackern.

"The current will flow from you to Innovator," it explained patiently, "so that it may taste you fully. Innovator, *now*, desires that no harm befall you. However, Dr. Mack-ern's regeneration procedure has subjected it to considerable stress.'' Was there just a hint of reproachfulness in that soft voice? ''The stomachs swim about in unnatural agitation. Were you to drift too near, they might digest you before Innovator could intervene.''

Water lapped over his feet. Coldness cut to the bone. Goose bumps kept pace with the water level.

He blinked. Memory images played across the insides of his eyelids. Waves breaking across his knuckles in the cock-pit of the manta. The swelling pressure in chest and throat of starved lungs as he swam down against inrushing ocean.

And an earlier memory, shocking in its vividness. Sweet blood from his nose trickling into his mouth. The ache of bruises crisscrossing limbs and torso. Water gushing in from the ceiling and exploding into superheated steam as it touched the burning deck.

He opened his eyes. The water reached his chest. The Speaker's nose/chest bags had inflated and tautened with shining good health as they entered their natural environ-ment. Straw-colored cilia waved happily in the flow.

The light dimmed. Waves washed over his face mask, closing in on him claustrophobically. He forced slow, even breaths.

When the chamber was full, ceiling and walls dilated open, sliding beneath floor level. Hickock floated above an open platform. A tug from his tether stopped his drifting. Cold water, gently insistent, flowed around him.

The Speaker lifted a meter-long vented cylinder. Its upper surface was broken by a complex series of buttons and knobs. Slipping its hands through the wrist binders at either end of the cylinder, it kicked itself free of the platform.

Hickock's pupils widened, drinking in dimness. There was just enough light to make out a large gray wall curving into darkness. In front of it, spherical masses of tentacles propelled themselves in seemingly random directions. A few had attached themselves to the wall. One that was pushing itself away from the wall appeared both smaller and more energetic than the rest. Humanoid figures—other Speakers? mers?—swam in silhouette. Using them for scale, he estimated the distance to the wall as less than twenty meters. If they were to converse with Innovator, the Shaper would have to be considerably smaller than Reeve and Mackern had implied.

The wall opened an eye. It had to be nearly two meters in diameter. Waves of color roiled out from the perimeter of the eye to the shadows. Three equally spaced depressions deepened around the eye. Flesh mounded into funnels around them. The funnels pointed at him.

". . . worry," Mackern was saying. ". . . unpleasant but not . . ."

A subsonic thrumming stirred the waters around him, drowning out the voice. It seized his face mask, vibrating it like a snare drum and almost shaking it from his face.

Abruptly the focus became sure of itself. Sonic fists massaged the inside of his chest cavity. They walked themselves up his spine, vertebra by vertebra, ascended the neck, and spilled into the hollow roundness of his skull. Sonic fingers defined teeth down to their roots and explored the twisting narrow cavities of his sinuses.

Then it went back down, doing a xylophone riff along his ribs, pressing against the solidity of pelvis and femurs brushing quickly to the end of tarsals and metatarsals.

The vibration ceased. He hung limply in the water, exhausted by an ordeal that could have lasted little more than a minute. His breathing rasped harshly in his ears.

A large round shape blocked the light. Hickock twisted around, forcing watery eyes into focus.

His first impression of tentacles had been . . . imprecise. The long, cylindrical extensions more closely resembled tubeworms. Their lengths were delicately tinted rose and jade. A primitive eye tipped each end.

The creature surged closer, stretching toward him. Hickock's mouth went dry. He reached back for his tether, remembering the Speaker's warning.

"This stomach is under Innovator's direct control." The Speaker's voice was calm. "You must allow it to sample you."

That, he thought, depends entirely on how big a sample it wants.

Long, flat tissues, pinkly translucent, extended beyond the tubes. One lolled out, like suddenly liquid ribbon candy, and wrapped itself around a leg. It was cool and rough, fine-grade living sandpaper. Long lines ran lengthwise along it. A sudden sting surprised his thigh. One of the lines pulsed red.

The tissue slid off and retracted. The tubes ceased the wavelike pulsations that had held the stomach against the current. It drifted back and merged with the wall of flesh.

"You taste . . . old." The Speaker's voice conveyed a sense of puzzlement that might have been its own or the Shaper's. Hickock wondered how even genetic modification and a lifetime of training could enable humans to decipher the chemical scents, the sub- and supersonics that were language to these creatures.

"Your genes are muddled," the Speaker continued. "I have never tasted any so unordered." There was silence. "Starfinder did." Another silence. "Your codons reveal no mark."

It changed the subject abruptly. "You have knowledge concerning radio astronomy. And thermonuclear fusion."

He knew enough to recognize that each answer could be a death sentence.

"Yes."

"What do you know of stardrives?"

Hickock shook his head helplessly. The question sparked
only shadow images: page after page of complex mathemat-
ical notation. Curved lines on a screen representing a flight
path through ten spatial dimensions. An instant's vertigo as
space-time was seized and *twisted* . . .

"You hide yourself. You respond with the greatest reluctance to my appendage Mackern."

"No." His voice was so small and dry that his microphone might not have been able to pick it up.

"The answer does lurk within you. It shall rise at my
command."

The thrumming began again, stronger and more strident.
Columns of water crawled up his skin.

"What are you? What is your purpose?" There was no
pause between the two questions, as if they were alternative
translations of one query.

"I do not know."

Sound formed a wall before him and thrust him back before it. An invisible barrier held him firm. The sound wave
thundered through him like a breaker crashing against a cliff.

"What are you? What is your purpose?"

"I don't *know*!"

Another sound wave broke through his body. Scores of
tendrils dredged his depths, creating a discomfort deeper than
pain.

"Whatareyouwhatisyourpurpose?"

The sound shredded nerve fibers. A scream ripped from
his throat.

The thrumming ceased. Hickock drifted, barely conscious.

"A Go'el. Explain the term."

Had that been in his scream? "A Go'el—" Astonishment
flooded him because, for that instant at least, he knew the
answer. "—is a champion. A protector."

"Protector of what?"

The memory block slipped back into place. "Protector of the group," he said desperately.

"What herd?" The thrumming recommenced, threatening, impatient.

"Innovator." Mackern's voice was loud and hoarse in Hickock's ears. "I have tried to force the subject's memory block. It is useless. He is programmed to self-destruct rather than reveal certain categories of information."

"You challenge my right to order his deletion."

"Of—of course not," Mackern said, voice quavering. "But as your appendage I am bound to recommend what I feel to be in your best interest. Hickock's value, though unquantified, is clearly substantial. He has had access to forbidden information. He is worth maintaining just to discover its source and its extent. Skybreaker has shown the value it places on him by risking—"

"If you had the intellectual capacity to understand my self-interest, you would be Shaper instead of appendage." The voice was devoid of bitterness or hauteur. Hickock could imagine using the same tone to a four-year-old while explaining why playing with an electric knife was forbidden.

"This creature has come close to involving the lineage group in a war I cannot presently afford. Its purpose here is destruction. It would delight in the death of all Shapers, in seeing these oceans boil into steam."

"That is not true!" Hickock protested. "I didn't even know you existed. How could I want to destroy you?"

He saw the flaw in his own position as soon as the words left his mouth. Without his memories, he could not be sure that he had not known of Innovator. Horrifying as it was, he could not *know* that he had not intended the incineration of the planet.

An amnesiac, he reflected bitterly, was at a double disadvantage when arguing with a possibly insane solipsist.

"You had no memories of Skybreaker," the Speaker responded, ''yet we know that your craft was involved in action against its space arm.''

''Skybreaker is your enemy. If my people are at war with it, we have a common interest.''

There was no response. Two stomachs detached themselves from Innovator, their tubes stroking in time against the current. At three meters, they swerved into the darkness on either side.

Innovator's eye closed. The current ceased.

''This audience is over,'' the Speaker said.

Slowly the tether reeled him back to the floor of the Nares.

ix

A FLUORESCENT DISPLAY SCREEN COVERED ONE ENTIRE WALL of Dalkan's office. At present, it showed a real-time—or as close to that as the continuous stream of incoming intelligence reports could make it—projection of the planet's surface, overlaid by colored borders indicating the domains of the lineage groups. Two such adjoining domains were highlighted: Seaking was carrying its war against Balancer into the latter's territory. Computer extrapolations predicted Balancer's imminent collapse.

At any given point in time, the map might show as many as a dozen such conflicts. Most ended indecisively, or with only minor adjustments to borders.

Seated across from Dalkan were Colonel Garrison and Jason Yader. The war minister lifted a paper from the whorled surface of his marbline desk and handed it to Garrison.

"The order for Hickock's deletion," Dalkan said. "I signed it two hours ago."

Garrison nodded, reading with satisfaction. "You won't regret taking my recommendation in this. However potentially valuable this Hickock may be, we simply do not have the time for Mackern to tease any more information out of him. Nor can we let another herd at him. This is the only logical result, distasteful as it may be." He glanced sharply at Yader, then rose from his chair. "I will have Yader carry—"

"Sit back down," Dalkan said. "I was giving you background. This order was countermanded less than fifteen minutes after I signed it."

He met Garrison's almost comical look of surprise with a grim smile. "By Innovator. It concurs with the first part of your own assessment. We do not have the time to break through Hickock's conditioning. Another attack like Skybreaker's may have consequences far more serious than the loss of Hickock. It might well reveal to the other lineage groups just how weak Innovator presently is.

"It notes that when Starswallower devoured Explorer, it eliminated all our assets in both herds. The thoroughness with which this was achieved suggests a psycho-probing capability exceeding our own. It is Innovator's command that we provide Hickock to Starswallower to determine if its techniques are in fact more effective than our own."

"How does it help us if they are?" Garrison asked.

"Hickock would, of course, be accompanied by one of our own men. As soon as the memory block was removed, Hickock would be abducted and returned to us."

Garrison wiped his neck with a handkerchief. "You make it sound so easy," he muttered.

"Now I understand why you asked for my presence," Yader said cheerfully. "You think that one of my 'siblings' can smuggle me past whatever psychological screening Starswallower's herd may use."

Dalkan nodded. "Yes."

"I think we have an excellent chance of pulling it off," Yader said seriously. "At the very least, we will learn whether Project Hydra has been a worthwhile investment."

"Neither of you realize how inconsistent you are being," Garrison complained. "If Starswallower's psychotechs are good enough to break Hickock's conditioning, they should also be good enough to see through Yader's 'siblings.' Conversely, if Yader is not unmasked, their luck with Hickock should be no better than our own.''

''In which case, we will be no worse off than we are now,'' Dalkan responded, ''while Starswallower will have to protect its new treasure from Skybreaker and others. Remember also that the only plausible hypothesis we have of Hickock's origin is that he comes from a herd that went rogue when Starswallower devoured Explorer. If that is the case, Starswallower's herd may be able to ascertain it without recourse to psychotechnics.''

Dalkan paused, wondering how much of what he would say next should be heard by Yader, since the agent might well be caught and broken under interrogation by Starswallower's herd. All of it, he decided. Especially if he were broken. Some truths would acquire credibility only in that way.

''My honest guess is that Innovator considers the situation urgent enough to be worth a long shot. It does not usually confide its motives to me, but I believe it was influenced by this piece of intelligence we received only twelve hours ago.''

He touched a button on his desk. The world map was replaced by a schematic of the star system. The point of view zoomed in on the primary planetoid belt. One irregular speck in a floating field of similar specks glowed red.

''Spaceswimmer's planetoid. Back before the Deliverance, the entire hundred and twenty-five cubic kilometers of rock was converted into a starship fabrication and docking facility by Spaceswimmer's ancestor. Since the readjustment of forces catalyzed by the presence of humans, it has been virtually deserted. Only in the last three years, in fact, has the situation planetside stabilized sufficiently for Spaceswimmer to think of living up to its name by restoring the base to operational status.''

Garrison shook his head. "A costly venture more likely to benefit us than itself. At least, while it puts its efforts into a high-risk enterprise like star roving, it has that many fewer resources to commit against us."

"Spaceswimmer may be influenced by the fact that the last major surge of interstellar exploration resulted in the rescue of the human race," Dalkan noted dryly, "an event that has done more to alter the balance of power among the lineage groups than any event in the preceding ten millennia.

"Moreover, some other group apparently fears that Spaceswimmer may discover something just as revolutionary as humanity was. Within the past week, the planetoid was attacked and taken. The crew, both human and S-spawn, suffered ninety percent casualties dead and missing. The manufactories were destroyed by low-yield atomics."

"Who was it?" Garrison asked.

"Nobody seems to know," Dalkan replied, compressing his lips. "Whoever it was, was able to take the base so suddenly that no distress call was sent, and to destroy the first courier ship that came to check out the situation. They retreated only when Spaceswimmer was able to assemble a battle group to retake the planetoid.

"Most of the damage was done then, not during the initial attack. As far as we can determine, the invader had only a secondary interest in demolition. Its main purpose in destruction was to disguise the fact that it took nearly all the software and substantial numbers of personnel. Both human and S-spawn."

"Why?"

"Nobody knows that, either. We would be ignorant of the basic fact except that Spaceswimmer's battle group chased off the invader before it was able to set all the charges it planned to explode.

"However, in the absence of definite clues, the problem

becomes: Who would have the capability of mounting that extensive an operation in deep space?''

Garrison considered the question. ''Starswallower, of course. Skybreaker, ourselves—''

''That is our most immediate problem,'' Dalkan interrupted. ''Spaceswimmer has commenced a full-scale mobilization. It fears that the attack on the planetoid was a prelude to full-scale hostilities planetside. If it could determine its opponent, it would almost surely launch its own preemptive attack.

''I need scarcely point out to you how vulnerable we would be in the event of large-scale conflict.

''We have been assuming that when Skybreaker ambushed Hickock's ship, all it left behind was the mystery of Hickock's origin. It now appears that an entire fleet remains to be accounted for. Resolving Hickock's mystery has assumed an importance far beyond satisfying Dr. Mackern's curiosity.''

''Excuse me, sir,'' Yader said, ''but it occurs to me that getting both of us into Starswallower's herd is likely to be easier than getting either one of us out. What are my instructions if, once Hickock's memory block is removed, I find it impossible to extract him?''

''That is an obtuse question,'' Garrison said sharply. ''In that case you will, of course, delete him.''

II. THE COUNTERFEIT SHAPER

X

THE TRIPHIBIAN BANKED, MAKING A LONG, SWEEPING TURN to keep its course precisely down the middle of the buffer zone. There were no lines of demarcation. Fungible waves wrinkled the surface of the sea to the sharp edge of the horizon. Columns of sunlight pivoted around the cabin, momentarily blinding Hickock before the craft put its nose to the sun and they narrowed themselves to extinction.

". . . the very latest, the best tested, the most *economical* products available today," the Eggman was saying. Effervescing with enthusiasm, he lifted his plastic case onto his lap. Nervous fingers punched the two-row keyboard. Obscure charts and figures appeared on the miniscreen to emphasize his points.

"Hulks, for instance," the Eggman continued. "Everybody uses them and everybody complains. They're slow; they eat too much; they die young because of Marfan syndrome, congestive heart failure, circulatory collapse; they get fallen arches and varicose veins and stress fractures. You've heard it all.

"Genemasters provides a total solution to the problem. We've redesigned the heart to allow it to pump more efficiently while lessening overall stress on the circulatory system. All veins in the lower extremities have been strengthened. The bone structure can accept fortifying plastic implants. The very metabolism takes full advantage of the square-cube law to produce hulks which require only slightly more food than the average ninety-kilogram man, have quicker reaction times, and are able to work comfortably without protective clothing in temperatures as low as zero centigrade.''

Hickock relaxed in his chair, letting the words wash over him. Beneath half-closed eyelids, he glanced quickly at the passenger to his left. Dr. Howard Yader. His voice was soft and guttural. He moved and spoke slowly, with almost painful precision. Much of the time, his eyes had an abstracted look. That, combined with the disarray of his hair and a general slackness of carriage, gave the impression that he wore his body like rumpled clothing.

Vaheri, still bruised from his encounter with Skybreaker's assault team, had introduced Hickock to Dr. Yader two days before. As Vaheri had explained the purpose of the Trade Talks and why they were most likely to find representatives from Hickock's herd there, Hickock had furtively examined his new keeper, trying to determine what about him was so disturbing.

It took ten minutes, bursting upon him suddenly as a question: In what way is this man different from Jason Yader? The name, of course, suggested a family connection. At first he had seemed different in every way: shorter, heavier, older. But isolating feature from feature, jawline from brow, nose from lips, he could discern no distinguishing mark, no concrete difference between the two men.

''Do you market clones?'' Hickock asked.

The Eggman's open mouth wavered as if trying to crunch an invisible nut while he grappled with the fact that his spiel had been interrupted by a question. ''Ah, clones . . . well, of course,'' he said, stroking his walrus mustache furiously. ''We can—and do, in fact—provide a full line of cloning services. But to tell the truth, the applications, outside of husbandry and aquaculture, are pretty limited.''

"Why?''

''Well, going heavily into clones is, in the old Earth phrase, putting all your eggs in one basket. It makes sense only if you know exactly what strengths you need, because you lose the flexibility that comes with a large gene pool. If the genotype you choose is susceptible to a disease that comes along—poof!—your entire investment goes up in smoke. And, of course, you are always locked into what looked like the optimal solution a generation ago.''

The Eggman had mentally switched data disks and was warming to his subject. "There have been some disastrous instances. Years ago, Wavelasher had in its herd a very, uh, aggressive commander named Hirohiko. It was so impressed with him that it had him cloned five hundred times in the succeeding generation.

"There were immediate problems. The clones had to be physically separated, because they would otherwise devote all their energies to trying to dominate or destroy each other. Even with the separation, only half of them survived until puberty. At that point, the original Hirohiko, still in his prime, feared the clones were being groomed as his immediate replacements, and so set in motion plans for their removal. The clones discovered this and naturally resisted. For a while Wavelasher's herd was torn by something much like civil war. When Skybreaker and Innovator divvied up the pieces, there were only the original and three clones left.''

Hickock glanced again at Yader, who was staring out the window with bored unconcern. The Eggman's analysis made sense. Moreover, cloning suggested no explanation for the complete disparity of behavior patterns and body language. Nor did it explain the scar on the right side of the jaw shared by both Yaders. Remnants of corrective surgery? Or the clue to some sort of cyborganic implant?

* * *

He had gone to Mackern before departure that morning. The doctor's geniality had been distinctly uneasy.

"Where is Jason Yader?" Hickock asked.

"On assignment. I'm afraid you won't see him again before you leave." Mackern's eyes darted nervously for a safe corner of the room.

"Why am I being sent away?"

Mackern gave a loud, rumbling bark, half throat clearing, half forced laughter.

"My boy, you are not being sent anywhere." The boisterousness rang pathetically false. Quick, involuntary glances pierced the facade, as if Mackern had to lower the mask to see how he was doing. "We have finally reached the limits of our usefulness to you. We have rescued you, patched you up, nursed you back to health, and made some crude beginning to restoring your memories. There our efforts have stalled.

"At the Trade Talks, you will see representatives of every major lineage group and most of the minor ones. And they will see you, which is more important. Your own group is bound to recognize and claim you."

The Eggman saw the glance and misinterpreted it. "Wouldn't you agree with me, Doctor?"

Yader turned away from the window, boredom penetrated by surprise. "Eh, excuse me, but I haven't been following your conversation all that closely." He seemed more than vaguely irritated at having his thoughts interrupted. His eyes focused with reluctance on the Eggman. "I'm afraid my own concerns are more theoretical, less grounded in commercial considerations."

The Eggman's smile became strained as he recognized condescension peering through a mask of self-deprecation. Hickock felt a momentary twinge of sympathy, imagining himself born into the intensely competitive environment of the herds, straining to climb to a position of at least moderate security, while being just smart enough to realize that he had no more than mediocre talents. And all the time receiving the smiling sneers of those who dismissed his efforts as vulgar simply because they were practical.

"My specialty is Shaper history," Yader continued, "a difficult subject since contemplation of times prior to their own existence is unnatural to Shapers and they are not introspective concerning events even in their own lifetimes. Therefore my tools are more those of a paleo-ecologist than those of a human historian. I sift through sediments, examine fossilized remains, and conduct long interviews with those Shapers who will humor us.

"Perhaps you have seen the series *The Sea Beneath the Sea*. It's largely fictional romanticizing, of course, but you may have remarked on the peculiar construction of the title. Perhaps you have also wondered why Shapers should consider such an icy world hospitable."

"I have seen the series," the Eggman said carefully. "As for the cold, I imagine between the mirrors placed in orbit to speed the melt and the genetic modification Shapers always work on their spawn . . ." His voice trailed off at Yader's smile.

"The Shapers sent to Snowball have needed almost no genetic preparation for the change of environment." Yader's voice was becoming animated as unfeigned enthusiasm for the subject melted his reserve. "The clue to why this is so is found in that series title. It parallels another phrase discovered in the earliest Shaper memories we have been able to retrieve: 'the sky beyond the sky.'

"Now, perhaps you might even dispute that such things as phrases can survive individual Shapers and be transmitted from generation to generation. After all, you would argue, until encountering humanity, Shapers had never conceived of language as we know it. All commands to spawn, all responses to Patriarchs, all defiances hurled at equals in other lineage groups, are transmitted by biochemical effusions into the surrounding waters. These compounds are not symbols of ideas as words are, but are rather organic catalysts that directly cause the recipient Shaper to experience the transcribed thought. Which, incidentally, is why Shapers find it almost impossible to distinguish between an 'exchange of ideas' and 'psychological warfare.' In the conceptual framework, ideas can be transmitted only by being forced on their audience.

"Nonetheless, because Shapers are capable of far more intense and abstract thought than human beings, they have to manipulate even larger blocks of unexamined concepts more quickly than we do. Therefore, certain key concepts are formulated in patterns every bit as stylized as 'the rosy-hued Aurora' or 'swift-footed Achilles.'

"One of the oldest we have been able to discover is 'the sky beyond the sky.' Ancestral memories of that time—which must have been more than a million years ago—are fragmentary, but what remain are structured in a form that is half epic, half survival manual. In these memories, the sky is associated with concepts of hardness, oppression, and suffocation. It blocks the light. Shapers' prey hide within and behind it."

Hickock felt himself mirror the puzzlement he saw on the Eggman's face.

"Ice!" Yader explained, his face illuminated with remembered epiphany. "This world was in the grip of an ice age so severe that most of the oceans were iced over, so severe that it gave the Shapers the evolutionary push that made them conscious, intelligent beings."

So much from such a little phrase, Hickock thought. Was Yader aware of the "thought" that Innovator had given

Mackern at the end of their audience? If so, what could he make of it?

> You are like oxygen
> Like capitalism
> Breaking down and building up
> Setting loose fire storms.
> What shall I do with this two-edged sword?
> Am I the hunter or the prey?

Mackern had recited those lines to Hickock as soon as they reentered the dry portion of the Nares. Although Mackern had clearly been both puzzled and disturbed, Hickock had the impression that Mackern could make a good guess as to what it meant but was looking to him for some sort of confirmation. Aside from the implied threat, it was totally opaque to him.

Another datum, perhaps, suggesting that Innovator had wandered beyond the borders of sanity.

Shapers, at least, were expected to be cryptic. There were humans whose speech was probably beyond even Yader's skills.

He had stepped onto the wharf that led to the floating triphibian. A haphazard pile of white cloth lay on one side of the wharf, dazzling in the sun. It stirred and unfolded. A dark head rose to regard him. Eyes danced behind the protection of cornrows.

"You're on your way to the big time now," Reeve said.

"Really?" Hickock asked. "I thought I was being given the bum's rush. To let me go after all the resources you have used in my apprehension and recovery seems rather a waste. From your point of view."

"I made my points when I predicted your arrival," Reeve said. Her eyes were shut. She seemed more involved in absorbing the warmth of the sun than in what she was saying. "Lost lots when I told them they would want to give you away. Just got those back. With interest."

"Any predictions for me?" Hickock asked. His eyes scanned the pier area, looking for Howard Yader. Water lapped gently at the hull of the triphibian.

Reeve's silence stretched so long that Hickock feared she had fallen asleep. "Take care of Jason," she said at last. "Put his pieces together and maybe you can put together the pieces of the big puzzle."

"I'm told I won't see him again," Hickock replied, wondering if that would nudge any elucidation out of her.

Reeve ignored him, absorbed in inner vision. "There's a—I don't know what to call it. I see it glowing around you. Sometimes it seems grand and important, like some sort of high destiny. Other times it's like a job you've done for twenty years, as simple and homely as saying your own name.

"It isn't your memories. They'll come back in time, but they're only about dead things, might have beens. This—thing—is alive. It's what you really are. When you know what that is, you will become a living key."

"Wonderful." On one level, that was so obvious as to be trivial. *Know what you are supposed to do, and do it, and everything will work out.* Reeve had once admitted to him that during dry seasons of her power she would gild ambiguities with pseudo-profundities. Was she doing that to him now? Why should she bother? On the other hand, if there was a deeper level, he certainly could not discern it.

A chime sounded from the cabin ceiling. "We are beginning our descent. Please make sure your safety harnesses are snugly fastened. There will be a slight jar as we intersect the surface."

Miniature suns flashed off the waves as they came up to meet the triphibian. Their crests blurred past the window and were suddenly lost in the huge unbroken wave splashing up from the craft's nose. Hickock involuntarily tensed himself against the deceleration.

The wave wiped out the sky. Its trough washed over the windows. For an instant the multipeaked, silvery surface danced above them. Then it disappeared. The light became a diffuse greenish-yellow, which faded quickly to total darkness.

Pulsating vibrations massaged soles and forearms. Rushing water surged along the sides of the hull with the sound of a strong, steady wind.

Light peeked through the murk below. One dot at first, then many. Circles of luminescent pearls, radiating lines connecting other circles in a pattern Hickock could almost grasp.

A dark line swept along the windows, erasing the lights. A dull clang penetrated the cabin. Brilliance flooded down from above as water drained out the bottom of the air lock.

xi

AIR WAS STILL ROARING FROM THE CEILING VENTS, BLOW-
drying the areas immediately beneath them, as Hickock and
Yader exited the triphibian. Starswallower's security personnel, diplomatically labeled guides, divided passengers into
groups of five for in-processing. Armed hulks lined the far
walls, obvious but unobtrusive.

The first steps were familiar. Hickock was directed through
portable sensadoors whose conflicting magnetic fields read
out the position of every molecule in his body and relayed
the information to a central computer. After several milli-
seconds of pondering the data, the computer decided that he
was harmless.

Vaguely sectoid medicomp units crouched just beyond
the sensadoors. Obeying his guide's instructions, Hickock
braced his thumbs on the scanning plates and pressed his
eyes into the rubber-lined stereoculars. Light exploded within
his eyes, leaving fragmented pink and purple afterimages.
He jerked his right thumb back reflexively and sucked at a
small pinprick that was already scabbing.

The hunched-over head of the medicomp belched out a
plastic card. A hologram of his own face gazed out at him
from the depths of the card. Next to it was a large green T^2.
INNOVATOR blazed across the card's balance line. Beneath

it, in smaller letters, was his own name. Bar coding covered
the reverse side like the guide marks for an irregular diffrac-
tion grating.

His guide handed him a leaflet. "This is a map of the
sections set aside for Innovator's herd representatives, as well
as all areas made public for Trade Talk members. Your identity plate, once it is validated, will grant you access to all
designated rooms and connecting ways. Always wear your
identity plate in full view. Otherwise, you risk arrest as an
unauthorized intruder. Repeated incidents will result in ex-
pulsion."

"When will it be validated?" Yader asked

"On successful completion of your interview. Over to the
booths, please."

Several lines had already formed. When it was his turn,
Yader took a seat; with poor grace he allowed the metal mesh
to be fitted over his forehead and hands.

"In all the meetings like this I have attended, I have never
before been subjected to such nonsense," he fumed. "You
have already inventoried my body down to the amino acids,
established my identity by the structure of my DNA, and
found me harmless. What more do you want? Or is this all
just a petty form of harassment, a way of letting members of
other herds know they are in Starswallower's territory?"

A woman in a black, form-fitting jacket and pants made
her way slowly over to Yader's station, glancing briefly at the
consoles manned by the other examiners. The two claws on
either shoulder meant nothing to Yader; likewise the three
rows of multicolored ribbons over her left breast. However,
the instant attention she was given as well as the minute
stiffening of postures of the seated examiners spoke elo-
quently.

A black coif framed a clear-complexioned, oval face.
Hickock found himself wondering about the color of her hair.

A curl escaping just below her ear gave the answer: brown, with rich red highlights.

Her eyes came up quickly, meeting his. He smiled, inclining his head fractionally. She made no answering nod, regarding him with thoughtful severity. After a second she tore her gaze away and picked up Yader's identity plate.

"You should be pleased with our precautions, Dr. Yader," she said. "After all, they should be nearly as effective in protecting you and your herdmates from inappropriate direct action from other herds as they are in protecting us.

"Once they have proved themselves, we may even be able to eliminate all other checks. The name you choose for yourself is really a matter of indifference to us. The sensadoors are useful in detecting weapons, but minds are the ultimate weapons. Our only real concern should be whether you intend to use your mind in a way hostile to our interests."

"And how do you accomplish that?" Yader asked sarcastically, shaking the wires trailing from him. "Mechanical telepathy?"

"You will see," she said, favoring him with a professional smile.

"You have probably guessed that this is a version of what our ancestors called a lie detector. It is, but in the same sense that our spacecraft can be considered versions of ancient Chinese rockets. The difference is not so much in the sensors, which were relatively sophisticated even when the first such devices were fabricated back on Earth, but in the interpretive software.

"Lying is a volitional act. The subject must evaluate a question, determine the true answer, recognize its danger to his interests, concoct a lie, test its plausibility, weigh its likelihood of acceptance against the penalties for being caught, and finally utter the lie. Quick as it may occur, all of this creates recognizable patterns of electrical activity in the brain and a biochemical response in the rest of the body. Our software not only picks out these patterns, it also learns the idiosyncrasies of any given subject so that it predicts when and about what matters the subject is most likely to lie.

"This may sound abstract and complicated, but it is working quite well. In the year since we began these procedures, we have eliminated no fewer than twenty-three espionage consortiums. Today Starswallower's lineage group is the only one in which there is no espionage penetration from other herds. We wish to keep it that way."

Hickock ran his tongue along the top of a suddenly dry mouth. That information confirmed, and to some degree explained, what Jason Yader had told him several weeks before. If his suspicions about Howard Yader were even approximately correct, it was time for an about-face and a march in quickstep back to the triphibian.

But for all his dark looks and muttered objections, Yader made no move to remove the mesh.

"Very well." The supervisor picked up a laminated card from the examiner's table. "Your name?" she asked crisply.

"Dr. Howard Yader." Resentment and irritation seemed to stretch each syllable to twice its normal length.

"Your patriarch."

"Innovator."

"Your purpose here."

"To participate in the Trade Talks. My studies concern the evolutionary and ecological relationships of Shapers. Most recently, my colleagues and I have devised a regimen that slows the aging process in Shapers, something your own Starswallower must need greatly." His eyes flashed as he added, "And that is all I am going to tell you about it. Any more, you will have to pay for!"

The supervisor's smile widened in genuine amusement. "If we can confirm your claims, I am sure you will be able to name your price. Now, tell me if you are familiar with any of the following names or terms.

"Dalkan."

"Our war minister, of course. Smart fellow. Tough, too." The last was almost a challenge.

"Garrison."

Yader was silent. Hickock had a moment to be thankful that he was not under examination. His heart was pounding so loudly it had to be audible even without sensors.

Yader shook his head slowly. "I don't seem to recognize the name."

"Hollings."

He was more emphatic this time. "No."

"Special Projects."

Yader considered. "Hush-hush group. Supposed to be as powerful as it is mysterious. I have nothing to do with it, and if I knew any more, I'm sure I wouldn't be allowed to tell you."

The supervisor glanced down at the console. The examiner looked up and shrugged.

"Mackern."

"Director of research. Almost as bright as he's said to be. Bit stuffy, though."

"Final question: While here, do you plan any activities that might be harmful to Starswallower, its lineage group, or their herds?"

"No," Yader said flatly. "I am here 'to participate in the mutually beneficial exchange of goods and ideas.' That is the official slogan, isn't it?"

The supervisor looked down at the console again and pursed her lips. She placed Yader's identity plate in the slot across from the keyboard. There was a slight humming. At her nod, the examiner began removing the mesh sensors.

"There. Perfectly painless, as you see. Your people will meet you beyond that doorway."

She turned away to resume her rounds as the examiner hooked up Hickock.

"Your name, please."

"Patrick M. Hickock. I presume."

That drew a perplexed look from the examiner, and a frown at the console.

"Your patriarch?"

"None that I know of."

"That's—" The examiner stopped, staring at the readout in obvious disbelief. The supervisor pivoted, took one look at the examiner, and strode quickly back.

"However," Yader said, from where he stood waiting, "Mr. Hickock is with me, and is traveling under the patronage and protection of Innovator."

"You said nothing of that!" the supervisor snapped.

"You didn't ask," Yader protested in aggrieved tones.

"Perhaps the question wasn't on your card," Hickock suggested.

The supervisor blushed furiously, but kept her eyes on Hickock. "What is your herd, then?"

"I have no idea."

Another quick, frustrated look at the console.

"Where do you come from?"

"Innovator's people . . . retrieved me from Seaking's territory. Beyond that, my origin is a matter of conjecture. I remember nothing before waking in the Freair hospital. Dr. Mackern speculates that I may be part of a hypothetical rogue herd. Possibly one that broke loose when Explorer was devoured."

Beneath the blush, the supervisor was in something near shock, though only her utter stillness for nearly three seconds disclosed it. Hickock's eyes narrowed. She was embarrassed at not having picked up his relationship with Yader while Yader was being questioned, and surprised that her instruments confirmed the truth of his unlikely story. Yet both of those together could hardly account for the depth of her disturbance. What had he said that could have shaken her so?

"So you know Mackern," she said, trying to get the examination back on track.

"Yes," Hickock admitted. "And Colonel Garrison, and Major Hollings. They have all had their crack at me. Unsuccessfully. Having thoroughly and vainly ruminated over me, they have spewed me forth as indigestible."

"Don't say any more," Yader warned. "That is all they need to know for legitimate security purposes. Any other facts that interest them they can negotiate for. Like everybody else."

"There is still the most important question," the supervisor insisted, glaring at Yader. She turned back to Hickock, clamping a firm hold on her anger. "Do you plan any activities that may be harmful to Starswallower, its lineage group, or their herds?"

Hickock's eyes were bleak. "I do not know enough about Starswallower or its enemies to have a position."

The supervisor quivered with exasperation. "Follow me. A more intensive interrogation is necessary."

xii

"RHEENA VAN ALSTYNE," THE WOMAN SAID, EXTENDING her hand in greeting. Carefully waved silver hair haloed a sharply lined face. Makeup so skillfully applied that it seemed not to exist blunted the marks of age, but it was the lively, inquisitive eyes that gave the face its deceptively youthful appearance. "You have made my job as leader of Innovator's trade delegation even more—interesting—than it had been.

"I'm sorry for the delay," she continued. "Sometimes I think Starswallower's security forces consider the entire Trade Talks to be a personal affront. It is unfortunate that you had to bear the brunt of their displeasure."

"I feel lucky to be here at all," Hickock confessed. "When that supervisor extended her inquisition, I feared I would be in for—" He caught "another" on the tip of his tongue and suppressed it. "—a long period of detention."

"They can't do that," Van Alstyne's companion said quickly. His identity plate gave his name as Jean-Claude Regala. "Under the protocols of the talks, the host's security force may admit or deny admittance to participants. No participant may be detained."

Hickock let himself be guided onto a moving walkway. It arced high over a room at least half a kilometer wide.

"If anyone could do it, however, it may be that young lady

you were talking to," Van Alstyne said. "Our preliminary assessment is that Rita Lieder, whom you term a supervisor, is actually number one in Starswallower's security executive."

Tables dotted the floor below them, stringing themselves around meandering, odd-shaped pools. Something long and dark darted through the depths of one of them.

"This place is large," Hickock said, surveying the far walls.

"It is *huge*," Van Alstyne corrected. "To waste all this space undersea implies wealth and power beyond the dreams of most megalomaniacs. All visiting lineage groups are to be firmly impressed with the fact that Starswallower's patriarchy is the oldest, the most extensive, and by far the most powerful.

"Even knowing all that," she said with a grim smile, "I must admit that I really am impressed in spite of myself."

They separated at the far side of the walkway. Regala led Hickock to his quarters while Van Alstyne and Yader went to the Great Hall to prepare for the opening session.

Fifteen access doors lined the mouth of the large corridor leading to Innovator country. Following Regala's example, Hickock fed his identity plate into the outside slot. The door whisked upward almost immediately, slamming noiselessly shut as soon as he had stepped through. His identity plate poked itself out of a lip in the short path divider to his left.

From their station behind a slit high in the wall, shadowed forms watched his entrance without apparent interest.

"I suppose they are there only to help us," Hickock said.

Regala followed his gaze. "Yeah. That's what they say."

They dropped three floors in a small, noiseless elevator. Hickock's door tasted the front third of his card, bleeped, and slid aside.

"Not all herds get, or even want, this sort of treatment,"

Regala observed. "Deepchurner puts all its herd members together in closely guarded barracks."

Hickock looked around quickly. The room was smaller than his part of the double he had shared with Jason Yader, and lacking windows, but in many other respects it was similar. The recessed latch for the flip-down bed was at wrist level. Opposite it stood a narrow closet, in which he hung his duffel bag. Next to that, a built-in work cubicle provided a movable keyboard, a wall screen, and a small, bare work space. The room ended less than three meters from the door with a toilet and shower stall.

"A bit spartan," Hickock murmured.

Regala looked at him closely. "When I was growing up, I would have killed for a cubby like this. I suppose," he continued speculatively, "that some of us come from more fortunate circumstances."

"Perhaps," Hickock agreed, forcing a crooked smile.

"If you would like to accompany me," Regala suggested, glancing at his watch, "we can get to the Great Hall in time for the opening session."

"Why not?" Hickock agreed, with a last look around. "Nothing to keep me here."

They went back out to the long corridor that was the trunk of Innovator country, through the checkpoint into the Concourse, which Regala called the Half Klick Common Room, and through a wide arch into the Great Hall. Hickock paused at the entryway, noting thick sliding bulkheads. Similar bulkheads had flanked the entrance to Innovator country. Even the door to his own room had opened with the hissing resistance of a vacuum seal being breached.

"It's a measure of the high value Starswallower puts on its human herds," Regala explained. "They breed too slowly to risk losing them if a section of the hull gives way. Each room seals automatically in the event of flooding. This whole complex is less than five years old. It has safety devices even Innovator has never dreamed of.''

Hickock stepped into the Great Hall—

—and staggered. Regala grabbed his arm to keep him from falling.

''What's the matter?'' Regala asked urgently. Members of other delegations stared at them curiously, then looked away.

Hickock blinked rapidly, gulping air. The floor seemed to spin and tilt. Impressions flew by almost too quickly to be apprehended: smells, shafts of light, a taste of bitterness, glowing dust motes doing their Brownian dance of almost stillness, golden-haloed dark-at-the-center clouds . . .

''The light,'' he gasped. ''It's so—'' He stopped, wordless for such terrible poignancy.

Regala guided him to a seat near Van Alstyne in Innovator's delegation.

''That should not bother you,'' Regala said with concern. ''The frequencies are those for which human eyesight evolved. Most of us find them quite comforting. In fact, Starswallower's delegation is offering the specs with the promise that human productivity will increase under such lighting.''

The rush of images and smells faded. Hickock was so shaken by them that he did not even try to fight the mental censor shutting them away from him.

He looked around. Desks spread out from the far wall like frozen ripples. At their focus stood a large, dark-robed figure chanting into a podium microphone.

''Thus do we give thanks to Thee, O undivided and ever bountiful Creator, for delivering us from the fires of Your righteous wrath and bringing us to Your fruitful womb, this world, to serve and be guided by Your Shapers.''

The voice was a deep contralto. Loose folds of flesh blurred any trace of sexuality in the face.

''Let us not seek to return to the days of old when we chose evil, calling it freedom. Let us not listen to those whose very name means babbling confusion. Rather, let us use this gathering as a time of rededicating ourselves to the service of those into whose infinitely intelligent care you have given us.''

There was a scattered chorus of amens. Most of the delegates appeared to be politely bored as the figure left the podium.

"What—" He reconsidered. "Who was that?"

"Mother Angela Gamorez, Church of the Deliverance," Van Alstyne told him. She waited for him to nod his understanding. His stare continued to be blank.

"The Church of the Deliverance," she explained patiently, "as you may have gathered from the last part of that invocation, believes the Shapers to be divinely appointed agents of mankind's physical and spiritual salvation. It is undeniable that they did save our race from incineration when the Sun flared up. Deliverance people take this a few steps further in considering the Shapers some sort of incarnate angels.

"To be like a Shaper is to be more like God," she said didactically. "Admittedly, striving toward perfection can take bizarre forms. For example, the Church of the Deliverance considers bisexuality to be a mark of humanity's divided, fallen state. The maphs—ah, you're familiar with them, at least—are one attempt to bring our reproductive biology into line with that of our masters.

"Mother Angela represents another way. Her faction considers females the least incomplete sex, since they—we—can reproduce parthenogenetically."

"Producing clones," Hickock observed.

Van Alstyne nodded, appreciative of his quickness. "For the moment. However, research indicates that even back on old Earth there were species able to produce genetically varied offspring without the aid of sperm. Deliverancers hope to produce a similar capability in humans within the next decade.

"In the meantime, they must content themselves with the greater mutability of language. Heads of lineage groups are referred to as matriarchs rather than patriarchs, as if any gender-based word could be strictly applicable to a unisexual creature."

"Just another damned heresy," Regala said in a flat voice. "It is the current variant of a recurrent lunacy going back to the Gnostics."

"Which, absurd though it may be, at least encourages loyalty to the herd and the lineage group," Van Alstyne responded carefully. "The Church of the Babylonian Captivity, however just the grievances it airs, does not. Furthermore, its belief in a messiah who will lead the faithful back to a miraculously reconstituted Earth is at least as ridiculous as any part of the Deliverancer's creed, while being politically far more dangerous."

She spoke looking directly at Hickock, yet he felt sure that the words were aimed at Regala. The words had a used feeling about them, as if they reprised an argument the two of them had had many times before. Underneath respect, underneath perhaps even affection, a warning was clearly given.

Hickock did his best to appear oblivious to the undercurrents. He filed them away as yet another puzzle missing most of its parts.

The actual business of the meeting began. The coordinator for this session gave a fifteen-minute introduction defining the excred, explaining how its value had been established by the pre-Talks conference, within what limits its value would be allowed to float, but ending with an admission that, for the foreseeable future at least, items of special interest, whatever they were, would probably be bartered.

Hickock's station had its own monitor, keyboard, and light pen. Also, somewhat incongruously, a stylus lay alongside a pad of paper. He tapped it, frowning.

"Why—" he began.

Regala placed two fingers on Hickock's lips. Shielding his own pad with his body, Regala scribbled:

Starswallower provides the data link. We assume everything going through it is monitored. It is also likely that fibercams are trained on each delegation.

That put a definite damper on any serious conversation. Furthermore, since Hickock could not be sure what was or was not serious, it effectively killed all conversation. Bored, he started playing with the keyboard, exploring the data link. A menu of menus appeared. A few keystrokes later, he brought up a listing of all the delegations, along with each item that had so far been officially offered for exchange.

Minerals, mineral rights, a bewildering variety of names for what appeared to be foodstuffs, only a small minority of which could be for human consumption. Manufacturers announced themselves in incomprehensible hierarchies of nomenclature.

Even as Hickock watched, the lists churned, expanding and contracting on half a dozen different lines simultaneously. Numbers in red appeared to the right of various item descriptors, burping upward at random intervals. After the numbers stabilized for more than a minute, they and their descriptors would sometimes disappear. The rest of the list would soundlessly crunch together, eliminating the gap.

Even books were on the block, some with surprisingly high opening bids. Hickock skimmed through the titles.

The Hero with a Thousand Faces by Joseph Campbell. A tour de force cross-cultural synthesis of mythic motifs, focusing on the role of the hero. Anthropologically interesting in that it documents early subconscious realization of the necessity for outbreeding to increase the diversity of local gene pools. A must for personnel managers seeking insight into historical psychology.

His cursor dived through a score of listings, coming to rest on:

The Call of Cthulhu by H. P. Lovecraft. Potentially the most important writing yet recovered from the pre-Deliverance period. Once superficially considered a series of horror fantasies. A growing body of scholars finds evidence in the "Great Old Ones" that Earth was guided by its own Shapers during crucial epochs. Absolutely crucial to understanding human-Shaper relations.

Hickock frowned and tapped Regala's arm, pointing to the screen. "Seriously?" he asked.

Regala grimaced. "No, but some people insist on pretending. Even some Shapers, who are certainly intelligent enough to know better. They find it inconceivable that creatures with brains as small as ours could develop atomic power or cybernetics on our own. So they are very receptive to any hint that we were civilized by our own Shapers, or by their own ancestors during some unrecorded pre-Deliverance contact."

Shaking his head, Hickock returned to his screen. People were for sale, both as individuals and in categories: mers, allegedly improved breeds of speakers, hulks . . . Hickock thought for a moment of the Eggman and wondered how he was faring in the huge, free-for-all marketplace.

Quite accidentally, he paged out of the list of ordinary offerings and on to the special interest section. These items had no minimum excred bids stated, but would have to be bartered for with items or agreements of like value. Most of the individuals in this section were managers, some were scientists, and a few were mercenaries. One name leapt out from the screen:

Hickock, Patrick M. Adult male Caucasian, roughly thirty years old, in excellent condition. Herd of origin unknown. This trained warrior and pilot combines superb reflexes with a high degree of resourcefulness. His one handicap is a memory block of such subtlety that it has defied the most sophisticated efforts of Innovator's lineage group. The opportunity to examine this unusual example of psychological engineering would by itself make this specimen a unique value. Indicators suggest that the specimen took part in armed action against a Skybreaker convoy destined for Snowball. Skybreaker's abortive kidnapping attempt directed at the specimen, which cost that Shaper an elite commando team, one light manta carrier, and four fighters, is independent confirmation of this specimen's high value.

There followed the communications code for Innovator's delegation.

Hickock's thumb jabbed the PRINT key. He ripped off the hard copy even before the paper ceased feeding out of the slot.

"Just what the hell is this?" he demanded.

Van Alstyne, who had been intently following a presentation being made from the podium, frowned irritably. "It's your précis, of course. What's wrong? Is part of it incorrect?"

"I was told that I was to be brought here so that I could be returned to my own people," Hickock said, his voice shaking with repressed rage.

"So you shall be," Van Alstyne said shortly. "Putting your précis on the data link is the quickest, most efficient way to make you known to the greatest number of lineage groups.''

''It puts me up for bid like a gross of cabbages!''

Van Alstyne bit her lip in perplexity. ''Your reference is to some sort of archaic Terrestrial vegetal matter, is it not? Which was of minimal value? If so, the metaphor is utterly misleading.''

''I really don't understand your problem,'' Regala said, impatience putting an edge on his usual amiability. ''You have engaged the efforts of some of our most important people for an extended length of time. During that time, if my briefing has been correct, we have brought you back from near death and even fought a decent-sized battle to protect you. Surely it is only fair that we get some return on our investment?''

''I was to be returned to my own people,'' Hickock insisted. ''Not to whoever put up the highest price.''

''The highest price will be information,'' Van Alstyne said coolly, ''and it is likely that only your own people will be able to pay it.''

''You should be flattered,'' Regala added. ''Two generations ago, herd members and all their offspring were considered the inalienable appurtenances of their Shapers. There was no way to be sold even within lineage groups, much less between Patriarchs. Individual worth was almost entirely a matter of a given Shaper's whim. Only when it became possible to buy and sell humans among various lineage groups could an objective standard of self-worth be established.

''I have served Innovator's interests well for more than a decade and have advanced quickly, but I am nowhere near important enough to make the special interest list. It is more than a little irritating to hear you scorn my highest aspiration.''

''Enough bickering,'' Van Alstyne commanded, holding

up her hand for silence. All her attention was directed to the front of the Great Hall.

One of Balancer's representatives was making a general presentation of a new method of herding and protecting sharphin. Using hunting spawn to protect the mouths of breeding bays was both inefficient and dangerous, he stated. Hunting spawn, even those specifically modified for herding, sometimes reverted to their basic heritage and turned predator. Other hunting spawn were ill equipped to deal with their own rogues. Sometimes the madness would spread through their ranks, resulting in a mass slaughter of the sharphin they were supposed to be protecting. The sharphin, having ancestral instincts of their own, would sometimes challenge and attack even nonrogue hunting spawn.

The solution proposed by Balancer's delegation was domestication. From prehistoric times, humans had shown a consistent tendency to form dominant relationships with other species to the mutual benefit of both. Dogs had been the first—

A hologram of a brown quadruped with large shapeless ears and sagging jowls materialized in the air above the rep.

—but within a few thousand years, horses, cattle, goats, birds, and even certain species of communal insects—

More three-dimensional images, some evoking gasps of horror and disgust from the audience, flickered through their ephemeral existence.

—had been added to the list. The habit of domestication was still strong. Children in widely separated herds had made repeated attempts to make pets of aquavians and various medium-size land herbivores.

''Sharphin promise to be the first commercially significant creature to be domesticated since the Deliverance. Sharphin are gregarious pack animals, used to following leaders. They are adaptable, flexible, and intelligent. Indeed, after the last period of overhunting, those sharphin who survived were measurably more intelligent than their ancestors.

"For more than five years, we have been training selected sharphin to obey human commands. No genetic, no biological modification of the sharphin has been necessary." The delegate paused, glancing around the Great Hall to emphasize his statement.

"We have learned how to recognize the natural pack leaders. These we train to our commands. Subsidiary leaders can be trained to aid in herding, alerting, and protecting the packs. As you will quickly realize, this allows effective shepherding even in mid-ocean. Despite the wartime conditions that have obtained, we have been able to more than double the size of our sharphin herds during the course of our project.

"Now, for those delegations willing to make meaningful—"

"Mr. Coordinator. Rule seven!"

There was a stir from the back of the Great Hall. A man nearly as tall as a hulk but more slightly built made his way forward, flanked by two guards on either side. Complying with the rules of the Talks, all were unarmed. Nonetheless, the two-piece formfitting suits and the suggestions of concealed body armor were to Hickock unpleasantly reminiscent of the Skybreaker assault team that had nearly succeeded in kidnapping him.

They were too far away for Hickock to see their identity plates. "Seaking," Van Alstyne said, looking at Regala with an air of tense significance.

Balancer's delegate appeared surprised and, Hickock thought, frightened. "Mr. Coordinator, please remind this unrecognized delegate of our rules against interrupting a delegate who has the floor. I can assure him that he will be given the same chance as every other delegation to make his offer."

"No one need make an offer for what his lineage group

already owns." Seaking's delegate advanced until he stood just below the podium.

"Mr. Coordinator," Balancer's delegate said quickly, "Seaking's motives for attempting to disrupt these talks should be obvious. Despite the agreements of the pre-Talks conference, it seeks to take its war with us within these walls—"

"The war is over." Seaking's representative had patched his throat mike into the Great Hall communications system. The voice came clearly from the speaker at every delegation's desk. "Less than three hours ago, Seaking devoured Balancer. All remaining members of Balancer's lineage group are being eliminated as I speak."

The room had become completely silent. "Traditionally," Seaking's representative continued, "human herds were considered inseparable from their Shapers, and so met the same fate as their defeated Patriarch."

Balancer's delegate regarded him with wide eyes, as he might a particularly dangerous serpent. Ceiling lights gleamed off his forehead.

"Our more enlightened practice," Seaking's representative continued, "recognizing herds as too valuable to be lightly destroyed, is to consider them the rightful property of the victor. This method of training sharphin, for example, displays originality well directed to a Patriarch's interests. I can promise that Seaking will find appropriate places of responsibility for all those involved in this project."

Balancer's delegate licked his lips and tried to speak. Nothing came out.

The Coordinator stood at his desk and cleared his throat, activating his microphone.

"The invocation of rule seven is acknowledged and must be resolved. In view of the extremely serious allegations brought before us and the far-reaching effect they will have if proven, all formal Trade Talks involving Seaking's or Balancer's lineage groups must be suspended until the rights of the trading parties can be definitively ascertained.''

His last words were nearly lost in the rising clamor. ''This meeting is adjourned.''

xiii

THE DELEGATES STOOD, PATIENTLY OR IMPATIENTLY, IN twisting lines that writhed away from each dining kiosk like cephalopod tentacles. Hickock had time to appreciate the full prismatic diversity of the delegations. Some stood in easily identifiable groups marked by common dress or skin coloring. Only a few places in front of him was one such group. Almond hands and faces poked out from stiff jackets of almost dazzling whiteness. Hickock heard a few stray words, liquid strings of vowels filled with near rhymes. Intrigued, he leaned forward to ask one of the group where they came from. A large, strong woman, her cuff girdled with silver stars, held up her hand warningly and ever so gently pushed him away, as if to protect them all from cross-cultural contamination.

Delegates, of all the hues of the rainbow in skin and clothing were scattered throughout the lines: pasty white flesh shining with unhealthy wetness; men and women staring at the world through egg-shaped, multifaceted insectoid lenses, their every abrupt movement speaking of strength and tension barely under control. In other groups, thin fingers moved like seaweed just beneath a storm-tossed surface. Hickock looked more closely. The ears showed no obvious sign of genetic tampering. Was the hand language for security?

Almost without realizing it, he had shuffled forward to the serving area. Attendants with cheerful smiles handed over the glass counter flat dishes of steaming red-and-green-tinged flesh, as well as moist purple puffballs and a grayish, spicy-smelling gruel. He accepted the offered plates and cups dubiously and looked around for an empty chair. After five minutes of searching, he found one at a small table whose other occupant was the Eggman.

The Eggman's identity plate listed his name as Urena. Discolored bags of flesh puffed under his eyes. He took long sips of steaming synstym as if he could suck vitality from the cup.

"Good morning!" Hickock said brightly. "You certainly look like hell. How is business?"

"Business." Urena gave a great gusty sigh. "Business is wonderful. I have never seen such demand in all my life. Yesterday's partial suspension of trade was actually a relief. It allowed me to catch up on my paperwork."

"That much call for hulks?" Hickock asked. He sampled a puffball cautiously. It tasted of mint mingled with a whiff of ammonia, which penetrated into the deepest recesses of his sinuses.

"Well, uh, no." Urena's face clouded. "Less than I had counted on, actually. Most of it is for generalized, defect-free ova/sperm—highest grade, of course—with chromosomal emphasis on intelligence, adaptability, and loyalty. Only my colleagues in body swapping are doing more business."

"You must wish you were a body swapper, then," Hickock observed.

Urena shook his head decisively. "Too many personality problems. When I first got into this business, body swappers were still splitting families, depending on which family member had assets attractive to which buyer."

"That doesn't happen anymore?" Hickock asked. The red-and-green flesh had a surprisingly light, delicate flavor.

Hickock let it dissolve against the roof of his mouth, savoring it.

"Sometimes," Urena admitted, "but for all practical purposes, the practice has died out. Someone brought to the Shapers' attention the fact that in Earth history, rival power groups often cemented alliances with marriages. They worried that having family members spread through different lineage groups would create divided loyalties. The simplest solution was to trade families en bloc."

"One might do away with the family unit altogether," Hickock suggested, "as Wavelasher did."

"Those herds failed to thrive," Urena said, tapping his cup decisively on his tray. "The few breeding pens that did well succeeded by turning themselves into extended families. At that point, most Shapers decided that biological families might create stronger ties, but were more manageable because they were smaller. It was very neat. If there really is a Council of Cooperation, it was a ploy worthy of their legend."

Hickock opened his mouth to ask a question, but was forestalled as the Eggman leaned forward conspiratorially. "The interesting thing is that almost all this demand seems to be originating from one source."

"How do you know?" Hickock asked.

"I know 'cause though a dozen lineage groups are buying these generalized types, a little asking around turns up that they are all fronts. For Starswallower."

Hickock frowned. "Why would Starswallower need such a large increase in that segment of its herd?"

"Could be trying to play games with the market: monopolize the current supply; sell it off later at a premium price," Urena suggested. "My real guess, though, is that Starswallower is getting ready to expand in a big way and needs personnel fast."

Hickock excused himself and deposited his tray on a con-

veyor belt. He braced himself as he entered the Great Hall.
There was only a momentary disorientation and quickening
of heartbeat. The churn of emotions and half memories subsided into a barely perceptible murmur.

"There he is now." Regala had spotted him. Standing
across from Regala and Van Alstyne was a short, stocky man
in a one-piece gray coverall. His identity plate revealed that
Wavechurner was his Shaper. Far smaller letters gave his
own name: Lucison 345.b2. On the table between them, a
palm-sized metal box hummed and crackled quietly.

"Why, so it is," Lucison said, his eyes momentarily alight
with forced enthusiasm. "And just as described."

Hickock felt the previous day's anger rekindle within him.
"Perhaps I should strip to fully display the goods on sale. I
seem to remember that to be the tradition."

"Not at all," Lucison said, oblivious to his tone. "Retinal
and blood checks will be sufficient."

"If your offer is accepted," Van Alstyne said.

Lucison tensed his cheeks into a quick salesman's smile.
"I'm sure it will be. If you look over the package I have presented you, you will have to admit that it is a most generous
offer for what you yourselves admit is an unknown and even
frustrating asset. As you see, we have included mineral mining rights for six months in the Trassic Bottom Range, and
entry into the Quintshap trading consortium for one year with
an option to extend the lowered tariffs for an additional year,
as well as . . ."

Van Alstyne listened to the proposal in seeming disinterest
as Lucison droned on. Twice Regala leaned over her shoulder
to point out something. Both times Van Alstyne nodded and
turned the page.

"If I may be so bold," Lucison said, concluding his spiel,
"the offer before you is replete with items of special utility
to Innovator's entire lineage group."

"It is indeed—replete," Van Alstyne agreed softly. "I

find it quite surprising that Wavechurner's intelligence section is good enough to realize just how much we do want certain items. That a relatively small lineage group like Wavechurner's can provide all this is incredible.''

"If you will just turn to the appendices," Lucison said quickly, "you will find documentation proving that the items we are offering can indeed be delivered within the specified time limits. Any further assurances you may need, I am sure we can provide."

"You mistake me," Van Alstyne said, over steepled hands. "I have no doubt that this contract would be fulfilled in every particular. What I doubt is that Wavechurner will be providing the items itself— or that it will take ultimate possession of Hickock, for that matter."

Lucison's smile faltered. "Delegate Van Alstyne, I—"

"You are a ten percenter," Van Alstyne said calmly. "Your principal wishes to conceal from Innovator the true identity of the Shaper who will take control of Hickock. That, in itself is a basic part of any price to be negotiated. Report to your principal that Innovator is quite willing to deal—with the real party in interest."

Looking extremely worried, Lucison left, in his distraction forgetting his static box. Regala leaned forward and picked it up. His hands pressed and twisted. The box sprang open along a diagonal. Regala peered within, humming tunelessly.

"A-*ha*!" Thumb and forefinger plucked out a small sectoid-like piece of circuitry. "As I thought. The noisemaker disrupts all listening devices . . . except its own."

He rubbed. Wires and circuitry fluttered down like snow.

Two other offers were received that afternoon. Both were from delegates acting, so far as could be determined, on behalf of their own Patriarchs. Both were far less generous than Wavechurner's offer.

Hickock had lunch with Van Alstyne and Regala in the

Concourse. They sat at a table four meters above one of the long, irregular pools. Walkways reached the edge of the pool, where they leapt gracefully into the air to meet at right angles and fuse into an oval floating island. Tall, thin-leaved plants provided privacy from the throngs below.

The floor was nearly transparent. Dark, powerful shapes swam just beneath the surface of the water. Dimpled wakes trailed above them until the creatures sounded.

Yader joined them, looking preoccupied. His stride was long and loose, odd and yet familiar. He refused to meet Hickock's stare.

Six men in arrow formation detached themselves and began the ascent to their table. They projected much the same relaxed arrogance as Seaking's guards. The uniforms, though, had unit markings almost identical to those Hickock had seen on the shoulder of the manta pilot.

The point man came even with Hickock and halted. "Herald Rodney 1.31C4.H619" flashed from the identity plate hanging just above Hickock's eye level. In the center of the formation, a chunky man with craggy Nordic features and the most irritatingly smug expression Hickock had ever seen pulled a chair over and sat himself down as if totally uninvolved with the event before him.

The herald placed a block identical to Lucison's on the table in front of Van Alstyne. "For the privacy of both parties," he explained.

Van Alstyne lifted a skeptical eyebrow but said nothing.

"Delegate Van Alstyne," the herald said formally, "Highman Rutger Chvartz, Mandible of Skybreaker, greets you and requests the prompt return of property belonging to Skybreaker's lineage group."

His eyes were fixed solely on Van Alstyne. Hickock could almost believe himself invisible.

"In olden day, possession was thought to be only nine-tenths of the law," Van Alstyne responded. "Between lineage groups, however, possession is ownership. Your statement is therefore self-contradictory."

Chvartz made a small but precise movement with his left hand.

"The particular item under discussion was misplaced during a period of confusion," the herald said evenly. "Skybreaker is prepared to pay a generous finder's fee to whatever lineage group can return it to us."

"The item is present in front of you," Hickock replied testily. "I have a name. I will even respond to questions put to me politely."

"Skybreaker's generosity is well known among all herds," Van Alstyne said expressionlessly, "but Innovator believes this matter to be more important than mineral rights." She fell silent, seemingly self-absorbed.

"What is it you want?" the herald asked unwillingly.

"Information. We want information about certain spacecraft that have disappeared during the past year. We want to know about a particular action that occurred on an acceleration curve to Snowball."

Chvartz's left-hand middle finger jabbed forward and down.

"That information is for Skybreaker's access only," the herald said. "It is not a subject for negotiation and is, moreover, entirely irrelevant to the transfer of this item."

"Look at me while you are discussing me," Hickock demanded. "I am not just your item. I am a free man. If you want me, you must deal with me."

There was an abrupt hand flutter from Chvartz.

"Madame Van Alstyne," the herald said through gritted teeth. "If you wish us to deal seriously with you, you must demonstrate control of what you claim to be your property. The Highman is not used—"

Hickock's foot shot out, neatly sweeping one of the herald's ankles out from under him. The herald seemed to topple in slow motion. There was more than enough time for Hickock to come up from his chair and slam his fist into the herald's stomach. He slid around as the herald doubled over, pressed the hard edge of his left wrist's radius against the herald's cricoid cartilage, then grabbed the herald's arm and forced it up between the shoulder blades.

There was abortive movement from the guards. Yader had stood up, arms straight out, hands clasping something too small for Hickock to see. It was pointed at Chvartz.

"As you can see, our description of Mr. Hickock's combat prowess has not been in the least exaggerated," Van Alstyne said smoothly. "His occasional violent unpredictability suggests that his personality derives from a decision-making caste of warriors."

Hickock and the herald lurched spasmodically across the floor like a pair of ponderously drunken dancers. Plants toppled away from them. The herald's foot swung over emptiness. There were no railings.

Blue-black splotchy flesh, looking hard and strong, broke the surface of the water. Waves splashed together as it submerged.

"Sharphin," Hickock explained, his cheekbone pressing painfully against the herald's. "Carnivorous pack hunters. Go a little crazy, sometimes, if they scent hunting spawn. Wonder what they'll make of you."

"Madame Van Alstyne," the herald gasped.

"Is not the one holding you," Hickock said. "Your guards don't dare help you for fear of endangering your precious Highman. He won't speak a word in your behalf. That would disclose possession of human vocal chords; show that he's not a diminutive Shaper after all.

"So I'm all you have. My name is Hickock. All you need do is ask nicely for your release."

The herald thrashed desperately. Hickock jerked the man's arm up higher, levering him another step closer to the edge.

"Please." He was bending farther and farther over the water. "*Hickock*. Let me go!"

"Certainly." He stepped back two paces and gently released his hold. The herald crumpled, sobbing, to the floor.

Hickock stepped back, gulping air. He looked up. There was commotion on one of the wall walkways, about twenty meters away from him. A black-garbed female figure was pointing at him. A hulk leaned over attentively.

"Perhaps you can explain this unseemly attack on one of my appendages?" Highman Chvartz asked.

"It speaks!" Hickock said.

Cold blue eyes appraised him. "That herald had been useful to me. He will now have to delete himself to atone for the degradation you have inflicted on him, as well as the insult to myself."

"Not here, of course," he said, flashing a charming smile at Van Alstyne. "He will restrain himself until in the proximity of facilities where his remains may be disposed of speedily."

The herald, coughing and blinking away tears, pushed himself to his knees. Hickock felt bitterness tainting the back of his mouth.

"This is not worth ending anyone's life," he muttered.

"You were not aware that that was the necessary result of your actions?" Chvartz asked incredulously. "I see that my reports were right. Ignorance is indeed your long suit.

"And it bothers you that this herald must die. How quaint. Fear not. You will soon be able to atone—at length—for my brother officers whom you have murdered during the past six months."

Hickock concentrated on the ground, trying to disguise a rising panic. There was no memory he could identify with certainty that went further back than three months.

"I think not." He raised his eyes. "You have already told

us that you are unauthorized to pay the going price. So it appears that you are reduced to ineffectual bluster.''

Chvartz flinched involuntarily.

''You see?'' Hickock asked the herald. ''It's child's play to make a fool out of him. If that calls for suicide, it's a wonder Skybreaker's herds aren't completely depopulated.''

''I may not be authorized to pay,'' Chvartz said in a frighteningly normal voice, ''but I assure you, you shall.''

He pivoted and stalked down the ramp, accompanied by his guards. The herald stumbled to his feet and ran after them.

''Not that I'm complaining,'' Regala said, breaking the silence that followed, ''but if anything could induce the Highman to provide the information we want, it would be the performance you just gave.''

''Perhaps.'' Hickock shrugged. ''More immediately important—'' He looked around quickly.

Yader had vanished.

xiv

"THANK YOU FOR COMING," LIEDER SAID.

The room was a uniform off-white, curved where walls met ceiling and floor as if all had been blown in a huge fiberglass mold. Scatter rugs and real-time visual displays—fountains erupting from pools in the Concourse; a circle of artificial light deep underwater, in which translucently pink tubeworms grazed delicately on ordered rows of wrinkled green leafage; sunlight flashing off rows of choppy gray waves, while on the far horizon clouds massed in an approaching storm—provided almost painfully bright splotches of color.

"It would have been churlish to refuse," Hickock said. "Especially when the invitation was delivered by two hulks packing nerve whips and laser carbines."

"You have been known to be unpredictably violent," Lieder said, taking a seat across from him. One of the displays shifted scene: Hickock watched himself wrench the herald across the floor toward the edge of the dining island. The camera shifted to Yader and focused on the dark, metallic mass clenched within his fist.

"My guards relieved Dr. Yader of his toy," Lieder said absently. "Since it was only a plastic dummy, he received no more than a reprimand. Nonetheless, the incident you triggered could have become serious. We might have been forced to expel either Innovator's or Skybreaker's delegation. The ripple effects might have led to a general suspension of trading. Starswallower would be very displeased were that to result.''

Swinging tables flanked their chairs. Hickock sampled spicy crackers from a small bowl, then quenched the burning with a cold glass of fizzing, bitter liquid.

''You are right to be concerned,'' he agreed. ''I am without doubt a dangerous lout. I myself hardly know from minute to minute what I shall do next. Obviously, everyone would be much happier if I was removed from the scene. Expel me.''

''That would bring a troublesome protest from Innovator. Besides,'' she said, leaning closer, ''you interest me.''

As Hickock had suspected at their first meeting, her hair, freed from the confining coif, was a mass of curls, as thickly textured as a storm-tossed sea. He inhaled a barely discernible scent. He jerked his head away, furious with himself for feeling aroused.

An old memory floated up to consciousness: communal showers, stinking of harsh soaps and chlorine, sprayed water that alternated from scaldingly hot to bone-chillingly cold. Men and women were hurrying through that part of the delousing procedure. Knobby knees, pear-shaped torsos, sagging breasts—it was inconceivable to that younger Hickock that mere nakedness could ever be sexually exciting.

So it was *unfair* that this woman, with only head and hands exposed, dressed chastely as a nun—

He seized on the image, intrigued by the fact that he knew what a nun was. Did nuns exist in either Innovator's or Starswallower's herds? Religious crazies like Mother Gamorez certainly did.

—should be so damned provocative. It was also terribly dangerous. Hickock needed all his attention focused on understanding the forces around him. He could not afford distractions.

His glance fell on his bowl and glass, both half empty. Aphrodisiacs? he wondered.

"Personally or professionally?" He sharpened each word with conscious insolence.

She colored in confusion. Her eyes fled his in momentary panic.

"Pr-professionally, of course." She forced a businesslike crispness into her voice. "Starswallower is aware that you are the focus of a recent series of skirmishes between Skybreaker and Innovator. It has recently derived a first-order approximation of why you are so crucial to both Patriarchs."

"You might let me in on it," Hickock suggested. "I seem to be the only party in ignorance."

"It would be imprudent to give you that much insight into our intelligence capability," she said frankly. "But I am sure you know very well the reason."

Hickock shrugged.

"More immediately important is whether you recognize this." A packet, roughly brick-shaped but twice as large, landed in his lap.

Hickock's lips twitched. "Should I give you that much insight into *my* intelligence?" he murmured. Then his curiosity overcame him.

A classically severe liquid crystal display showed the correct time. Black and white insulated wires ran from the housing behind the display to a cluster of metal cylinders the size of his hand. He pressed a button at the corner of the display: 99:60:60. The seconds column launched into a leisurely countdown.

He turned the unit over. A metallic rectangle extended the length of the cluster. Its top edge was coated with a white, sticky substance. Burnished sawteeth ran along the inside edges.

Hickock's smile vanished. Gravely he handed the unit back to Lieder.

"It appears to be a limpet bomb, which I have just set." He looked at the ceiling. "Not my weapon of choice for use in an underwater installation."

Her fingers danced quickly across the setting buttons. The display zeroed and the time reappeared.

"Limpet bomb," she mused. "I am unfamiliar with that term. We call them clampers, after certain voracious marine parasites. But you are basically correct. This is a small chemical explosive. My people disarmed it, and the twenty-four other units discovered with it, six hours ago. It doesn't have enough punch to be truly dangerous. The lethality radius is just over two meters. It could not knock through one of our outer pressure walls. Nor does it have the fragmentation sheathing for antipersonnel use."

Hickock frowned and reexamined the device. "It's too big," he said, disturbed. "You could package that sort of power in something no larger than the LCD."

She was watching him intently, nodding slightly. "So you could. Unless the idea was to ensure their discovery. That is Highman Chvartz's explanation, in fact. He says that these were planted in Skybreaker's trade goods by your agents."

"Mine?"

"Innovator's."

He took another sip, letting the small bubbles abrade the roof of his mouth. "Perhaps."

"Or Chvartz could have planted them himself, either to ricochet suspicion against Innovator or to give my searchers something to find in hopes that they would go away happy and leave undisturbed whatever he really wants hidden. If the latter," she said smugly, "he has been very disappointed."

"Life is possibilities," Hickock agreed.

Lieder lowered her voice. "For you, possibilities are narrowing at an alarming rate. So far, luck and resourcefulness have allowed you to survive. Even that combination may not suffice against the Highman. Damaging his self-esteem as much as you did may cause him to react in ways not entirely rational. Given my doubts on the source of the explosives, I do not have just cause to expel him. But if he decides to move against you, I may not be able to react quickly enough to protect you.''

"You are concerned with my protection?'' The insolence sounded tentative even to his own ears.

"Yes.''

He stood, suddenly uncomfortable. "If there is nothing either of us can do, we have no more to say to each other.'' He scanned the walls for the thin lines that might be gun ports or the doors behind which guards would be standing.

He turned quickly at a humming behind him. A doorway shaped like a rounded cone opened on an empty corridor.

"You can go,'' Lieder said. "But you do not have to. You owe Innovator nothing. Our Patriarch, Starswallower, is the most powerful Shaper on this planet. If you come over to us, we will be able to protect you. If you cooperate with us, the rewards could be considerable.''

Hickock inclined his head, as if considering the proposition.

"But can you pay the price?'' he asked.

XV

ATTRACTION IS A MATTER OF APPETITE, HICKOCK TOLD HIM-self, staring up at the darkness. Love is a matter of will. My will can control both.

There was hard-won reassurance in that thought, backed up by memories almost available to him. A ghostly twinge in his stomach, associated with a long trek through a baking landscape of volcanic rock. Polarized goggles shielded his eyes. Spongelike material pressed gently against both mouth and nostrils, recovering exhaled water vapor. He would be three days without food.

"Pain is a good thing," some shadowy mentor reminded him. "Normally, you should pay attention to it: it carries important information. But sometimes some things are more important."

Rita Lieder's image formed before him.

Blessed are the pure in heart.

Well, of course! Single-mindedness was essential whether one was training to be a saint or an assassin. Even the Shapers knew that. Hadn't the Eggman . . . something about body swapping whole families . . .

His door clicked open, blackness giving way to blackness. His eyes were suddenly wide open. He tensed to swing as silently as possible onto the floor. A hand clamped over his mouth, forcing his head back down onto the pallet.

"A warrior team is advancing down the corridor. It has already knocked out the power on this level. I'm pretty sure it's after you. Unless you want to stay and negotiate, I suggest we move."

Though the words were whispered, the phrasing and cadences were immediately recognizable. Hickock forced himself to relax. The hand fell away from his mouth.

"Yader. *Jason* Yader. And that was you this afternoon, as well."

"Yep. Hold on to my shoulder and shut up, and maybe I can get both of us out of here."

They edged outside the door. The darkness was absolute, textured only by retinal feedback. Hickock forced himself to breathe slowly, straining for some sound beyond the pounding of his own blood.

The air vents were silent. Stale, warm air collected around his mouth.

His right hand was on Yader, his left hand trailing behind, brushing the wall. His soles brushed the carpet almost inaudibly.

Yader stopped. They waited. There was a slight movement of air, an aural sense of openness. Hickock imagined a cross corridor in front of them.

He counted his pulse. More than a minute passed. Then Yader leapt forward, out of his grasp. There was the sound of three blows landing in quick succession, followed by a grunt. Then Yader's hand tugged urgently at him.

"Run!"

Hickock ran. His right hand speared the air, searching for obstacles. Part of his mind continued to tick off the seconds. Four, five, six— A flash of white light froze the corridor in a lightning still life. The shock wave hit Hickock's shoulder blades, lifted him into the air, and dropped him to the floor.

He staggered to his feet. Darkness seemed to tilt around him.

"This way."

He strode after the voice. Walls loomed out of the darkness twice and hit his side, sending him reeling back to the center of the corridor.

Far ahead, diffuse circles of light splashed off a side wall. There was the sound of men conversing in low tones. Weapons stocks rasped dully against body armor.

Yader pulled him back the way they had come. "Sky-breaker's thugs have blocked our way out of Innovator country," he whispered. "We will have to go to ground."

They retreated into a farther corridor. Red light glowed from Yader's palm. He ran it slowly along the base of the wall. After four meters, he raised the light to waist level. Hickock could just barely discern a ring, less than two fingertip widths in diameter, recessed into the wall.

Yader placed a small metal box next to it. Five rows of bright yellow digits began a methodical race through all possible combinations. One, then two more, then all five digits froze. The wall sighed. A dark vertical line appeared. Yader grasped the edge with both hands and leaned. He vanished inside.

Following him, Hickock found himself wedged in a cramped space barely deeper than he was. Yader jostled him as he pushed back into its position in the wall.

"Keep quiet. I don't know if they have fredeyes or sniffers to track us here, or lectropicks for the door, but I would rather not make it easy for them."

Sensors picking up their presence switched on fiber optics. Rows of minilights, alternately amber and green, stretched upward and curved out of sight. Clusters of pipes vibrated as the fluids flowed within them. Color-coded wires twisted around each other like thigh-thick clumps of rainbow spaghetti.

"Watch your head," Yader warned as he started up a small ladder. "I'm afraid these tunnels were designed for maintenance midges."

"Where are we going?" Hickock asked.

Hickock stopped at the top of the ladder, swiveling his head as he tried to orient himself.

"Out of Innovator country. Out of the Trade Talks section. Starswallower's people are the only ones who can protect us now."

"So we're defecting." And just what sort of offer did Lieder make you? Hickock wondered.

Yader picked a tunnel. Knotted pathways of piping, running both with and at right angles to the tunnel, forced him into a crouch.

"I wouldn't call it that. Innovator sent you to the Trade Talks because it wanted the best deal it could get once it realized it couldn't get past your memory block. Now your presence here has endangered the Trade Talks themselves. Hard though you may find it to believe, you just aren't worth that much. So it is time to cut losses."

"Starswallower is going to allow Skybreaker's thugs to cut its power trunks and rampage through this habitat at whim?"

"Starswallower will probably throw Skybreaker the hell out of the Trade Talks as soon as it has its act together. Unfortunately, by that time both of us would be long gone."

Rings of light brightened before them, extinguished behind them. Cross tunnels intersected at varying angles. Some were so small that even midges would have found it hard to crawl through.

Twice the tunnel they followed was interrupted by huge vertical openings. Catwalks took them around the rims. Wind roared up from the depths.

The third time, there were no catwalks.

Yader knelt, surveying the edge. After a few seconds he located a ladder and swung himself over. Hickock followed.

After the first few meters, he lost all sense of perspective. The ladder became a treadmill, moving upward through slowly winking circles of light. Arms and shoulders tightened into quivering, aching knots. He forced himself into a slow, deliberate pace. With each step down, he carefully stretched every muscle he could. Glancing at the circle of shadows below, he could too easily imagine what would happen if his muscles began to spasm.

Without warning, his heel slammed into flooring. The pit seemed to spin around him. He slouched against the ladder, unable for a moment to pry his nerveless fingers from the rungs. Only then could he turn and realize they had come to a dead end.

The floor was a dark-metaled semicircle. No part of it was exactly level. Instead, gentle slopes swirled around drains spaced roughly three meters apart. Vibrations from far below shook the floor, died away, and came back with renewed force.

Open ducts and grillwork covered the curved wall. Yader examined dials seemingly scattered at random among the jumble of pipes that was the straight wall.

"Hell of a way to come to do a systems check," Hickock complained.

"There has to be a way through," Yader said. "We should be just below the Concourse. Most of the machinery around us helps circulate water from the ocean through the waterlocks, up to the sharphin pools, and back outside again."

"Waterlocks?"

"We are more than five kilometers below the surface," Yader explained patiently. "The differential between the water pressure outside and the air pressure in here is tremendous. If any part of the hull was breached, the jet of water that would thunder in would rip these walls like paper."

He resumed his examination of the wall. Hickock wondered if the basic premise might be wrong. His ride to Lieder's quarters, which were some distance beyond, had been through magna-tube, crammed in a capsule between two wordless hulks. Maybe that was the way one had to travel to get out of the area set aside for the Trade Talks. It would certainly discourage unauthorized incursions like their own.

Frowning, Yader placed his lectropick box below a seam almost out of reach above his head. The numbers began their race, stuttered, zeroed, began again, stuttered again, zeroed again. . . .

He reached up to detach the box. There was a hiss of displaced air as the wall vanished into the floor. Yader toppled into the darkness with a splash.

Hickock rushed to the edge. Yader thrashed to the surface less than a meter below him. At first he thought Yader was gasping for air. Then he realized that Yader's explosive exhalations were laughter.

Hickock extended an arm, braced himself, and pulled Yader up onto the ledge. His arm came away with a dark, sticky wetness. The lights in the chamber shed a reddish-purple radiance, almost useless for human eyes. Squinting, Hickock brought his wrist up to his face. He sniffed. His tongue confirmed the salty sweetness of blood.

It came from an incision in Yader's forearm, straight and razor thin. The agent's laughter died abruptly. "I didn't even feel that," Yader said wonderingly. He tried awkwardly to help as Hickock ripped off the already torn sleeve to fashion a makeshift pressure bandage. "I could have bled to death while laughing my head off. Thank God it didn't hit an artery."

"The ledge doesn't look that sharp," Hickock observed.

"It isn't."

Their eyes had adjusted as much as they could to the strange, dim lighting. The chamber before them was enormous. Although the ceiling rose no more than twenty meters, it extended farther than the combined sharphin pools in the main level above them. The water was smooth and oily.

Rough spheroids floated in clusters of eight. The nearest of these was less than a meter from where Yader had fallen in. A thin sheath of translucent jelly, occasionally thickening into milky globules, covered the entire area exposed to the air. Beneath the jelly lay the suggestion of a gnarled surface, of limbs folded tightly together.

"Crushers," Yader said, sounding a little uncertain of his own identification.

"Which are what?" Beneath his unease and exhaustion, Hickock felt again the old frustration of not being able to carry on a conversation for five minutes without having to have the simplest terms explained to him.

"They were specially bred amphibious warrior-spawn during the first generation after the Deliverance," Yader replied. "They were not very intelligent. Worse, they were unable to communicate in any human tongue. Most of the time, a show of force followed by a threat is enough to make people do what you want. Crushers couldn't make the threats intelligible. It was inefficient to send a Speaker with each one."

"What are they good for?"

Yader shrugged. "Nannies get a lot of use out of them in threatening their charges to be good. Beyond that . . ."

"No idea why Starswallower wants so many all of a sudden?" Hickock insisted.

"No," Yader said. His lips pressed into a thin, disturbed line.

The ledge extended only a few meters to either side of the opening. There were no walkways and no other tunnels. Straining his eyes, Hickock thought he could see a similar ledge far across the water. There was only one way to get there.

The water was painfully cold when Hickock slipped into

it. Luckily, it came no higher that his bottom ribs. The floor was solid but slippery. Hickock followed Yader, sometimes walking, sometimes dropping into the water to breaststroke for a few seconds before the aching cold in his bones forced him upright again.

The clusters of larval crushers crowded closer together as the men approached the center of the pool. The jelly, according to Yader, was what remained of the soft eggs originally laid by the Shaper. Its thinness suggested they might wake to adulthood in a week or less.

Hickock's lower limbs had become so numb that he could not feel his feet hit bottom. Only the slight shudder the impact sent to his upper body assured him that there was solidity beneath the water. Fits of shivering swept through him, disrupting his coordination. A strong current tugged him insistently sideways.

Two-thirds of the way across, Hickock slipped and fell. The current grabbed him. His arms scythed air and water in a powerful crawl stroke. His legs hit something hard well above floor level. He twisted, trying to see what it was.

A Crusher's slick, gleaming carapace loomed over him. It was rolling over slowly, unbalanced by his kick. A long, multijointed arm swung free, splashing the water in front of him. The front of the claw was as straight and sharp as a unicorn's horn. Behind that it broadened. Double rows of backward-slanting stiletto-sharp teeth lined each inner surface. The claw by itself was more that half the size of his entire body.

An eye, yellow and unblinking, rotated out of the water. Hickock froze, instinctively trying to blend in with the watery dimness. The eye peered incomprehendingly through the translucent jelly protecting it, then slid back beneath the surface.

Hickock regained his footing, and as quietly as he could, made his way from the uneasily sleeping monster.

They reached the far side of the pool a few minutes later. Hickock pulled himself onto the ledge. Forcing his body out of the heat-conserving fetal crouch it demanded, he rubbed arms and legs vigorously to restore circulation. Starbursts of pain rewarded his efforts.

Access to the service corridors were easy from that side.

"We should be beyond the sections set aside for the Trade Talks," Yader said. "As soon as I find an entry hatch, we will step into the main corridors. It is likely that we will be picked up immediately. That is nothing to worry about. In fact, we want an escort to Starswallower's security executive. So stay loose even if the hulks nudge you a bit."

They found a hatch only a few minutes later.

"Only two things to remember," Yader said. "The first is my name: Howard Yader. The second is that you are here requesting asylum because Innovator's herd hasn't been able to protect you from Skybreaker's thugs. Since both are true, you should be able to maintain them in good conscience."

Yader hit the punch plate at the sides of the hatch. Hickock followed him through, expecting to hear a quick shout and to feel rough hands thrusting him against the wall.

For a moment he thought Yader had made a mistake and opened a hatchway into another set of service corridors. The lighting was still dim.

But the hallways were wider and higher. Metal paneling covered the inner mechanisms of the walls. It was also quieter: there was only the barely perceptible rustling of air sifting down from the vents.

Yader pivoted, seemed to consult an inner sense of direction, and pointed. "That way."

They followed the hallway to where it joined a main artery, ten meters high by twenty-five wide. The stillness was unchanged.

Yader licked his lips uneasily. "When Lieder had you

picked up for questioning, did everything over here seem . . . all right?''

Hickock thought back. ''I was under close guard all the time. Between the private magna-tube station and Lieder's quarters it was less than fifty meters. Nonetheless . . . I passed several people, both going and coming. They all seemed intent on their own business. There was no particular tension that I can remember.'' He looked sharply at Yader. ''We couldn't have taken a wrong turning, I suppose, and come to an abandoned quarter, one temporarily evacuated for renovation?''

''No,'' Yader said, shaking his head impatiently. ''Besides, this is Starswallower's main submarine habitat. The human herd it quarters here has to number over a million. Just setting aside room for the Trade Talks should have severely strained its space resources. There certainly should not be anything like this much unused space.''

''Suppose those weren't Skybreaker's thugs?'' Hickock suggested. Yader started around and stared at him. ''Suppose we were wrong in thinking that action was directed against me. Could it have been part of a larger action directed against the entire habitat?''

''Nonsense!'' Yader said, not bothering to justify himself.

They strode on in the same direction. Double rows of footprints stretched far behind them in the light dust.

The walls on the left gave way as they crossed a large hallway. Stools surrounded round tables in what had once apparently been a food kiosk. Star-shaped scorch marks reached from floor to ceiling. On the stools and on the floor beneath them, a differently textured darkness had flowed into dark, deeply staining pools.

Hickock picked up a hand-sized box of carbochips, brittle with age. ''It happened while they were eating,'' he said. ''Quickly, violently, thoroughly, to little or no resistance.

Then there was a perfunctory cleanup. But where are the victors?''

Yader's eyes darted nervously from corner to corner. ''Herds are sometimes culled of defectives or undesirables. Usually, though, that is done at an examination station or while the victim sleeps. Perhaps an incipient revolt . . .''

Without thinking of it, they had both lowered their voices. As they walked on, Hickock adjusted his stride: ankle muscles tense, heels rolling to the balls of his feet so smoothly and noiselessly that walking seemed to have become an extended dance step.

A snow-white rectangle, looking new and out of place, covered half of one wall at the next cross corridor. Multicolored lines wrapped around each other on a score of levels. To Hickock, it looked like the exploded diagram of a highly complex piece of hydraulic machinery.

''I haven't seen one of these since I was in the crèche,'' Yader said slowly. ''Youngsters haven't had time to memorize all the routes, and it helps them visualize the habitat as a whole.

''See.'' He pointed to a black dot. ''There is where we are. That is the route we have been following, and this is the way into the central complex.''

Thereafter, each cross corridor was emblazoned with a map. The black dot made slow but steady progress into the interior.

A low murmuring reached them. The hallway brightened ahead. Another ten meters, and it was as if they had crossed an invisible barrier. Workmen were busy threading large strands of intestine-like tubing through a disassembled floor. The moving walkways that formed the spines of the main hallways were functioning. Off them, workers rolled packets of paneling and tools.

A matronly superintendent looked up from her clipboard,

took in their expressions, and laughed. "You boys look lost. You part of a swap team that got separated?"

"Yes," Yader said. "I don't know how it happened. I thought we were following the right directions, but . . ."

She nodded indulgently. "There's still a lot of confusion. Probably not even your fault. These team leaders may look seasoned, but some of them are nearly as raw as you are, you know?

"Here, take this." From her clipboard she gave them a leaflet, which Hickock recognized to be a smaller version of the wall map they had been following. "In-processing is only five levels up. Somebody there will have your assignment."

Hickock thanked her.

"And stay out of the deserted sections," she warned them. "The last of the defenders were flushed out of the west bulkheads months ago, but there are so many levels that if you got really lost, you could starve to death, you know?"

It took them fifteen more minutes to find a hulk and make him understand that they were surrendering themselves.

xvi

BEYOND THE GLASS, DUAL ROWS OF COLOR MONITORS EX-
tended out of sight in either direction. Each shifted scenes at
approximately three-second intervals. Most seemed to be of
the Concourse from various angles. Occasionally a blue-
uniformed observer leaned forward in his chair and tapped a
few keys. Lips moved in utter silence.

This must be the herd's central security complex, which
gathered the scenes Hickock had seen displayed in Lieder's
apartment. The place was run with a quiet efficiency Hickock
found impressive. He relaxed in a padded chair so comfortable that he could almost bring himself to ignore the narrow
slots from which, at the appropriate electronic signal, bands
would shoot forth to clasp wrists and ankles in place.

Yader paced in front of him, radiating ragged aggravation.
"I am simply unable to understand why we are being treated
in this manner. We come to you for protection. We bring
with us information that I know you find valuable, as well as
what may be the most avidly sought prize among all lineage
groups today. Yet you do not welcome us. You do not use
us. Instead, you subject us to repeated sessions of puerile
questioning."

He knotted his brows together, glaring at Lieder. "If you
really think that we are spies, or you simply lack the imagi-

nation to utilize us effectively, then send us back where we came from. I have no desire to fall under Skybreaker's control, but at least its herd understands that man's importance.'' He jabbed a finger in Hickock's direction.

Lieder regarded him impassively, saying nothing.

The interrogator, a bald, round-faced man whose voice rarely rose above a monotone, looked up patiently from his notes. ''I understand that you have had a trying time, Dr. Yader, but you must appreciate that habitat security is of primary importance. Your very appearance here has been a rude surprise.''

''One I have repeatedly explained. You have the lectro-pick, something I would never have given you voluntarily if I was a spy. It was handed to me by a member of our delegation with the suggestion that I might use it to enter areas reserved for the other delegations. But as I explained when I was admitted to this habitat, I am a scientist. I have no time for these games.''

A young boy winked into existence above and behind Lieder. Clothed in a loose-fitting robe, he floated in lotus position: the Buddha, even down to being surrounded by a glowing nimbus. The face, hook nose jutting from angular cheekbones, cut through the illusion. Sharp brown eyes raked quickly over Hickock, dismissed him, and focused piercingly on Yader.

Yader's eyes shifted uneasily. Neither Lieder nor the interrogator seemed aware of anything extraordinary.

''You have said you were attacked by Skybreaker's warriors,'' the interrogator said patiently. ''It is a serious charge to accuse any delegation of breaking the Trade Talks truce. You were in the dark all the time. How can you be sure the attackers came from Skybreaker?''

''Well, I can't, of course,'' Yader said, exasperated. ''I can only make those inferences obvious to anyone who has not undergone a lobotomy. Skybreaker's forces made one costly and nearly successful abduction attempt of Hickock. I presume even your security section is aware of that. This afternoon their delegation made two attempts to purchase Hickock. The only reason the last attempt failed was their refusal to share the basis for their interest.

"However, at that meeting, Hickock gravely humiliated two of their party, including Highman Chvartz. Less than eight hours later, we were attacked. The inference does not require a genius. Save for that lectropick, both of us would probably have been shipped out under your noses in a commodity canister by now."

"The lectropick specs have been in our data banks for three years," the floating boy announced. "Innovator's security forces apparently consider the design obsolete, having issued more sophisticated devices to their agents during the last four months. This may be their last effort to get some use from them before disposing of them entirely."

"If we have had the specifications for three years, why is it that we have not yet instituted effective countermeasures?" Lieder asked.

"Physical accessibility was the main impedance until eight months ago," the boy said blandly. "Since then, as you are well aware, our resources have been considerably extended. The necessary implementation involves not only rewiring every hatchway in the habitat, of which scores remain unmapped, but also an extensive rewriting of the software in our access control computers. An optimum projection for such an effort would be four months from date of initiation.

"You may remember that I was tasked with presenting an estimate of the likelihood that our defenses would be breached. I assessed the likelihood as forty-eight percent and recommended that the Trade Talks be postponed. I was overruled."

Hickock had been covertly studying Yader during the exchange. The phrasing, the stride, all the physical mannerisms were close to those of the Howard Yader whom he had met on the triphibian—but they were not genuine. None of Starswallower's herd had the personal acquaintance necessary to see through the deception, or any reason to suspect it. But if that truth helmet was to be placed over his head and the right questions were to be asked, Hickock might well compromise the entire operation. Never mind that he had no idea what it was.

"What exactly is the nature of your relationship to Hickock?" the interrogator asked.

"He's my patient," Yader said. "He has not been aware of it, of course. He was assigned to me by Dr. Mackern. It was his hope that the stimulus of seeing so many different herds represented at the Trade Talks, including, we hoped, his own herd, would serve to loosen his memory block. Failing that, I was to be available if his original herd tried to regain him. If we captured one of their agents, I was to be part of the interrogation team with the mission of learning any clues to the operation of the memory block."

For the first time, the interrogator allowed himself to look interested. "You are saying that Hickock was under your care?"

"Not directly. I was part of an advisory group. We suggested approaches to be investigated and evaluated the resulting data. I never dealt personally with Hickock. That was reserved to Mackern and Vaheri. Therefore I would be able to observe him during his sojourn here without him recognizing me or my purpose."

Hickock kept his eyes straight ahead. It would be well to show no reaction to anything Yader said, no matter how unexpected.

"You were high enough in Innovator's herd to be trusted with such an assignment, and yet you now say you are defecting?" The skepticism was undisguised.

"I am not saying that. I am saying that Innovator has aban-

doned both Hickock and me. Mackern's jealousy kept my
treatments from serious implementation. When his own had
come to their necessarily sterile conclusion, and Skybreaker
began putting pressure on us, he just threw up his hands in
despair and had Hickock bundled off here to fetch the best
price he could. When I protested, he had me sent along to
prevent me from going over his head and exposing his in-
competence.

"Even that I was willing to abide. But when it became
apparent last night that Innovator's control had so broken
down that we could not be protected from attack, I ran to
what appeared the most logical haven for safety. Now I—"

The floating image interrupted him. "I have just accessed
the corridor cameras in the sections reserved for Innovator's
delegates. Playback follows. *Guards!*"

Two hulks who had been standing massive and motionless
as twin monoliths snapped into quick, almost daintily precise
movement. Hickock felt, rather than saw, the barrel leveled
at his head.

A sphere of darkness engulfed the boy, expanding until it
touched floor and ceiling. Luminous, seemingly disjointed
figures moved within it. Hickock squinted, trying to adjust
to the unusual perspective. He was looking down on himself
and Yader. Hands and faces glowed brightly. Their clothes
appeared light gray. The rest of the corridor was dark, save
for a ghostly billowing whiteness flowing from a vent.

Hickock was letting Yader guide him, brushing his fingers
against the wall for added orientation. His eyes were wide,
unseeing. Yader moved surefootedly in the blackness. He
halted Hickock at a cross corridor. Two men crouched to
either side, fixing clamper bombs to the walls. One looked
up, gave Yader a hand signal—

A breath of air was the only warning Hickock had. The
barrel beside his head pivoted quickly and crackled. Yader
froze, halfway up from his chair, right arm fully extended.

The tips of his fingers traced a rapidly widening spiral in the air.

He toppled like an overbalanced statue. The hulk whose rifle he had briefly knocked aside brought it down to port arms. Hickock's hulk brought his rifle back to bear on Hickock. Not that there was any need to. The straps from his chair bit unyieldingly into his flesh.

He lay back, forcing himself to relax. Obligingly the straps retracted into their slots.

A blinding flash ripped across the holo-sphere, sending the images of himself and Yader tumbling down the length of the corridor. The sphere shrank and became once again a boy floating in midair.

Lieder bent over Yader's rigid form, a thin, transparent rod held between thumb and middle finger. Very gently she let its end touch his staring eye. She rotated the rod, then pulled it back. She lifted an almost invisible disk off its end and held it very close to her right eye.

"Infrared converter lenses," she murmured. "I had no idea they could be made so thin."

She looked up at the nearby hulk. "Relax him immediately!" she ordered. "I don't want him going into hypoventilation shock."

The hulk unholstered a pistol that appeared ludicrously small in his huge hand. He placed it at the base of Yader's ear and depressed the trigger. Yader's body jerked. Abruptly he seemed to deflate like a punctured tire. The hulk lifted him onto a shoulder and carried him from the room.

Lieder turned, meeting Hickock's stare. "Forgive us," she said, "In the confusion, we have shamefully neglected you. I think the time has come to remedy that."

XVII

THE DEBRIEFINGS WERE AS POLITE AS THEY WERE PRO-
longed. Nearly every morning, a new interrogator would pick
up a thin sheaf of typed pages or a wrinkled set of index
cards, or would simply glance over his desk comp screen,
and begin precisely where his predecessor had left off. Each
session averaged ten hours.

There were no overt signs of coercion. Any weapons stayed
well concealed behind gun ports. Hulks entered only to bring
food and drink, which Hickock could order at any time.
During a session, he could sit or pace as he pleased.

Much of the time he preferred to pace.

A basic understanding had been achieved almost immediately. There was no reason to believe that Hickock's loyalties, if they could be uncovered, would coincide with those
of Starswallower's herd. However, it was just as unlikely that
they would coincide with Innovator's. Therefore, while the
questioning concentrated on his detention by Innovator, there
was no reason to be other than truthful.

Only once was the air of cool pragmatism strained. The
interrogator that day was an enormously fat man of indeter-
minate age. His hands, which tended to flutter about indecisively, were soft and pudgy as a baby's. The shining

pinkness of his head thrust up from a shapeless mound of flesh that seemed to pool beneath it.

Yader was the subject under discussion. The interrogator was visibly disturbed that Yader had been able to lie without detection during in-processing. He nibbled incessantly around the problem of personae: Jason or Howard? Which was which? What did Hickock mean when he said that the Yader who had presented himself to Starswallower's security was Jason pretending to be Howard? Was there ever a time when Howard was not a pretense?

Hickock answered as truthfully as he could and then asked his own question. "What has happened to Yader? Under either name."

The interrogator glanced guiltily at Lieder. His head hunched down into his shoulders, withdrawing turtlelike into his shell.

"Mr. Yader has been undergoing interrogation even as you have been," Lieder said briskly. "In his case, there have been unforeseen—complications."

There was an uneasy silence, in which Hickock could hear himself inhale and exhale. "Torture?" he wondered. "Or have you ordered his execution?"

"Of course not!" Lieder said with unconvincing impatience. "We have just found his defenses surprisingly unique. Our next step with him requires considerable forethought."

There would be no further explanation.

"Would you be disturbed to learn of his execution?"

Hickock considered the question. The purpose of this test was impenetrable. He was thrown back on the ambiguous resources of truth.

Yader had held out a cup to him. *If you were perceived to be a threat . . . you would be instantly eliminated.* With some regret, perhaps, but no less efficiently or finally for that.

"Yes," he said, surprised at his own answer. "He was

both a pleasant and interesting companion. His Patriarch was not allied with yours, but I know of no way he harmed you so as to deserve death.''

Lieder's expression seemed curiously vulnerable. ''We have no intention of killing him. He shall be hurt no more than is absolutely necessary.''

On that subject, there was nothing more to say.

There came a morning that broke the pattern of interrogation. The hulks escorted him to a garden with a high blue ceiling. Rows of fan bushes blocked line of sight to the walls, making the room feel larger than it could possibly be. Interlacing fountains swept through the air, prisming bright beams of polarized light. Notes from a string quartet competed almost successfully with gently splashing water.

The effect was to emphasize the silence. There was no constant murmur of voices, no ceaseless tread of feet or hum of moving walkways. None of the maze of piping he knew to be present between the walls made itself heard. Even the air vents were far enough away that the sighing from their lips and the rumble deep within their throats were lost in the distance.

The plants caught Hickock's attention. Thick, symmetrically spiked stalks, purplish red in hue, stretched vainly toward the electric suns above them. Iridescent, almost microscopically small petals formed a translucent haze over the surface of dark green mounds. Mosslike mats covered all otherwise bare ground.

''Our ancestors felt an almost sacred attachment to the flora of their native planet.'' A man of medium height stood behind Hickock. A closely trimmed beard, coming to a point just below his chin, outlined the bottom edges of his face. He had been an observer at several of the interrogation sessions. ''I do not deny a practical aspect to the garden: new food sources are always being discovered; medicinal compounds even, greatly beneficial to the well-being of our Shapers. Still, if you pay attention to the arrangement of the garden and note how through several generations the emphasis in breeding has been on form and color, you might conclude that our genetic memory was trying to re-create our planet of origin.''

''Are you familiar with neRoses?'' Hickock asked.

The stranger frowned. ''I think not.''

''Look for them on Innovator's trading menu,'' Hickock suggested. ''You will find them quite interesting.''

The hulks had disappeared. The stranger led him down a path to a white table. Lieder was seated in a chair, sipping a long black drink. Next to her, in a white lab coat, was the boy he had last seen floating in the air. Seeing Hickock's look of recognition, the boy grinned and plunged one hand noiselessly through the surface of the table.

''Excuse me for not introducing myself,'' the stranger said, taking a seat directly across from the hologram. ''I am Dr. Hans Heiliger. Security Director Lieder has put me in charge of your most interesting case.''

Hickock seated himself on the fourth side. Two drinks were in the center of the table. At Lieder's invitation, he took one of them—the one farthest from him. Heiliger smiled, took the one that remained, and sipped.

''You will excuse me for not returning your introduction,'' Hickock replied. ''My name you already know. Much more than that I am not able to tell you.''

''That is a matter of concern to both of us,'' Heiliger said. ''From what we have been able to piece together, we believe that Innovator transferred you here because it realized our—may I be so immodest as to say 'my'—superiority in the area of psychological engineering. It hoped to dangle you before us as on a fishhook. We would bite, find a way through your memory block, and then Innovator would jerk you back.

''That plan fell apart when we realized Yader's true role.

Still, the basic perception is valid. We do have resources beyond those of Mackern and company. I have spent the last two weeks gathering as much data as possible about the extent of your block, as well as the trigger mechanism that causes your parasympathetic nervous system to shut down. Now I think we are ready to remove the block.''

There was a low buzzing in Hickock's ears. His lips felt thick. ''You believe my answers without putting me under that snake-wired helmet you used for in-processing?'' he asked carefully.

Heiliger looked amused. ''The wires are necessary only because of the number of people we were handling simultaneously. And as convenient misdirection. Microphones picked up your voice for stress analysis. Most of your other bodily responses were monitored by the chair you sat in. Low-power infrared laser pulses kept tabs on you while you paced.''

Hickock found that he was nodding and stopped himself. ''How do you propose to get by the memory block?''

''I begin by considering how selective the block is,'' Heiliger said. ''So far as I can tell, you have access to all the skills, to all the abstract knowledge you have acquired throughout your life. At times surprise or just intense concentration on this general knowledge has managed to trick out information from behind your block. Thus Mackern was able to learn that you were proficient in unarmed combat and in piloting fighter-class spacecraft. That the name of the larger vessel to which you were assigned was the *Vengeance*. That by the death of the previous holder, you assumed the rank or office of Go'el.

''We see a recurrent pattern whenever we pursue those memories. Your palms perspire. Heartbeat and blood pressure increase. Your breathing becomes fast and shallow.

''Only then, *after* we see these physiological indicators, do we note this dramatic shift in your brain-wave patterns.''

Graph paper unrolled like a herald's parchment. Eight jagged columns made it look like a mental seismograph.

"You see, these two here are almost totally suppressed. That is your block kicking in. Your anxiety has triggered it. If we wish to get to your hidden memories, we must suppress your programmed anxiety."

Heiliger's voice had gradually become deeper and softer. It rose and fell in gentle waves.

"How—" Hickock began. He took a deep slow breath, closing his eyes in order to better concentrate on the tremendous effort it took to think through a sentence. "How do you propose to cut off the anxiety reflex?"

"I have already done so," Heiliger said quietly.

Hickock followed the direction of his gaze and saw, without surprise, that the glass had slipped from his hand. A dark, wet stain spread along his thigh.

"You see? We have already embarked on the voyage whose prize is the full restitution of you to yourself. In the next few minutes I will guide you into your shadowed depths. You will be whole again. You will remember your duties and loyalties and will have the knowledge to act in their behalf."

In a way neither threatening nor even perceptible, Heiliger's eyes had grown until they merged with the blue of the ceiling and expanded outward until they became the cobalt sea in which he floated, amniotically content. Below was darkness. Light filtered down from high above.

An oval appeared in front of him. It grew, turned toward him, and became a face. His own face, smiling, with eyes closed against the golden light that washed over it.

"Please state your name."

The smiling face parted its lips. "Patrick M. Hickock."

"What is your rank?"

"Commander. Go'el."

"To which Patriarch do you belong?"

"None."

There was inward hissing of breath, then Lieder's voice, tense and excited. "A rogue herd. We were right!"

"To what individuals or institutions do you owe obedience?"

"The Noram Defense Forces. The Institute for Racial Survival."

The boy's voice spoke, crisp and emotionless. "Our data base contains no reference to either organization. Be sensitive to possible relationships with the Council of Co-operation."

"You were part of a battle group that attacked a Sky-breaker convoy. What was this battle group?"

"Allied Expeditionary Force, third attack wing. I was detailed to the flagship *Vengeance.*"

"Where was the expeditionary force based?"

Silence.

"He's fighting you," Lieder said.

"Nothing like that shows on the readouts," Heiliger replied. "It must be that he doesn't comprehend the question. Let me try to work around it.

"Where were you born?"

"Wister, in Winglend."

"No correlative for either reference," the boy said.

"On what planetary body, in what stellar system, is Winglend?"

"Earth. The solar system."

This time the silence extended so long that, to the extent that he could think of such things, Hickock thought the voices had gone away. He tumbled slowly in the blue stillness.

"Earth was destroyed more than three hundred years ago, when the Sun went nova," Heiliger said sharply. "How do you reconcile this fact with your statement?"

"Three hundred twelve years ago, severe solar flares raised the average global temperature ten degrees. It dropped back to its preflare average within five years, after stressing the biosphere to the point of near ecological collapse. At the time, many feared that this was the prelude to the explosion of the Sun. Even back then, however, enough was known of the thermonuclear reactions that powered the solar core for it to be realized that there were no conceivable circumstances under which such flares could occur naturally. It took seventy years for civilization to recover enough for an international group of physicists to confirm what the paranoid and xenophobic had long maintained: the flares had been caused artificially, almost certainly by the same aliens who had abducted an estimated twenty million humans from the world's population centers.'' And even in the submarine blueness, he could taste the bitter dust on his tongue, could feel the warm sunlight streaming through the window as he sat down from reciting his history lesson to a grudgingly approving instructor.

"My God." The voice, a hoarse whisper echoing through azure caverns, could have belonged to anyone.

"You actually believe that story." Scorn sharp enough to etch steel dripped from the high, precise tones.

"He is telling the truth!" Near hysteria spiked a high quaver into Heiliger's words. "The instruments are unambiguous."

"He believes he is telling the truth." The boy paused to let the distinction dampen the dangerously high play of emotions. "Do I have to spell everything out for you? Explorer was shaped by Starswallower because it recognized Innovator as its most dangerous, most unpredictable opponent. For the past decade, Innovator has been served by Dalkan, the most aggressive and efficient administrator its herds have ever had. Dalkan has promoted Garrison and Mackern as his two primary tools. Both have put us repeatedly on the defensive.

"Now there comes to us from this most successful adversary an individual who tells us that he has spent more time than he can account for in the hands of our adversary's most effective instruments. An individual placed in our hands by a man who happens to be one of Garrison's agents. An individual who, on being subjected to your special questioning techniques, disgorges a story which any sensible person would consider a joint hallucination of the Church of the Captivity and the Council of Cooperation.

"Tell me, what would result should this fabrication be circulated generally?"

"Civil war," Lieder said in slow horror.

"You are overly optimistic. No Shaper would ever let it go that far. That information would be treated like a contagion and eliminated. If the elite of our herd leaders were suddenly replaced, who would benefit most?"

There were more words, falling like rain upon the swell. Among them were words of power. At their sound, the light above faded. Darkness coiled up and extinguished him.

xviii

THERE WAS NO INTERROGATION THE NEXT DAY. EXCEPT FOR the two times when hulks appeared with food trays, Hickock's door remained locked. He hardly noticed it. Hour merged into hour as he dived deep into his past, linking memory to memory, forming coherence—forming identity.

Each time he looked into the mirror above the sink, he saw a new face.

The day after that, questioning resumed. Lieder, Heiliger, and the light ghost were the only ones to speak to him. The boy stayed in the background most of the time. Heiliger probed the extent of his "false" memories. His patronizing air irritated Lieder more than it did Hickock.

The questions themselves were carefully constructed, much more so than would have been necessary to determine the consistency of an illusion.

"So far you have been vague on the exact number of ships in this expeditionary force of yours," Heiliger said. "List the various classes of vessels comprising it, the number of each class, and each vessel's total complement."

Hickock was reclining in his chair, his lids half covering his eyes. "I think not."

"What?"

Hickock's eyes opened fully. Placid blueness regarded

157

Heiliger. "You heard me. If my memories are factual, I am disclosing information that may be damaging to my shipmates, and conceivably to everyone on Earth and its colonies.

"If, on the contrary, these memories are implants, it is a waste of your time and my own to pursue them."

Heiliger radiated an astounded anger. "It is necessary to measure the extent of your false memories before embarking on the next stage of your treatment, even as it was necessary to measure the extent of your ignorance before making our first breakthrough.

"Even if you do not come from Earth, you are clearly linked to the destruction or disappearance of a dozen spacecraft belonging to four different Patriarchs. It is quite likely that at least some of the memories you ascribe to Earth are links to your true masters.

"Let us proceed, if you don't mind. I am not used to being questioned by either patients or prisoners."

Hickock's gaze was untroubled. It flicked quickly to the image of the boy and back again. "On the other hand, you find being a ventriloquist's dummy quite congenial.

"Let's go beyond these games. You already know most of what you need to know about me. The major gaps that remain are there because you have not had the imagination to ask the right questions.

"I will suggest one: Just what do I know concerning the fate of Starswallower?"

There was silence. Congealed tension held all three figures motionless. That was when he knew he was right.

"We have overindulged you." The boy's image enlarged, glowing with a crimson nimbus. His skin luster changed to a dull, metallic gray. Sharply triangular fingernails flashed with reflected light. Green fire flared in his eyes. "Dr. Heiliger. Demonstrate to the subject why he should want to cooperate fully with us. Try to do no permanent damage. He may yet prove of value, with the proper chastisement.''

After Heiliger finished and departed, Lieder supervised the technicians who removed wires from Hickock. Then they undid the straps, releasing the bruised flesh beneath.

He tried to stand. As if bereft of bone, his legs folded beneath him. The technicians supported him across the room and propped him up in a shower stall. Hot, soapy water drummed into his body, sluicing away crusted salt and filth.

Hot air roared in through the top of the stall and moved down either side of him, pushing the water down and off. A power chair was wheeled next to the stall. A robe was draped across the back, spread open on the seat. The technicians helped him seat himself and folded the robe over him.

Lieder held out a small cup. Shadowed eyes gleamed. Hickock bit back a wisecrack. Conceivably, her distress was genuine. Almost conceivably, no one else had noticed it. Nothing could be gained by making her own people suspect her.

''Do not drink this,'' she said. ''Use it to clean your mouth out. You can spit into the shower drain.''

A few drops slid down his throat by mistake. Without warning, he found himself half out of the chair as his stomach tried to squeeze itself out of existence. The contractions went on for five minutes without result. Every portion of his digestive track had been thoroughly emptied more than an hour before.

Finally the convulsions weakened to little more than sporadic flutters. He collapsed back into the chair.

''You should not have angered Iqbal,'' Lieder said. It was the first time anyone had mentioned the boy's name. ''He is our information clearing point for policy matters. You must not treat him lightly at your next meeting.''

Her voice was clear and completely steady. Perhaps he had imagined the wetness in her eyes.

His vocal chords functioned on the third attempt. "When—will I see him again?"

She frowned, surprised that he had asked that question. "Tomorrow. If you have recovered enough."

Hickock nodded, satisfied. Iqbal would need all of that time to prepare.

xix

THE SMALL WHITE BALL HIT THE TABLE WITH THE SOUND of a bone cracking. It ricocheted to the right with sidespin. The young girl in gray threw herself almost horizontal to get her paddle on it.

"Out. Nice try, though."

The far side of the table was a third smaller than the near side. Iqbal Ali sat in a power chair twice the size of the one that had carried Hickock the day before. Wires and tubes sprouted from him like a cloak of seaweed. Sweat coursed down the face wherever it was not covered by metal or plastic. Precisely defined, diminutive muscles knotted the forearm of the hand clutching the paddle.

"We must cut short our session, Rochesalana," Ali said, spotting Hickock standing just beyond the bulkhead, flanked by two hulks. "I will see you all the earlier tomorrow."

"You are doing very well, sir," his opponent said. "Six months ago you didn't have nearly the strength to return that last shot, much less the coordination."

Ali gave a tiny nod. "Two more months, and we shall enlarge my side of the table. A year, and I shall play this game standing. And beat you."

Rochesalana smiled. She flipped the table over on its side and collapsed the legs, carrying it over to the wall.

"Till tomorrow," she said. She brushed by Hickock as she left the room.

One of the hulks nudged Hickock. He moved forward into the room. The hatch slid quietly into place and sealed with a dry hiss. To his ears, the room felt suddenly smaller.

"Take a cushion."

Hickock selected a cushion, placed it before Ali, and slowly lowered himself upon it. His muscles protested almost audibly as they stretched, each one sliding abrasively over its companions.

"I did warn Heiliger not to impair you," Ali said, watching him closely. "However, the procedure he employed requires careful monitoring, as well as an unscientific quantity of luck. Tendons are sometimes pulled; bones have been known to snap. I regret having to use such methods."

"It was a necessary misdirection," Hickock conceded, not to be outdone in graciousness. "Though I do wish you had been able to come up with something that did not leave me so clearly aware of where each chest muscle attaches to each rib, every time I inhale."

Ali's face was expressionless. "I suppose I should be more sympathetic to other people's pain. Unfortunately, I find it difficult to look past my own.

"You undoubtedly consider these—connections—bizarre, though you are too polite to stare." His gesture took in the snake's nest of wires and tubing extruding from head and torso. Not all were opaque. In some, red and brown fluids of various consistencies churned furiously or flowed slowly through transparent plastic.

"The transparency is functional. Much of the technology necessary for my life support has never been more than inspired jury-rigging. Blockages tend to occur. Were they unnoticed for more than a few minutes, they would certainly prove fatal. It is not a matter I care to entrust to mere machines." The words had a quiet, savage irony.

"You were in a serious accident?" Hickock asked.

"On the contrary, what you see is the result of scrupulous consideration. Several decades ago, our Patriarch encountered difficulty when it tried to breed a human-computer interface. The neural mechanics of linkage were simple. The problems arose from the personalities of the subjects. Some were addictive. They tended to completely dissolve themselves within the cybernet. Nonaddictive personalities suffered a revulsion so severe that it manifested itself in an autoimmune response at the site of the neural implants. This was diagnosed as psychosomatic, but they died nonetheless.

"At roughly the same time, certain pre-Deliverance writings came to the Patriarch's attention. Either fantasies or very odd philosophy, they suggested that the human race would at some future epoch evolve into purely rational disembodied intelligence.

"From these hints, the Patriarch inferred that the human brain was unable to integrate a rapidly changing data stream while coping with the constant tumult of demands made by the body.

"Its solution was direct. In its womb tanks, it cultured fetuses from which everything was removed except the brain."

"Was this exercise in Gnosticism successful?" Hickock asked.

Ali was expressionless for a second. Then his eyes sparkled with delight. "What an odd—yet exact—metaphor. I would never have made that connection.

"No, its efforts failed miserably. Most of these floating brains never attained the size of the top joint of your little finger. Brain/body—perhaps mind/body as well?—had proven a false dichotomy. A necessary feedback loop had been cut. Merely having protection and the proper nutrients was not enough. Without the stimulus of directing a body's growth, the brains never developed much beyond a mass of disordered neurons.''

"Except in your case," Hickock observed.

"In my case, a unique balance was achieved. I was allowed to develop something of a body, but it was made dependent on the cybernet for every sort of sustenance and vital function. My very blood sugar and urea concentrations are controlled through these wires.

"It is no exaggeration to say that this entire room is a necessary extension of my body. If I appear to ruminate or to need time to digest a point you make, I may perhaps be doing that more literally than you at first imagine.''

"You are the only success?" Hickock asked skeptically.

"There were partial successes," Ali said. His gaze seemed to turn inward. His breathing deepened and became more audible. "Their output was—sporadic, often incomprehensible. I alone was able to make direct contact with them, through the cybernet.''

Ali paused. After more than a minute, Hickock wondered if his presence had been forgotten.

"If there is a God," Ali began. Hickock leaned forward to hear the faint voice. "If there is a God, and if this God is just, then I expect that my killing of those shattered creatures will weigh significantly against all the evil I have done.''

"Why are you telling me all this?" Hickock asked.

"It is important that you understand with whom you are dealing." Ali's eyes measured him precisely.

The moment had come. "Are we safe from eavesdroppers?''

Ali gave a small measured nod of approval. "We are now. Anyone who attempts to tap into this room's surveillance system is now listening to me lecture you concerning my importance to Starswallower. I am warning you that my access to the cybernet, as well as Heiliger's methods of lie detection, make useless any attempt to evade my questions.''

"Then let us talk about your real importance," Hickock said. "Let us discuss the Patriarch of your story, whose real name is Explorer. Let us consider in detail how you and your associates aided Explorer in devouring Starswallower. And how you have managed to keep this secret from all the world."

Ali's expression was of mild curiosity. "Why should I respond to such a fantastic series of allegations?"

"Because of who I am," Hickock said urgently. "You have learned that I am Go'el. You have no idea what that means.

"Three centuries ago, the Shapers departed the solar system, leaving nine-tenths of the human race dead and the Earth teetering on the edge of ecological collapse. The survivors made the rebuilding of Earth's life net their first priority. Over the next three generations, more than a dozen organizations and societies with similar aims merged to become the Institute for Racial Survival.

"Rebuilding the Earth was the first step. The second was to make sure that the survival of the human race would never again be so threatened. We had to find our enemy. For that, we needed a stardrive. Now that we knew it was possible, we would have come up with it eventually. Fortunately we did not have to start from scratch. Shapers had quarreled with each other over the spoils of their raid. They left wreckage. Even after the starships had been blasted with lasers strong enough to turn most of the hulls into abstract sculpture, even after they had buried themselves in impact craters, we were able to find enough of the drive mechanisms of seven of them to give us the necessary clues.

"We have had starships for the last eighty years. We have built an armada. For ten years we hunted for the Shapers' home world. Three years ago, a scout reported success."

Hickock paused to let his words sink in. He wondered if the gesture were necessary or effective. He had no feel for how quickly a cybernetically linked human could think. On Earth, neurologists had encountered the very same problems Ali had detailed. Only on Earth, no experimenter had been so callous or so driven to succeed as Explorer had been.

Ali was serenely expressionless. Hickock could almost ignore the tangle of life-support equipment and see the idealized Buddha that Ali had projected at their first meeting.

"And now that you have found us, all you do is make furtive raids against the interplanetary commerce of—what? Half a dozen Patriarchs. It seems like an anticlimax."

"We are here," Hickock replied evenly, "to destroy the homeworld of the Shapers; to engage in preplanned, thorough, and complete genocide; to eradicate from the universe every single member of the species that is the greatest danger our race has ever encountered."

Ali's eyes had closed. Save for the ventilators, the only sound was a muted throbbing from the life-support machines.

"How?"

"Much the same way the Shapers made Sol flare. Collapsars sown just beneath the convection layers. Incandescent gases pour in at multiples of a million atmospheres until the collapsar is saturated. The splashback can lift twenty thousand square kilometers of stellar surface at a speed exceeding escape velocity. Set enough collapsars in a reinforcing geometry, and the splashback becomes an artificial nova. Not a supernova. The star will settle back into its old sequence, robbed of a million or so years of life, burning with a slightly redder light. But everything out to two light-hours will be sterilized."

"Yet your people have not done this yet. Why not?"

There had never been any real choice. Heiliger, given enough time, would have dragged it all out of him. The only choice he had was how to present his own facts, how to sell a viewpoint that might, just possibly, save all their lives.

Ali showed no reaction, no visible signs of emotion at all. Hickock's next statement had to be akin to a leap of faith. He had to hope that he could convince the machine-child, that he would not become the greatest traitor the human race had ever known.

"The mission of the Institute," Hickock began, "of any Go'el, is the survival of *all* humanity. From the fragmentary records we could reconstruct, we estimated that nearly twenty million humans were taken from Earth during the Burning. It was considered possible that they might have descendants. A policy decision was made, more of a conscience-salving gesture than anything else, to search for them before we disrupted the star. Most of us were sure none would ever be found."

"The latest estimate, including the new interstellar colonies that the Patriarchs are trying to keep secret from each other, is five hundred million," Ali said.

Hickock nodded. "Once we were able to partially decode the radio transmissions, we knew the number was substantial. Our raids were intended as a sampling technique. That was when we got our first hints of what had been done to you.

"It put us in a quandary. To destroy the Shapers' homeworld, we would have to ourselves become the second greatest cause of death to our own species."

Ali looked sympathetically curious. "How did you resolve your dilemma?"

"At the time the *Vengeance* was destroyed, no resolution had been reached."

Ali pursed his lips. There was little doubt what the resolution would be if Fleet Command realized Hickock was still alive and disclosing its existence—worse, disclosing the existence of a regenerated, human-controlled Earth.

"It seems harsh," Ali suggested. "The Shapers could have

destroyed Earth had they wished to. How do you account for their restraint?''

"Given how close they came to destroying all life on the planet, there was little restraint to account for!" But that was an emotional reaction, inculcated by listening to stories of the Burning passed down from generation to generation, from seeing the blackened remains of forests rising from deserts, from making pilgrimage through surrealistically melted cities.

"The main school of thought is that the Shapers simply made a mistake, that they had no idea we would be able to recover as quickly as we did. Shaper history seems to support this. As individually brilliant as Shapers are, their overall advancement seems to have been both slower and more erratic than our own.

"Howard Yader suggested a different answer. His research indicated that Shaper populations went through wide swings brought on by overhunting their food sources. Maybe they have learned from that. Maybe they realized that, having no idea of how to breed humans, they would be well advised to allow a residual population to continue on Earth. Just in case all their samples died and they needed to replenish their supply.''

"Never foreseeing that the introduction of humans would so disrupt Shaper society, if you can call it that, that all interstellar travel would cease for most of three centuries. By which time humans would not only have refilled their world but have discovered the stardrive.'' Ali considered the scenario. "It is plausible.

"Enough. We have strayed from our first point. Why do you insist that Explorer devoured Starswallower, when all the world knows the contrary?''

It was Hickock's final card. Ali gave no indication that he would give anything in return. Hickock chose his words carefully.

"From the moment I entered this habitat, everyone I met marveled at how much *room* there was. Not just in the Great Hall, which assembled volumes of empty air in such magnitude that even I realized it extravagant, but even in the quarters set aside for the lowliest delegates. But all the delegates seem to have dismissed this with the supposition that Starswallower meant to impress them with its wealth, and they were duly impressed. If anyone considered the matter further, he probably imagined that the regular inhabitants were crammed close as circuit boards into the areas off-limits to the delegates.

"Then there was the odd response to Starswallower's trade delegates to Innovator's offer of life-extension techniques. Not disbelief, not a demand for proof, not hard bargaining to get the price down. Simply—disinterest! Yet Starswallower had the most powerful lineage group precisely because it was the oldest Patriarch. It had to be approaching critical size, the point at which it would soon 'engulf the sky.' Why wasn't it at least interested in some sort of fact-finding?

"These things bothered me, but so did a hundred other things just because your entire world is so strange to me. Only when Jason Yader and I emerged from the ductwork did I begin to realize the significance of these questions.

"We found ourselves in kilometer after kilometer of deserted tunnels. Once that space had been densely inhabited. Indications were that the population had been destroyed, or at least forcibly removed.

"Jason was surprised by the wall maps. Even with body swapping allowed among herds of different lineage groups, the overwhelming majority of each herd lives in the same habitat for life. Since each adult easily memorizes the full extent of its own work space and can ask for directions in an unfamiliar area, there is no real need for maps. Yet here there was a map at every intersection.

"The clincher came when we finally found your herd

members. We had expected to be arrested immediately. Instead, the woman we first spoke to noticed nothing odd in our dress or our accents, or even in the fact that we were obviously lost. Her response was to give us a hand map and tell us not to worry about 'defenders.'

"It could not have been made much clearer. All humans were strangers in this habitat. They probably came from many different herds. They were here now by right of conquest.

"Shapers don't allow fights of that sort between their own herds. Patriarchs don't allow battles between herds of Shapers within their own lineage group. So one Patriarch had displaced another—Starswallower, in fact. How could that have been done without becoming common knowledge? As far as I can tell, each Patriarch spends most of its time watching all of the others for some sign of weakness. If nothing else, the carnage caused by Starswallower's death when the lineage group dissolved at the first-generation level into a free-for-all would have alerted everyone to what had happened.

"Then I remembered hearing how Starswallower had supposedly summoned Explorer to its destruction. For months, all trade, all communication with Starswallower's herds had been cut off. Even the spy nets went silent. A counterintelligence breakthrough bordering on the supernatural was rumored."

Hickock shook his head in rueful admiration. "Heiliger's computerized lie detection is good, but not that good. The spies weren't discovered; they were replaced. As were all members of Starswallower's herds.

"One thing I haven't figured out. Did you have them all killed?"

"No." As Ali continued, Hickock let himself breathe again. "That was neither necessary nor desirable. Only the few who realized what actually happened were eliminated. The rest have been reeducated. They have been told that their leaders intended to murder Starswallower and set themselves up as a rogue herd.

"The survivors have been split up, sent to other habitats both on this planet and on Snowball. A few contingents are preparing for interstellar colonization. My agents report that, almost without exception, the herd members are grateful for being treated so leniently."

"How many people know?"

"Less than a hundred. Even that is too many, but it is unavoidable. Let me fill in a few gaps in the story.

"It is no secret that for several generations Starswallower has regarded Innovator as a constantly growing menace. As a result, it shaped Explorer to counter Innovator, to exceed it in flexibility and originality.

"Explorer interpreted this shaping to mean that it should remove all constraints upon its freedom. Chief among these constraints were the genetic inhibitions implanted by Starswallower. It could do nothing about them directly. It *could* ask its herd to look for ways around them.

"It budded off dozens of immature selves for our experiments. We soon learned that a thorough purging of inhibitions would have required complete regeneration of the brain and the entire nervous system. It would have taken twenty years to acquire the necessary skills. Explorer would never have trusted us to carry out such an operation in any event.

"Instead, we came up with an effective half measure. We isolated and decoded the structure of the pheromone Starswallower used to make its commands irresistible to its offspring. We also learned the structure of the related pheromone that triggers the dissolution of the main blood vessels, causing the Shaper to hemorrhage to death.

"We planted clues, some of them legitimate. Starswallower's agents dutifully relayed them to their master. Starswallower budded a squad of messengers, their sacks distended with obedience pheromone, and dispatched them to demand

Explorer's immediate presence. When Explorer arrived, Starswallower swam up-current, releasing clouds of dissolution pheromone.

"It had no idea anything was wrong until Explorer launched the torpedoes it had concealed within its body. The first salvo severed Starswallower's main tentacle complex and destroyed its speaking ducts.

"Then Explorer released its stomachs and began its victory feast.

"Starswallower's chemical words had gone—unheard? Unsmelled? Even after all this time, I am not sure which word is misleading. We had been able to bind an artificial molecule to Explorer's receptors. Until they were removed, neither obedience nor suicide pheromones could affect it.

"Survival and freedom were necessary. Neither was sufficient. Explorer wanted power, the power that had accrued to Starswallower by virtue of its unusually long life. The power that would now fragment as each first-generation offspring became Patriarch of its own lineage group."

"Unless Explorer became Starswallower," Hickock said.

Ali shrugged. "To all other Shapers, the result was foreordained. There was no reason to question it. Even those in the same lineage group keep to their own hunting seas, separated from each other by a hundred kilometers or more. The Patriarch is known through his messengers to other Shapers. Which is to say, through the obedience pheromone, which we controlled."

"Yet your victory is not complete," Hickock observed. "You had to have me tortured when I merely hinted what I had deduced. Whose attention were you diverting? Does Explorer resent its dependence on you? Or, having destroyed Starswallower, does it feel that that dependence is obsolete?"

"Its feelings are almost entirely irrelevant," Ali said blandly. "We still control the two pheromones. Explorer has been taught that certain actions, certain directions, are prohibited.

"Your main point is correct, however. A large and powerful minority, the Deliverancers, regard Shapers as close to divine. Controlling one would be regarded as blasphemy."

"Why haven't they gone the way of Starswallower's herds?" Hickock asked.

"They are both too numerous and too talented. We need them. We have given them a variant of the story we gave Starswallower's herds, though. They believe that we invaded this and other habitats because the herds were in revolt against Starswallower. We have explained Explorer's pretended death as a ruse to trick Innovator."

For the first time since he had entered the room, Hickock felt himself able to relax. "I think we have a basis for negotiation. Your people are what I—what all Go'els—hoped to find. Not only are you humans who deserve our protection, you have been resourceful enough to gain control of your captors.

"Despite which you *need* us. You've admitted the precariousness of your situation. Starswallower's offspring may discover your imposture and revolt. Explorer may learn how to bypass your conditioning. If the Deliverancers realize that you had Starswallower killed or that you have constrained Explorer, they may launch their own crusade.

"I can help you. Give me access to communications equipment, and I can ally you with a fleet that will lay your enemies at your feet."

"A fleet," Ali observed, "that has the incineration of everything in this solar system as its sole reason for existence."

Hickock frowned. "That was before we learned how many humans were in captivity. Everything is changed now."

"Is it? Your long-term goal is still extermination of the Shapers, is it not? Ship-to-ship battles would be too uncertain and too costly. Worst of all, they would give the Shapers time for a counterstrike at Sol. Splashing this star is the obvious answer. Those Shapers in the outer system, or in the nearby star systems, could then be taken care of in mopping-up operations."

Hickock licked his lips, conscious that he was hesitating too long. So little time, so much missing information! Against that, the certainty that Ali, behind his impassive eyes, wanted to be convinced.

"That might have been true if you had not learned to synthesize obedience and suicide pheromones. With those tools we can be selective."

"Your fleet commander may choose to live with guilt if it will buy him safety."

"I am now Fleet Go'el. That decision would be mine," Hickock insisted. "*I* would not allow it. But unless I am able to contact my fleet, I will not be able to exercise my authority. Unless I can plead your case before the fleet commander, tell him of the millions of humans on this world who have fought so long for their lives and their dignity, he may well decide that the safety of Earth outweighs the lives of the captives, of whom he knows next to nothing."

Ali was hunched over, his eyes shut as if in prayer. "Perhaps so," he said at length. "You must understand that we have a more basic problem. I am by no means a Deliverancer. Nonetheless, I tell you that neither I nor my friends would ever support extermination of the Shapers."

For a moment Hickock was speechless. "After what they did to Earth? *After what they did to you?*"

Ali sighed. "My knowledge of human history is necessarily spotty," he said, "but from what little I have been able to put together about my own people, it seems that we spend most of our time plotting to avenge ourselves on whatever group wronged us last, no matter how long before that may have been. Turks, British, Jews, Americans, Sunnites,

Shiites, Russians . . . Our wounds were too precious to be allowed to heal, so we constantly abrade them, as you would polish fine silver to keep it bright.

"I am delighted to learn that Earth survives, that there is reality behind such legendary words as *dolphin* and *dragonfly* and *orchid*. However, I shall not be ruled by romantic nostalgia. *This* is our world, as wonderful to us as Earth is to you. I would think the Institute and its Go'els would intuitively understand that.

"As for the Shapers themselves . . ." Without warning, his expression softened. "The Shapers are very dangerous," he conceded quietly. "Yet if they do not constitute the whole of creation, as they sometimes imagine, they are clearly close to its crown.

"Do you fully comprehend their achievement? This race has no society, no culture as you and I understand those words. One of our greatest geniuses said, 'I see as far as I do because I stand on the shoulders of giants.' Such a sentiment is almost literally incomprehensible to Shapers.

"Nonetheless, this race has produced individuals who invented the stardrive. The best we could do was devise ingenious proofs that such a thing was impossible."

"My presence," Hickock interrupted testily, "proves we did considerably better than that!"

"Your presence proves that after several generations' study of wreckage, humans can copy and adapt matrix stressor engines. Can you seriously tell me that you would have even the basic mathematics by now on your own? Or do you have the mathematics?"

"I have no idea. I am not a theoretician," Hickock said. "I am just sophisticated enough to know that no amount of technological cunning can balance out the solipsistic amorality that is the one trait these creatures cannot breed out of themselves."

Ali bit back a retort. "We are both tired and under stress," he said. ''We can meet again when we are both feeling better.''

The locks unsealed. Two hulks entered to escort Hickock back to his quarters. For the first time he noticed the purplish-red welts where the wires tapped into Ali's skull. He wondered if they would ever heal.

XX

THE MONITORS HAD SHOWN HIM PACING FOR MOST OF AN hour. Rows of images, variously distanced and angled, strode, pivoted, and collided with each other in the imaginary space between the screens.

"You would never know that you have been given the most luxurious suite of rooms in the entire habitat," Lieder complained when she could stand it no longer and had come to see him in person. "You have been given all the honors of a full ambassador, yet you charge the walls like a netted sharphin searching for points of weakness."

Hickock halted, suddenly aware of her presence in the doorway. "Your analogy is exact," he said, holding up his index finger. "Call it what you like. I am a prisoner, as I have been ever since landing on this planet. My captors have changed, my cell has become more commodious, but my basic status has altered not one whit."

"Nonsense," she replied, disturbed by his anger. "If you were being treated like a prisoner, you would still be in Heiliger's care. He would be busy extracting data we very much wish to have: the exact strength and armament of your fleet, its communication frequencies, ASCII code words. . . . Now that you have access to your memories, Heiliger could force that data out with relative ease. We don't, because we have determined that your goodwill is valuable to us.''

Hickock lifted a skeptical eyebrow. ''As ambassador, I should have freedom of more than this room.''

''Until we have fully formulated our own policy, we cannot allow you to contact your fleet. Nor can we allow you the freedom of the habitat until the Trade Talks end tomorrow. We can't have either Innovator or Skybreaker trying to grab you away. Aside from that,'' Lieder said, ''you can do pretty much as you wish.''

''Can I have questions answered? Oh, excuse me. Your job is to question, mine is to answer.''

''You are being needlessly difficult,'' she said. ''You have a data terminal—''

''Restricted access.''

''—and I will answer your questions myself. Within reason.''

''A lawyer's answer. I didn't know you had them here. Let's see then . . .'' He saw that she was already angry. He cast about for something that might catch her off balance. The claw insignia, the—

''Tell me about the ring you wear. The cobalt stone is very distinctive. Heiliger wears one nearly identical, though not so elaborately set. Why?''

Wariness gave way to something like amusement. ''Almost one in ten members of the herd hierarchy wear such a ring. It's not what you may have been thinking. It is the mark of the familial society I belonged to while in the crèche. I was elected secretary of my graduating group. We have managed to keep in touch since then. Our society now has members in various leadership positions in all of Starswallower's herds, and even in some completely outside his lineage group.''

''Quite a convenient network for the head of Security,'' Hickock observed.

"Security is not an adversary to loyal herd members. My greatest achievement has been showing how cooperation with Security benefits everyone!"

"I'm sure. Just as it has benefited Yader. Speaking of whom, whatever happened to him? The last time I asked, you were evasive."

Her face twisted. Even though it was the sort of response he had been probing for, he felt obscurely guilty at having triggered it.

"We made mistakes with Yader," Lieder said heavily. "We are still not sure what they are. Heiliger will not admit it, but he has run out of ideas. Perhaps, because you have known him longer, you might have an insight."

That surprised him. "I might at that. Take me to him."

The room was just large enough for the four of them. Rolled-up clothing pushed out untidily from almost closed drawers. Dishes and cups of brightly colored plastic littered a small fold-down table.

A figure hunched on a bed in the corner, regarding them apprehensively. His hands clenched tightly together just below his chin. A thumb glistened.

"You're not here to hurt me again, are you?" he asked.

Lieder forced a smile. "We don't ever want to hurt you, Jimmy. We have brought a friend of yours today, Mr. Patrick Hickock. Do you remember him?"

"That metal band around his head," Hickock said. "Another one of your toys, Doctor?"

"Merely a relaxicisor," Heiliger said defensively. "He has become very upset, really irrational at times. With the controls in my pocket, I can soothe him back to sleep before he harms himself."

Jimmy peered up at Hickock uncertainly. "I don't know you."

"I think I know you, though," Hickock said, seating himself on a corner of the bed. "Or someone like you. Let's talk about where you come from. Maybe we can figure out where we met.''

Jimmy fought back a snuffle, glancing fearfully at Heiliger. ''I kind of have trouble remembering things.''

Hickock smiled. ''Me, too.''

''This persona remembers nothing worth knowing,'' Heiliger muttered. ''Its whole purpose is to dead-end any interrogation effort. All you will learn is that it was raised in a crèche in Freair. We know more than we need about the child-rearing practices in Innovator's herds.''

''You still know less than you need about the right questions to ask.'' Hickock turned back to Jimmy. ''Tell me about home.''

''Well, we all live in the dorms, o'course. All the guys. Most of them are pretty good. A few are shits, though.''

''You take care of yourselves?'' Hickock asked.

''Pretty much. The monitors think they run everything, but that's just because they've been around two years longer. The nannies have to sit on 'em sometimes.''

''The nannies?''

''Yeh. Nanny Kit takes care of me and my sib group.''

''Do you like her?''

''Nanny Kit?'' A look of affection and awe passed over his face. ''Sure. She's *beautiful*.''

Hickock paused, remembering. ''What does she do?''

''Makes sure we eat right.'' He flashed an embarrassed grin. ''Makes sure we wash all over. Checks our lesson papers. Goes to the proctors with us when we get in trouble.''

''She must care a lot for you.''

''Yeh.'' His face became troubled. ''She cries a lot sometimes. After they've hurt me. Then she hides in her room from me.''

''Who hurts you?'' Hickock asked.

''I know it's not her fault,'' Jimmy said, becoming more

and more agitated. "But she feels real bad. Nobody can do anything against them. Everybody knows that."

"Who?" Hickock repeated.

"You didn't report any of this," Lieder said.

"There was no use in following it up," Heiliger insisted. "We gain nothing in learning that Dr. Mackern was a sadist at an early age."

Jimmy was rocking back and forth on the bed, arms clasped around his knees.

"What did they do?" Hickock asked.

Jimmy shook his head. "I don't know. It started here—" He pressed his temples. "And it spread down and around, like fire. Each time it was worse. I was sick a lot, between times. Then once, when it was so bad I didn't think I could stand it, I . . ." His voice trailed off. His expression took on a dreamy, disconcerting quality.

"You what?" Hickock prompted.

"I ran away to a place they couldn't find." Jimmy had become almost serene. "But there was a man there. He said he would take my place. So I let him."

"Induced multiple personalities," Heiliger breathed. "I thought Mackern had just taken advantage of a natural condition. I had no idea he had the techniques to bring it about on command."

"Personali*ties*," Lieder said. "How many?"

Heiliger shook his head. "Half a dozen, that's only a guess. There's Howard the scientist and Jason the spy. There's a woman called Janet. There's Jimmy here. There's somebody called Cord that Howard and Janet, at least, are aware of, though we haven't been able to call him up yet.

"It's really quite clever," he said with grudging enthusiasm. "How better to get an agent through hostile interrogations than by creating a cover personality who really believes everything he is saying? And how could you be more flexible? Mackern could switch his personalities the way you would switch computer spools."

Lieder bent down closer to Jimmy. His eyes widened as he saw her shoulder insignia. He hugged his arms tight against his sides. His breathing quickened again. A low moan pulsed through clenched teeth.

"Something's wrong," Lieder said tensely. "Help him, Heiliger!"

Heiliger's hand worked inside its pocket. The rhythm of the moan slowed. The clenched arms relaxed. Almost in slow motion, Jimmy straightened, then melted into the contours of the bed.

"Hold him there!" Hickock said suddenly. "Don't put him completely under. I'd like to try something."

"There's no point." Heiliger's voice was peevish. "I have already told you that this persona was constructed with an absolute minimum of information just in order to be a dead end to any interrogation. What we have to do is break out of this persona."

"And such is the esoteric subtlety of your technique that pain is the only lever you have," Hickock said.

"It has worked well so far!" Heiliger replied, stung. "Far be it from me to remind Security of its responsibilities, but it should be remembered that the original purpose of Jason Yader was to put Hickock into our hands and then pull him back to Innovator once his memories were restored. To the extent that *you* have an idea of how to recall Jason, it is likely to be dangerous to us."

"There are two of us in this room," Lieder said. "There are hulks guarding the outside door. And we are under electronic surveillance. We have already proved sufficient to handle the pair of them under similar circumstances."

"Then I may proceed?" Hickock asked.

"Satisfy my curiosity first," she said. "When you were

talking to Jimmy just now, you had the warmest, most natural smile I have ever seen on you. Why?''

There were questions behind that question. But there was no full answer he would even attempt with third parties present.

He shrugged. ''I promised his nanny I'd take care of him.''

She was expressionless for a second. Then she nodded. ''Go ahead.''

Heiliger emitted a snort of incredulous disgust.

''Try to lower him just to the edge of consciousness,'' Hickock said.

''There are no less than nine states of consciousness,'' Heiliger said, ''and I can position him precisely within any one of them. What I cannot do is interpret the imprecisions of layman's terminology.''

''I need him to be conscious enough to hear and respond to me. At the same time, he should be close enough to sleep that the images and situations I suggest will seem real to him.''

Heiliger took the control unit from his pocket and fussed with three dials and a bank of buttons. ''Tr.S B3. *If* that is what you want, good luck with it.''

Hickock ignored him, concentrating entirely on Jimmy. ''Jimmy, can you hear me?''

''Yes.'' The voice was soft with sleep.

''I want you to remember the Golden Days Crèche. You are back there.''

''Yes.''

''It is the end of the day. Your lessons are over; your chores are done. You have time to play. What do you do?''

''Kickball, painting, hide-and-seek—''

''Hide-and-seek. You are in the maze. It is dusk. Someone is after you. Someone nasty.''

Jimmy moaned. Lieder looked at him curiously.

"There is someone in the maze you must find. Someone who will protect you."

"Nanny—"

"No, not Nanny. A grown man. He is your friend. He is what you would like to be when you grow up. He has protected you before. He can do so again, if you can find him."

Lieder's eyes widened with sudden comprehension. Heiliger showed interest despite himself.

Jimmy's breath came in short, irregular gasps. Hickock could feel within himself the rhythm of the running steps, the long straightaways, and the hairpin switchbacks.

"They're getting closer," Hickock said. "You must find him soon!"

The gasps became little cries that accelerated—then abruptly ceased. His breathing slowed and deepened.

"You have found him," Hickock surmised. "We need to talk to him. Can we do that?"

"Yes." The voice was deeper, more mellow than either Jason's or Howard's. The eyes opened, and cheeks and lips flowed into a face Hickock had never seen before. "I have wanted to talk to all of you for quite some time."

xxi

"I THOUGHT I WAS CALLING UP JASON," HICKOCK SAID, RE-
garding the stranger warily.

They were in Lieder's quarters. As soon as she had realized what had happened, she had commanded the guards
outside Jimmy's door to be their escorts. Discussion on the
walkways had been discouraged. Even the interrogation
rooms, Hickock suspected, might be too public for her lik-
ing.

She left the guards at her own door. Hickock remembered
the study beyond from his previous visit. At her work desk,
she flipped several switches in rapid succession. The stranger
looked on in silence until she finished.

"I know," he said to Hickock. "You nearly got him.
However, it seemed the good doctor Heiliger would find Jason's reappearance alarming. There are also aspects of this
situation I feel I can best handle myself. Unfortunately, the
drugs being used on Jimmy prevented me from reasserting
control on my own. Jimmy had to be led to call me up. For
which, my thanks."

"Do you have a name?" Heiliger asked shortly.

"Excuse me. I thought you had guessed. I am Cord."

"Who is Cord?" Lieder asked.

Cord's laugh was pained. "That is a difficult question. Dr.

Vaheri would say that it is based on improper assumptions, that Cord is not so much a personality as a housekeeping program, useful in making sure none of the other personas harm each other.

"I hope," he said with an unintentionally comic earnestness so reminiscent of Jimmy that Hickock thought for a moment that he would segue back to his younger persona, "that you will agree with me that such reductionism is unrealistically oversimplified."

"Each of the other personas I have examined seems to have been cultured for a particular purpose," Heiliger observed. "Jason is a spy. Howard may act as a cover for Jason, but he is a qualified biologist in his own right. Janet concentrates on artistic creativity and interpersonal sensitivity. Jimmy . . ." He frowned.

"Jimmy is no more or less than what he seems," Cord said. His voice was hoarse. "He is a small, frightened boy who has seen more than his share of pain."

"And you?"

"I am the Ur-block," Cord said in a brooding voice. "I am the original tangle of talents and desires from which each of the personas is carved and cultured. I have Jason's daring, but not his reflexes. I have Howard's curiosity, but not his methodical thoroughness. I have Janet's sensitivity, but not her grasp of nuances. I have all of Jimmy's fears."

"Will they slice away at every feeling you have until there is nothing left of yourself?" Hickock asked.

Cord smiled sadly. "I used to fear that. I have found, however, that through them I can experience my own powers at their fullest. At a remove, of course."

"You said there were certain aspects that called for your personal attention," Lieder said.

Cord nodded. "I've noticed a number of disturbing facts— or, rather, Jason and Howard noticed them, but I made the critical cross-associations."

"I think we noticed the same things," Hickock said. Despite warning looks from Lieder and Heiliger's outright astonishment, Hickock outlined the steps by which he had deduced Starswallower's death and Explorer's subsequent imposture.

Cord frowned as he finished. "Well, yes, that's a good part of it."

"Part?"

"What about those buying patterns your friend the Eggman pointed out to you? Why is it that Starswallower has no interest in ova or sperm, no interest in body swapping save for young generalist, technician through executive classes?

"Maybe my imagination is deficient, but the only thing it suggests to me is that Explorer is getting set to expand in a big way very soon. It is about to take over a new herd, perhaps even an entire lineage group, and wants to expand its management teams so it can put its own people in the top positions."

"Nonsense," Lieder said impatiently. "We have no immediate plans in that direction. I can assure you that I would know if we did. More important, we do not have the ability even if we had the desire. Far from being in a position to take over any other groups, we needed these Trade Talks to consolidate our own position with Starswallower's herds."

Cord seemed to be studying the floor. "Then the pattern the Eggman noticed makes perfect sense to you," he said expressionlessly.

"The pattern is an artifact of limited date and even more limited intelligence," Lieder said. "I have not been specifically overseeing our trade representatives, but I know for a fact that our needs are much more varied than what you describe."

"Was there anything else?" Hickock asked.

Cord raised his eyes to meet Lieder's gaze. "I seem to

remember that Jimmy flinched away from you less than an hour ago.''

"Yes." Lieder said, disturbed by the memory. "He should not have. I have done nothing to cause him fear or pain.''

"Not you," Cord replied. "Your insignia." She frowned. "The claws," he explained. "Jimmy has only partial access to the memories of the other personas, but he usually picks up on anything sufficiently traumatic, even though he may not be able to understand it. When your crusher nearly sliced my arm off''—he held up his forearm and ran his fingers along the still-red scar—"that was sufficiently traumatic.''

"That happened recently," Lieder said, examining the scar.

"Less than two weeks ago," Cord said, "within two kilometers of where we are sitting.''

"Starswallower has not bred crushers for more than two generations," Heiliger said. "Explorer has never bred them. Their inef—''

"We know all that," Hickock interrupted. "Nonetheless, you have a chamber filled with hundreds, maybe even thousands of them. If they are some big lineage group secret, we can accept being kept in ignorance. Yader, after all, belongs to one of your rivals, and my own allegiances are even more alien.

"However—" He regarded Lieder speculatively. "If you really do not know what we are talking about, I think you should be quite disturbed.''

"Have Heiliger put us under his truth probes again," Cord suggested.

Lieder glanced from one to the other and came to a quick decision. She flicked three switches on her desk in rapid succession.

The lights went out. There was a moment of complete silence.

"Hickock—" Lieder began.

Ali's image exploded into the room, washing over them in a nova-burst of light. His form pulsed and rippled. Static crackled like thunder.

". . . alertALERTalert . . . avebeensubverted . . . ontrolslipping . . . pletelinetakeover . . . temscrashing . . . UMUSTESCAPEBEFORE—"

Wires and tubes became visible an instant before they ripped away from his body. Blood gushed in impossible torrents.

The image froze. Large, rectangular pixels of emptiness hollowed it out. It faded to nothingness.

Almost tentatively, the lights flickered back on.

Doors at either end of the room slid open. Hulks crouched to enter. Laser rifles never wavered from their chosen targets.

"Madame Security Director," the squad leader rasped, "you and your guests are to come with me immediately."

Lieder looked from the muzzle back to the squad leader. She seemed perfectly calm. "What is your authority for this intrusion?" she demanded.

"The Coordinator has discovered a conspiracy against our Patriarch. Assassins have been dispatched against our loyal herd leadership." Dull eyes dared her disbelief. "You must come with us for your own protection."

xxii

THERE WAS JUST BARELY ROOM FOR ALL OF THEM IN THE shuttle. The rifles had to be upended next to the hulks, but the passengers were all wedged together so tightly that any thought of escape was impossible. A hulk who stayed behind had locked the door from the outside. As far as Hickock could tell, there was no way of opening it from within.

An oppressive heat radiated from the hulks. The smell, though less overwhelming than Hickock might have imagined, was not pleasant. His glance fell on the hands of the hulk to his right. Veins bulged thicker than his own fingers.

Lieder leaned forward, trying to get a glimpse out the window. A station flashed by, instantly replaced by a blur of featureless tunnel.

"This isn't the route to Ali's quarters," she said angrily.

The squad sergeant put his hand to the metal ovoid embedded just below his ear. "The Coordinator has been moved to a place of safety following an attempt on his life," he said woodenly. "You are being taken to his new command post." His fingers tightened on the stock of the laser.

Hickock looked over at Cord. "Jason."

Cord nodded and concentrated on the floor. The hulk between them frowned but said nothing.

Deceleration pushed them even more closely together as

the shuttle slowed and stopped. The door slid open. The sergeant motioned them out.

More hulks stood to either side of the shuttle, lasers at port arms.

"The Coordinator cannot see you just now," the sergeant announced. "Step forward into the elevator. You will be taken to a safe holding area until the Coordinator can brief you."

Hickock flicked his eyes quickly left and right. There were too many hulks with too many lasers.

He stepped onto a bare platform. Cogs at each corner ran it up and down tracks fixed to metal scaffolding. There were no railings. Emptiness extended into the darkness on all sides. Clusters of people milled about on the floor one hundred meters below. Hickock looked up. The curved ceiling was featureless save for grillwork and the spotlights that illuminated the floor.

Lieder, Heiliger, and Yader came in behind him. Hulks stationed themselves at each corner. One pressed a button on an upright attached to the floor. The platform thrummed and began a slow descent.

Above them, the massive door sealed itself shut.

"What is this place?" Hickock asked with growing uneasiness.

Lieder licked her lips. "It's an aquarium. The biologists use it as a controlled environment for plants and animals they wish to study. It's large enough to support an entire ecology."

"Why is it dry?"

"They're drained periodically for cleaning."

Half a dozen hulks formed a semicircle on the floor, keeping people away from the spot where the elevator would come to rest. Small figures, too far below to be heard, gesticulated in the direction of the elevator.

Everything fit together. Yader's wide stare showed that he had reached the same conclusion.

''Now!'' Yader said. Without turning, he kicked back against the ankle of the nearest hulk. It staggered and grabbed Yader, who bent forward and pivoted. With Yader shielded from view by the hulk's body, it appeared as if the hulk were clumsily attempting a dance step. It skipped, slipped, and abruptly disappeared over the edge.

The hulk near Hickock raised his laser. Reflexes took over. The heel of Hickock's left hand swept the muzzle aside just far enough for him to step in too close for the hulk to bring the weapon to bear. He kicked up hard into the hulk's crotch, following up immediately with a power punch to the solar plexus.

Foot and fist met concealed body armor. Grinning slightly, the hulk grabbed Hickock's shirt and slammed him against a girder. Hickock's breath exploded out of his lungs. The girder scraped upward along his spine and the back of his head.

Hickock's hands encircled the hulk's wrist. Somewhere, beneath all the muscle and tendon sheathing, there should be a pressure point—unless genetic engineering had taken care of that, too.

The hulk drew him forward and threw him against the girder again. Through a red haze, Hickock saw the hulk's smile fade into a look of pained puzzlement. The hulk's hand loosened its grip. Hickock fell. He had just enough strength to tumble forward, away from the edge.

''Grab that laser!'' Lieder shouted.

The stock dropped five centimeters from Hickock's cheekbone. He grabbed it before it could follow its late master to the floor far below.

Shaking, he pushed himself to his feet. Lieder faced him, holding a thin, blood-stained blade. The lifeless body of a hulk lay diagonally across the platform. Jason punched a button on the control stand. The elevator halted its descent. Another stroke and it laboriously began to rise.

"Heiliger?" Hickock asked..

"Got brushed aside by one of the hulks coming after me." Lieder grimaced.

Jason rolled the hulk's body over the side. "Stay back from the edge," he cautioned. "Any moment now, those bone-heads below will realize what is going on here and will start shooting."

Hickock obediently moved closer to the inside edge. Yader had also secured a laser rifle. From butt plate to muzzle, it was almost taller than he was.

"When we get to the entryway," Hickock said, "are we going to be met by—"

All lights went out. The elevator motor died with a decre-scendo groan.

There was an instant of silence punctuated by scattered shouts from below. Then a roaring erupted to either side. Hickock was abruptly flat on his stomach, his palms sliding frictionlessly across wet, cold metal until the metal gave way to an uprush of air. Bullets of spray spat down on him. Through the roaring, he could hear screams from the faraway floor.

A hand fumbled across his back and grasped his shoulder.

"Follow me up the girder," Lieder yelled.

"To the entryway?"

"No! Above."

On hands and knees he felt his way across the platform. He stood, carefully, when he reached the corner, grasping a girder for support.

"I'll go first," Lieder shouted. "Follow closely. Make *sure* you don't lose that laser!"

Wet curls brushed his lips and cheeks as she turned away from him. The watery cacophony swept away most of her words. "Ya . . . fol . . . ickock!"

Then her body moved up past him in the darkness.

Irregular triangles in the girder provided hand and foot holds. They were slick with spray. For a few moments Hickock feared he would have to climb straight through a cataract. But then, he thought, the girder would shudder under the impact of tons of water, and constant rivulets would cascade down the steel. After what he gauged to be three more meters of climbing, the sound of roaring separated to either side.

Steel pressed harshly into his palms. The hulk's laser, cinched as tightly around his shoulder as its oversized strap would allow, seemed to double in weight with every meter. The slant of the holds wedged his feet at awkward angles.

If he stood on his toes instead of his insteps, he would be able to move more quickly.

His toe slipped. For an instant, only his fingers, moving over the oily metal millimeter by millimeter, held him suspended above the void.

If I drop, I'll take Yader, too, he realized.

A flailing foot hit the girder. Hickock's body rebounded. The laser swung below him in an opposing arc like a deformed bell clapper.

His fingers slipped again. The next-to-last joint of three fingers of each hand were all that held him.

He forced his body to relax as it swung back into the girder. His foot moved lightly up the metal, found an opening, and pushed itself in. Step by step he ascended.

The guttural thunder of the waters gave way to a higher-pitched, more constant clamor. The updraft became so strong that in his fatigue Hickock imagined launching himself and gliding through the darkness like a bat.

His head ran into Lieder's heel. "Up here," she shouted. "On the other side."

He swung around and clambered up, careful to avoid dislodging Lieder from her holds.

"The laser!" she demanded when he was even with her.

Carefully bracing himself, Hickock unslung the laser and handed it around to her, holding on until he was sure she had a firm grip on the strap.

There were two sharp snaps. A red dot of light strobed across an unexpectedly close ceiling. Light, dark, light, dark, light . . . It was a grating, presumably one of many set into the ceiling, large enough to suck out huge volumes of air to make room for the floodwaters. Where such immense quantities of air went, they should be able to follow.

"Are we going to burn through that?"

"No."

Plastic scraped across metal. Again the laser came on. The sighting dot flickered across the wall, coming to rest behind him. Reddish reflected light gave definition to the girder, to Lieder's form perched across from him, and to the laser balanced in one of the triangular holes in the girder.

"Don't turn around," she warned him. "As soon as I get this steadied on the lock of the access hatch, things will become uncomfortably bright— There!"

Yellow brilliance bounced off the massive curved grating above them, flashed off Yader's eyes where he hung wrapped around the girder, and died in the roiling chaos far below, in which dots, which might have been people, were tossed in rising crests of darkness.

"That's it," Lieder said. "Now you get the fun part. I burned through the lock, but you have to open the hatch. It is about half a meter directly behind you. It should open from your left to your right. If you swing out, you should be able to move it aside."

Hickock thought for a moment. Pulling his belt off with one hand, he passed one end through a hole in the girder, the other through a single belt loop, and cinched the belt together. He checked his footing. Holding tight with his right hand, he swept behind him with his left. Air rushed between outstretched fingers.

He pulled himself upright. He released his right hand and shook it, trying to get the blood flowing again. Then, bracing himself, he extended both arms as far as he could, leaning out until he was nearly horizontal.

Fingertips brushed smooth metal. It burned. He must be very close to the lock that Lieder had melted through. He threw his weight against it, in the direction she had said it should open.

It gave way suddenly. Hickock lost his handhold. The belt tautened, curving his fall into the side of the girder. The belt loop ripped apart. Arms and legs embraced metal. It took him a few seconds to realize that he was not falling.

Yader was muttering curses.

"Sorry if I came down on your knuckles," Hickock said.

"Glad to hear that."

Hickock climbed back up. The hanging belt brushed his hand. He undid it. Holding one end, he snapped it like a whip. Even through the din of cascading water, he could hear and *feel* the buckle hit the wall. He snapped it again. There was silence as the buckle passed through the open hatch.

Five more snaps, and he had defined the size and position of the opening.

He moved up another step, positioning himself just above the level where he imagined the deck of the hatch to be. The rest should be easy. The gap was narrow enough that he could almost step across it.

But he was trembling with strain. It was no consolation to remember that the standing broad jump had always been his worst event.

He leapt, throwing himself flat. Elbows struck first, numbing his hands. His legs swung through emptiness, hit the wall, slid down, and—

—stopped on a rung. There was another, level with his knees. Two steps, and he was in the service corridor.

"No problem," he called to Lieder, hoping the noise

would drown the quaver in his voice. With the belt, he guided first Lieder, then Yader, across the gap.

It was perhaps fifteen minutes since the lights had been extinguished.

"We have to find the control room," Lieder said, gasping to recover her breath. "It takes more than half an hour to fill that chamber. If we move quickly, we can have it drained before everyone in there drowns. Ali—"

"Is dead," Yader said. "He tried to warn us. We saw him pulled apart. Everything the hulks said about him was just to keep us quiet while they herded us into the drowning tank."

Hickock waited three breaths for an angry refutation. "Right," Lieder agreed at last. "As soon as we shut down the pumps, we'll try for the escape pods. Follow me, now. I owe my colleagues this much, at least."

Their forms acquired a shadowy definition as they moved away from the hatch. Around a corner, yellow-orange light-strips outlined the service corridor. Lieder found a vertical tunnel. They descended thirty meters.

The exit was less than ten meters from the control-room door. The two hulks standing guard collapsed almost silently as Hickock and Yader fired quick laser bursts.

A telescreen voice seeped around the edges of the partially open door. It rose and fell rhythmically, almost in a chant. Sharp syllables conveyed a vindictive anger. The words were indistinguishable.

". . . could drain it now," a man's nervous voice was saying. "I'm sure you have frightened them enough that—"

"You have not been listening." The hulk's voice was blurred and gravelly. "They have been sentenced to death. Be thankful you were not judged one of their number."

Lieder bent over a slumped figure and silently pulled from a holster a pistol so heavy that it required two hands. She looked up and nodded.

Yader kicked the door open, firing on the first hulk before

he could turn away from the consoles. His partner had just enough time to turn and raise his muzzle before Hickock's blast hit him.

Lieder strode into the room. Its sole occupant was a small middle-aged man in a white coat.

"Drain the tank," she commanded.

He bobbed his head and hit a series of black buttons on a panel to his right, in a top-to-bottom sequence.

"If you destroy these cables," he said, pointing below the panel, "it will be impossible to flood the chamber until they are repaired."

"Good idea," Lieder said. Hickock triggered two bursts. The cables melted into something resembling middle-period Dali.

The controller cleared his throat. "It would be much safer for me," he said, without turning around, "if I were found bound and unconscious."

At Lieder's nod, Yader pinched off the man's carotid artery. He shook him out of his white coat, ripped it into strips, and used them to bind and gag him.

Mother Angela Gamorez glowered down on them from video screens near the ceiling. ". . . the long-awaited cleansing that our pride and blindness have made necessary. Yet the Shapers are more merciful than we deserve. This time, there will be no Burning. Even as I speak, those most guilty of exalting themselves above Shapers are being purged from our system. Their suffering expiates our . . ."

Lieder seated herself at a keyboard. Her fingers rippled across the keys. She studied the monitor carefully.

"They have taken total control of the communications networks," she said in a low voice. "I can break through that for maybe five minutes, but then they'll be able to trace us." She bit her lip, then abruptly came to a decision.

Her finger brushed the record button. A status light at eye level cycled green to red.

"This is Security Executive Rita Lieder speaking. As many of you have already realized, the Church of the Deliverance is attempting a revolution. Its claim to be acting as authorized agents for Starswallower is, of course, completely false. All of these traitors will be brought to justice within thirty hours. Since some violence will be needed to reduce their positions, I must advise you all to evacuate the habitat. Further instructions will be provided in relocation centers on the mainland.

"All Trade Talks delegates are hereby notified that the Trade Talks are indefinitely suspended pending disposition of the revolutionaries. You are all advised to return to your herds until further notice."

The light went out. Her fingers played quickly over the keyboard. "In ninety seconds, that message will start broadcasting on a continuous loop. It will take them a few minutes to override my priority code and a few minutes more to trace the origin of the message. By then, we should be long gone."

The corridor was deserted. Lieder found an elevator and punched in a destination.

"Explorer was very safety conscious when this habitat was being constructed," she explained. "Escape capsules were embedded at regular intervals all over the exterior hull, to be used in case of a rupture. Most everyone has forgotten about them by now. But they should be our ticket out of here."

The elevator stopped. Hickock lowered the muzzle of the laser as much as he could in the cramped confines, half expecting to confront a squad of hulks. The doors parted, revealing a corridor as deserted as the one they had just left. Lieder's face relaxed into a smile.

"Just a little further," she said. "Around that corner and—"

There was no sound to warn them. Only a rumble felt first through the ankles, then in the chest. Displaced air accelerated past them, forcing them to stagger to keep their balance.

Hickock had just an instant to glance over his shoulder and see the raging chaos exploding through the corridor behind them before the wall of water hit them.

xxiii

THERE HAD BEEN POOLS IN THE CONCOURSE, CONNECTED
by locks with the surrounding ocean. The locks were necessary because the pressure at this depth was so great that
any direct opening would instantly become an inwardly
erupting geyser that would flood the entire habitat.

But if one were to open the locks, while sealing off the
interior bulkheads, except in the target area . . .

". . . are being *flushed* from our system . . ."

Hickock's head broke the surface. Air rasped through his
throat in an inhaled scream. The current swept him past a
lighting panel, surprisingly close overhead. A door came
within reach. He grabbed it. Water eddied in whirlpools all
around him.

Stupid creature, he thought light-headedly. It's already
failed to drown us once. If this is all it can do . . .

Water boiled off a mottled brown shell at the end of the
corridor. The thing submerged again before Hickock could
decide why it looked familiar.

A surge of water broke over his head. By the time he could
clear his eyes, the creature had completely disappeared.

His right shoulder was being dragged under. To his surprise, he found he still had the laser strap wrapped around
his arm. Bracing his feet on some underwater projection—a

door handle?—he pulled the stock above the surface. The electronics housing appeared waterproof.

The crusher's claw knifed up from the water in front of him, its edge translucently sharp. Hickock ducked to the right. The claw whistled past his ear and embedded itself in the wall behind him.

He let the muzzle fall, reflexively squeezing the trigger. Superheated water boiled up in a frothing mound, scalding him. The water vibrated as if to subsonic bellows. Massive bone plates jammed him against the wall.

Waves broke over his head. He forced his chin up, gasping for breath.

The pressure eased. The crusher rolled up, staining the surface mauve. The current caught it and sent it tumbling away, blood streaming ahead of it like the tail of a comet.

Hickock fell away from the wall. The laser slid from his grasp. Feeble strokes kept his head above water.

The current caught him, sweeping him into a main hallway. At its far end clustered at least six more crushers.

Hickock struck out for the side, desperately looking for a handhold. With each stroke, he reviewed everything he knew about crushers, everything he had seen of the jelly-covered forms in the cavern, trying to think of any vulnerability.

One of the crushers, apparently spotting him, moved out effortlessly against the current, its claws held before it at a forty-five-degree angle like a swordsman brandishing a left-handed dagger.

A streak of gray hurtled past Hickock, tumbling him helplessly in its wake. Hickock felt the impact as it rammed the crusher. The crusher staggered and twisted thirty degrees.

Three more gray forms sped through the flood, one so excited that it threw itself into the air, impatient with the drag of water. Hickock had an instant's glimpse of razor-sharp fins, teeth like rows of interlocking needles, and a blunt snout bludgeoning through spray.

Crushers were modified hunting spawn. Someone had told him that. And sharphin *hated* hunting spawn.

The other crushers, apparently sensing the disturbance, moved apart, almost as if fleeing. They were not fast enough. Cartilage impacted on bone plate in a triple stutter that was almost unison. Even through the rushing liquid cacophony there was something joyful in the sound of shattering shell.

"Hickock!"

He looked around. The wall slid by, chopping the water to foam. Spray clouded his eyes.

"Up here!"

Twisting his head up, he saw a hole in the ceiling ahead of him. A blurred face peered out; a hand gestured.

The ladder was almost invisible, no more than a vertical series of indentations in the wall. He grabbed the slippery plastic and pulled himself up from the flow that gurgled and sucked at him.

At the top, his strength nearly failed him. Strong arms pulled him up and through. He tumbled into something much like an acceleration couch.

Lieder loomed over him, frowning with concern.

"You're bleeding," he said, touching the wet stain on her cheek.

She looked at him strangely, her smile twisting into something else. "It's your blood."

He lifted his hand, suddenly conscious of the line of pain along the left side of his head. The palm came away wet and red. The crusher had not completely missed him.

Yader dogged the wall and hull hatches shut.

Lieder began flicking switches and checking readouts. "We are pressurized, we have power, the radio—damn!"

"What's the matter!" Hickock asked.

"There is a locator set to go off as soon as we hit the surface. Unfortunately, we do not want to be spotted."

"Let me at it," Yader said. He twisted himself beneath the console and began pulling out clumps of wires.

"Strap in!" Lieder instructed. "We are casting off—" A loud clang made the hull ring like a great bell. "—now."

The pod lurched free. Viewscreens came on in front of Hickock. Shadows moved through the dimness, too vague to be resolved. There was a hint of light from the top of the screens.

"You are in the pilot's chair," Lieder said. "When we hit the surface, the ground-effects system will come on. I'll direct you to the mainland."

"I've never flown one of these things," Hickock objected.

"Neither have I," Lieder said. "The controls are designed to be simple enough for anyone to operate. Your reflexes are the reason I want you in that chair."

Shafts of faint green light illuminated the waters around them. Above, the surface folded into multiple peaks that looked like great translucent tents seen from inside. The brightness increased, seeming to come from everywhere.

The pod lurched through the surface, rolled, then righted itself as the air jets roared into life. Color exploded across the screens: yellow-orange sunlight flashing off the rectangularly textured surface of a thousand wavelets; the sky, shading from a dark purple at zenith to a haze with only the slightest blue tint at the horizon; the water itself, catching each hue from sky and sun and charging them with its own essence, adding shades of brown and green in myriad combinations that even through the screens overwhelmed rationality and left the rest of the mind in something like an exalted drunken stupor.

The pod slid down the side of a long, gentle swell, churning the surface behind it into a salt contrail. It came to rest in the trough. Mountains of water bulked to either side.

Lieder had been squinting into the screen, trying to orient herself with the sun. "Thirty degrees right," she directed.

Hickock rotated the wheel appropriately. After a second, as if having thought it over, the craft responded and began ascending the swell.

Something like a vine sprouted from the crest above them. Others broke the surface at equally spaced intervals, their tips writhing, twisting, searching.

The swell passed beneath them. And then they were skidding down the slope. The structures elongated and thickened. Distance had deceived him, Hickock realized. The base of each was as thick as the pod.

The tips curved over, converging on them.

"Don't let them grab us," Lieder commanded.

There was no way the pod could turn and run. The stalks were slicing through the water, were *falling* on them too quickly. Hickock boosted the acceleration to the maximum and aimed for the nearest gap.

The pod impacted on an obstruction, then careened in a half circle. Huge, greedy suckers covered the screens. Hickock pulled the wheel over as far as it could go, putting all the pod's power into increasing its whirling. The air jets, meeting resistance, dug the craft under the water. White froth blotted out the sky.

A low, almost guttural tearing sounded from the back of the cabin, leaping in a second around the walls to a spot just over Hickock's controls. The pod spun free. It bobbed sickeningly back to the surface. A water-veiled sun lurched diagonally across the screen.

The pod jetted across the waves, spray erupting behind it like a mane of wild white hair.

XXIV

A LINE OF BRILLIANCE FLOODED IN FROM THE THIN, BARRED opening that ran along the top of the cell's back wall. The light almost washed out the neatly stenciled words painted just below the opening.

PASSIVE VENTILATION AND LIGHTING SYSTEM

Hickock frowned, wondering if it was some engineer's idea of a joke. On the other hand, for an architect who was the product of more than fifteen generations of living underwater, the idea of illumination by sunlight and ventilation by wind may have seemed revolutionary.

He crouched and sprang. His fingers grasped the ledge and held. Slowly he pulled himself up until his head brushed the ceiling.

The bars were about seven centimeters apart, of two-centimeter-thick steel. The height of the window was scarcely larger than his fist. Even without the bars, there would have been no way for him to squeeze through.

Hickock dropped back to the floor. He paced the rest of the cell. There was a cot. A toilet. A door with a bolted peephole—a passive observation device? It felt as solid as the concrete walls.

They had so nearly been free! Dark water had given way to light as the pod sped beyond Explorer's shadow: blue to green to yellow as the sandy bottom swept up to two meters below, one meter, then thrust up above the water. The pod roared up a sharply retrograde beach, bursting through a standing wave of sand.

A line of nondescript single-story buildings lay before them. At Lieder's direction, Hickock set the pod down ten meters from the nearest building. Yader threw the hatch bolts, and they climbed out onto the vine-bound sand.

Workers ran from the buildings. "Are you from the habitat?" "What's going—"

"Shaddup!" Quiet fell as two hulks lumbered awkwardly through the sand.

Lieder's eyes ran quickly along the rank slashes on the sleeves. She strode toward the more distant hulk, not letting her eyes drop from his even when she stumbled.

"Sergeant!" Hickock stiffened involuntarily at the whip of command voice, even though it was not directed at him.

"I am Security Chief Lieder. I have just escaped an assassination attempt by rebels attempting to take over the habitat. Take me to the station director."

Hao Vu, the station director, gnawed his mustache uneasily as he listened to Lieder. Head down, he paced the length of a long window overlooking short rows of hemispherical dendritic bushes irrigated by salt water.

"The situation in the habitat is very confusing," he temporized. "For a few hours today, we lost all contact. Since then we have received a series of contradictory messages, none with the proper validation codes. Our comm center has been inundated with requests from foreign herds that we contact their Trade Talks representatives, something quite out of the question even if it was possible."

"That is why I need immediate access to your comm center," Lieder said, impatience edging her voice. "The rebels have already discredited us among the other lineage groups.

They have nearly consolidated their hold in the habitat. It will take all our outlying forces to retake it.''

She turned and strode to the door, not intending to give him a chance to disagree.

''Contact was reestablished less than an hour ago,'' Hao said. ''A list of traitors still at large was broadcast. Your name headed the list.''

Lieder whirled, contempt blazing from her eyes. ''You choose to believe a message that you admit lacks all proper validation codes, and to disbelieve your own chief of security?'' Her gaze darted to the two hulks who had entered the room with them. ''Do your men intend to join the traitors as well?'' The hulks shifted uneasily.

Hao himself was sweating, but he persisted. ''The message said that the real traitors were former herd members of Explorer, as deranged themselves as their Shaper had been. You *were* prominent in Explorer's herd, were you not? Yet soon after Explorer was devoured, you became the new director of security.

''While I, who had worked loyally for Starswallower from the time I left the crèche, found myself—out here.''

The bleakness of Hao's voice told Hickock all he needed to know. Casually he glanced at the nearest hulk. The hulk met his eyes and grinned, shifting the laser so that Hickock could see that the safety was off.

There was a knock at the door. A technician entered, wires trailing from an electronics module held in his fist. He presented it to Hao for inspection.

The station director looked sharply at Lieder. ''Your locator was disabled. Recently, it appears.''

''Y-yes,'' Lieder improvised. ''Sabotaged by the rebels. We were lucky the drive mechanisms worked.''

''Very lucky,'' Hao said flatly. ''I think, given the current confusion, you should stay here until things settle down.

Where I can protect you from further contact with subversive elements.''

Meals came in a shallow bowl shoved through a slot in the base of the door. The slot flap was hinged on the outside. Hickock's probing fingers only shut it more securely. Not that opening it promised to gain him anything. At three by twelve centimeters, it was smaller than the window.

Nor did the bowl itself offer possibilities. Of soft red plastic, it had barely enough tensile strength to maintain its own shape when filled with gruel. There was no way it could be used to chip or cut, or even to cause a concussion.

Too soon, there was nothing to do but contemplate his captor's plans for him.

Hao was only an incidental problem. The real problem would be the Deliverancers. By now they must have consolidated their control of the habitat. Within a few hours, at most a few days, Mother Angela would send a detachment to the surface to collect the traitors. If he was able to convince them that he came from Earth, it might buy him time. On the other hand, they might just consider that a second good reason to eliminate him.

For Lieder and Yader, there would be no hope at all.

Sunset slanted through the slit. Three irregularly spaced peals of thunder shook the cell. Sonic booms. Belatedly, a klaxon began to pulsate.

Hickock jumped and grabbed the bars to hold himself up. A blood-red sky reflected itself in the waters beyond the beach. Something glinted at the far horizon. A speck dropped into the ocean.

He dropped back to the floor of the cell. Footsteps echoed hollowly in the far distance.

Three times more that night, the klaxon sounded. Once there were sounds of muffled thunder. Even at the distance, Hickock could tell that they were not sonic booms.

Four detonations in as many seconds woke him. The stars were dimming with approaching dawn. People ran across the grounds outside. Then there was silence for nearly five minutes. It was broken by the harsh, brittle rasp of a stutter-laser exploding a shallow path across rock. Or concrete.

There was a small explosion at the far end of the building. The thick door clattered as it fell into the hallway. Hickock thought quickly. He positioned himself directly across from the cell door, his hands away from his sides, palms outward.

Bang! It was the sound of a boot sole kicking open a door. Then the same set of sounds came again, closer.

Even though he was expecting it, the incandescent flaring of the lock made him jump. A drop of molten metal fell onto his pants and sent up a thin wisp of smoke. Hickock batted at it, trying not to burn his hand as he put out the smoldering fibers.

When he looked up, he was facing a soldier in a black-and-brown one-piece and face paint. The stutter laser was pointed directly at his midsection.

"Identify yourself!"

"Patrick M. Hickock. Under the charge of Jason Yader, herd member to Innovator."

"Well, I knew we'd find you if we just kept knocking on enough doors."

At first Hickock did not recognize the man who had stepped in behind the commando. The shoulder pips indicated a major, at least, in Innovator's armed forces—

"Hollings, is that you under all that grease?"

A quick grin split the man's face. "Right enough. Good to see you, and all that. Double time with me back to our platoon carrier. Explorer should be tied up for some time with the little presents we've just dropped, but it won't hurt to be safe. This Shaper has surprised us before."

XXV

THE DEBRIEFING WAS OVER—AT LEAST UNTIL SOMEONE thought of more questions to ask. Hollings had begun it in the triphib platoon carrier as it raced after the retreating night. The triphib hugged the wave tops, dodging Explorer's radars, thermally mimicking the water below. An open speaker relayed radio traffic into the aft cabin. Even though it was coded, Hickock built up a picture of scores of individual actions taking place over an undefined area: fighters being attacked, unspecified loads being dropped, enemy movements being monitored.

Beyond the viewport, an eye-searing pinpoint illuminated the entire horizon like day. Night reclaimed its own in ten seconds. Static clogged the radio for another fifteen minutes. Hollings kept asking questions in the same steady monotone until he noticed that Hickock was tensing for a shock wave which refused to come.

"Explorer's main satellite complex," he explained. "More heavily protected than we thought. Not that it did it much good.

"Now about this crushers' breeding pen you and Yader found . . ."

The sun caught up with them as they landed at Freair. Mackern relieved Hollings as interrogator. Twice that morning Colonel Garrison walked in, asked a few questions of his own—mainly about what sort of defenses Explorer might have—and walked out. As he left the second time, Hickcock heard Lieder's voice coming from a room down the hall.

By early afternoon, his voice was blurring with fatigue. An orderly brought a mug of steaming, bitter liquid. It was so full of stimulants that, for a few seconds after he gulped it down, his heart did its own imitation of a stutter-laser.

Then, as if they had abruptly lost interest in him, it was over. He was escorted from the sterile formality of the interrogation chamber to an outside terrace. A small buffet was set up. One plate held crackers about the size of his palm, adorned with variously hued leaves apparently meant to be eaten with them. Broiled ichthys fins, salty and crisp, were displayed in sunburst patterns.

Next to the buffet was an open bar. Hickock allowed his glass to be filled with the bartender's suggestion. Dark-brown particulates floated in brownish-amber fluid. It was distilled from something that, as much as he could understand it, vaguely resembled seaweed. It looked and sounded nauseating. But if he closed his eyes and sipped, he could imagine bourbon.

Small groups of military and civilians drifted onto the patio, staying mostly with their own cliques. Several glanced in Hickock's direction but kept to themselves, for which he was profoundly grateful. Many, both military and civilian, wore blue rings nearly identical to the one he had seen on Rita's hand.

A great bellow of laughter erupted onto the terrace. Mackern stepped out of the doorway, his entire torso convulsed with gargantuan mirth. Even Vaheri, a step behind his supervisor, managed a sickly smile. He murmured something in Mackern's ear.

"And why shouldn't I celebrate?" Mackern asked loudly. "That is what we are all here for." His hands swept in everyone on the terrace.

"Consider our plight," he went on. "We held a piece of inestimable value, but we had no idea what to do with it. In our despair—no, don't hush me: all this boasting about our subtle long-term planning is the merest opportunism—in our despair we handed this piece over to one of our main rivals in the slim hope that it would be able to decipher the piece's worth and that our agent would be able to get that knowledge back to us.

"We succeeded beyond our wildest dreams. Not only was the secret more important than we could possibly have imagined but, almost in passing, we destroyed Innovator's most dangerous enemy."

"A reasonably decent piece of work," Yader agreed, coming up behind Mackern.

"To which you made an invaluable contribution, my boy," Mackern said. "But the true founder of our fortunes is this young man here."

Hickock had been reclining in a lounge chair, allowing the warm, setting sun to gently push his eyelids closed. At Mackern's words he forced a reluctant eye open.

"Recount, please, how I performed these marvels," he said. "An excess of humility has repressed the relevant memories. Or perhaps my mental blockage has been reactivated."

Mackern forced another glass into his hand. The new drink gave off a minty exhalation that scoured the insides of his sinuses. Mackern's breath was nearly as potent. Hickock sipped very carefully.

"My poor boy," Mackern said, heaving a gusty sigh as he settled himself into a nearby chair. "All this excitement, all your exertions, all the questions you have so generously and completely answered, yet I will wager that no one has informed you of the revolutionary developments of the past thirty hours.

"First, imagine how we felt scarcely a fortnight ago. You and Yader had gone over to what we thought to be Starswallower's herd on schedule. Many of us feared that was the last we would ever hear of either of you. Then there were vague reports of unusual activity. Nothing, however, could have prepared us for Mother Angela's insane ranting. Nor did our observers have time to assess her claim to be suppressing a revolt before the security director broke into the circuit, accusing the Deliverancers of being the revolutionaries.

"That was more than enough confusion for our delegation. Ms. Van Alstyne called all the members together and engaged a triphibian for their departure. They had barely boarded when the entire Concourse was flooded."

"Speaking of Lieder," Hickock interrupted, "where is she?"

"With Hollings and Garrison, learning the ropes of our security organization," Yader replied, taking a chair across from Mackern. "Anyone who can help conceive and carry out the murder of a Patriarch and its cover-up deserves a high station in any hierarchy. Under strict supervision. We wouldn't want her to make a habit of it. I don't doubt that I'll be reporting to her in less than a month."

Mackern cleared his throat. "Our forces were already on secondary alert when we received Yader's coded message."

Hickock frowned.

Yader grinned at his puzzlement. "You were rather busy at the time, and I didn't get the opportunity to tell you afterward. I didn't just disable the escape pod's locator. I was able to convert it into a crude radio. Capable of sending only short and long bursts, but that was enough to get about thirty words in code to an overhead relay satellite."

"Your names," Mackern said. "Your approximate location. The fact that Explorer had devoured Starswallower and was somehow ruling the lineage group in its name.

"Dalkan and I nearly dismissed the message as a fake. Only, if we accepted that one incredible premise, a score of other misfit facts suddenly fell into place.

"Dalkan made the recommendation to Innovator. It gave immediate approval. We launched missiles aimed at the seas immediately surrounding Explorer. Most were destroyed. Enough canisters of chemo-messengers got through that each of Starswallower's first-generation Shapers knew within three hours that their Patriarch had been killed and replaced with an impostor."

"How can that make a difference?" Hickock asked. "Explorer still has control of the compulsion pheromones. Even if every Shaper in the lineage group knows Explorer to be a fraud, not one of them can defy it."

"All they had to do was to stay beyond the reach of Explorer's messenger spawn for a few brief hours," Mackern said, with a crafty grin. "Innovator gave them an unprecedented safe conduct into its own territories. Innovator's Shapers moved among them with their full deployments of warrior spawn and human soldiery. They reached Explorer about the time Hollings was picking you up. That engagement terminated about three hours ago. We now have official reports that Innovator has devoured Explorer."

Scattered applause rose from a handful of eavesdroppers.

"I still don't see what I had to do with that," Hickock objected.

Mackern barked laughter. "How like me to become so involved in the telling of a tale that I forget its point! Well, of course, your being, ah, who you are, undoubtedly caused Explorer a great deal of agitation. It clearly did not like being dependent on, much less controlled by, part of its own herd. The possibility you offered, of a totally different loyalty for its humans, was too dangerous to be allowed to continue.

"Much more immediately, however, you and all the herd members who knew of you had to be killed at once. You and Yader had seen the crushers Explorer was growing. There was only one reason why Explorer would need such servants and would need to keep them secret from Ali and Lieder."

"It had been planning to eliminate them before it knew of me," Hickock said slowly. "It wanted to kill everyone who knew that it was not Starswallower. It especially wanted to kill everyone who knew the secret of command pheromones, who could control it."

Mackern nodded. "So you needn't feel guilty about Ali or anyone else. All you did was force Explorer to act prematurely. That may have caused its failure."

Vaheri, who had been looking increasingly nervous, pointed to his watch.

"Yes, yes, we'll be late for our meeting if I don't hurry." Mackern heaved himself out of the chair and stood looking down on Hickock. "I have to help advise Dalkan on whether we should support each of Starswallower's prospective heirs in turn until they completely annihilate one another, or whether it is more in Innovator's interest to keep a rump Patriarchate as a buffer with Skybreaker."

"What will you advise?" Hickock asked.

"I have no idea. The prospect is quite unprecedented." He stumped after Vaheri off the terrace.

Talk swirled about Hickock, most of it dealing with promotions and bonuses, rumored or confirmed.

"What is your bonus?" he asked Yader. "Quite substantial, I should imagine."

Yader's glass stopped halfway to his lips. His eyes were unreadable. "Reintegration. If I want it."

Hickock considered the implications. "Do you?"

"It's—hard to say. In a way, it terrifies me. It sounds so

much like dying, without even the possibility of an afterlife. Janet is even more frightened than I am. Howard tries to put on an air of scientific objectivity, saying that he needs more data before making a judgment. Cord is the one pushing it. I suppose he thinks he will be center stage all the time.

"But when I dream . . . It's like finding I'm ambidextrous. All of a sudden I can do things I would never have been able to imagine before. I can look at the vegetation growing along the bluff and tell you that there are fifteen separate genuses represented, what each one is, and how each one contributes to their miniature ecology. I hear old music, highbrow stuff, some even from Earth, and I can tell you the name and the composer. Smells are sharper and more subtle. Colors are brighter and more clearly defined.

"When I dream . . ."

Yader was silent. Frivolous talk washed around them like spume from the ocean.

"What does Nanny Kit think?" Hickock asked finally.

Yader's grin made him look, suddenly, ten years younger. "I suppose that *is* the ultimate question." He thought only a moment. "She'll be for anything that brings her Jimmy back," he said softly.

A steward came by, refreshed their drinks, and provided them with plates of small pretzels. Except for being black, they looked and tasted just like the pretzels Hickock had eaten on Earth.

"What about me?" Hickock asked. "Do I get a bonus?"

"Being important can have its drawbacks," Yader said slowly. "Take Reeve, for instance. Are you surprised that you haven't seen her yet? Coming back as you did, with the information we had, validated her entire existence. However, it also made it necessary to review every trance statement she has made within the past ten years. Especially any that might concern you. So her debriefing is just starting.

"They want any clue she can give them because, now that

they know who you are, they have less idea than ever what to do with you. Right now, most of their attention is absorbed with the task of consolidating Starswallower's territories, so you are a matter of only secondary importance. Be grateful. It gives you freedom.''

"Freedom?'' Hickock asked, surprised by the bitterness in his own voice. "To go wherever I want, I suppose.''

"Of course.'' Within, as they both knew, a reasonable proximity of Freair. Accompanied by whatever monitoring devices had been inserted in his clothing—or perhaps in his body, perhaps in the drink he was at that very moment swallowing—and by the observers, self-effacing to the point of invisibility, but never absent.

"I shall do that,'' Hickock said. He swung to his feet and walked to the edge of the patio, expecting the barked order followed by the hand on his shoulder.

"One thing,'' Yader said. Hickock stopped. "Enjoy the next few days. Soon you will be back at the center. The deep space raids are increasing. This—'' He gestured. "Maybe it's not much of a planet compared to old Earth, but it seems pretty special to a lot of us.''

Hickock turned and descended the stairway. It switched back and forth across the cliff face as it made its way down to the beach.

Colors bannered the waters: orange brown where the waves churned up the shore, living green farther out, and finally a cobalt blue deepening almost to black at the horizon. Children, finished with the chores and studies of the day raced across the sands like aquavians, their laughter drifting up to him.

A breeze gusted off the water, cool with the approaching dusk. It cut through the warm drowsiness he had been fighting, cleared a film from his eyes, and heightened all other sensations.

Once before he had trekked across sands. During his Go'el

training. Then the sands had burned the soles of his feet, and the puffs of wind had been breaths of flame. For a week he had made his way across the Cauldron, avoiding the melted cities, learning survival skills in the vast wasteland of scorched rock created by a sun gone mad.

But learning how to live off that land had been secondary. Observation—and with it, the learning of a certain wisdom—had been his main purpose. Even there, in that land of ashes, there was life, an abundance of life, if one knew how to look. There were seeds buried under the dust, almost indistinguishable from it, waiting for the infrequent rain to wake them to evanescent life. Easily overlooked holes led down to subsurface coolness, the dens of snakes and desert mice. At night they darted between the shadows, ears straining for the almost silent swoop of owls' wings.

Bleached, mummified grasses. Squat cacti, looking comically dumpy and unshaven. Even, in the rare pools bubbling up from the depths, frogs and small, silvery fish.

Life. In the desolation of the Cauldron, there was an abundance of life, competing, adapting, cooperating, working in a slow, seemingly haphazard manner to make the desert its own. For the student, the desolation was necessary. Only there was there little enough life that each organism could be seen by itself, the way one would hold a jewel to the sun, before discerning the context of delicately webbed interrelationships.

All his training came back to him, but richer, more powerful than he remembered, as if somehow honed in dormancy. Dark layers sandwiched in the cliffside hinted at surface life hundreds of thousands of years before. He reached out and scraped some onto his fingers, then brought it close to his face. A slight oily smell spoke of compressed hydrocarbons.

More than five meters of shiny, rubbery-looking flesh lay half submerged in sand at the waterline. A young crèche-nurse waved her charges back: hidden stingers might yet discharge, even though the creature itself was clearly dead.

"But what *is* it?" a high voice demanded.

"I have no idea," the crèche-nurse admitted. "That doesn't surprise me, though. I read the other day that less than one percent of the life on this planet has been catalogued. Maybe some of you can study creatures like this when you grow up."

"Aw, the sea can't be that full of strange things," a young skeptic objected.

"It certainly can," Hickock said from behind him. "I was washed up by the waves, just like that, and I'm the strangest thing I know."

The crèche-nurse gave him a strained smile, grateful for his support but half suspecting that he was mocking her.

Farther down the beach he came to a dune overlooking a tidal pool. He settled himself with his back to the dune. His mind became as light and empty as cloud wisps driving across the sky.

Two girls stood waist-deep in the tidal pool beneath him. Aquavians dived beside them, then burst through the surface in explosions of spray. As he watched, he realized that the older girl was training one of the aquavians. She took a sectoid husk from a pouch hung around her neck and threw it as far as she could. The aquavian darted away from her, kissed the water the sectoid had just touched, and flew back. She rewarded it with a second husk as it settled into her arms.

"Now you try it, Marti," she said.

Marti threw her own sectoid husk. Her arm motion was awkward; the husk went hardly half as far as the first one. Nonetheless, a nearby aquavian burst from the water. Marti grabbed another husk and waved it to get the aquavian's attention.

It turned obediently, but as it was settling into her arms for a second treat, its wings blurred into an angry buzzing.

Their force knocked Marti over backward. The aquavian arced high into the sky and plunged into open ocean.

Marti came up, sputtering. The older girl floated helpless with laughter.

"You have—to keep—your arms wet," she explained between gasps. "The quavers *like* our warmth. That's why they come to us so easily. But our dry skin is rough on them, especially after they have lost their own skin moisture to the air."

They tried a few more times before going in for the evening.

Stars sprinkled the dark blue vault with white pinpricks. Their reflections scattered across the almost-mirror-smooth surface of the sea. Then the surface seemed to disappear, and the lights were countless cities hidden on the ocean floors of the planet.

Starlight was gleaming off his face when Rita Lieder found him. She bit her lip and sat down next to him. "What's—wrong?"

He brought his hand to his face. Wetness surprised his fingertips.

"I used to think it was so simple," he said, his voice hoarse. "I wanted to protect the Earth. I got a commission in the Noram Defense Forces. I felt the calling to cherish all life. The Institute gave me a fellowship. A few radicals claimed this was a contradiction, that the Grabbers—that's what we called Shapers—were living beings and so had as much right to our protection as any other species. I always dismissed that argument. It seemed so obvious that any creatures which had come so close to annihilating our entire planet had forfeited any rights they might have. We would see if we could rescue any descendants of human captives. Then, for our own safety, for the safety of all other life in the galaxy, we would destroy the Shapers.

"It is a good argument. I think I could have defended it

against any amount of evidence to the contrary. Only the mind block, which was supposed to protect my secrets from the Shapers, deprived me of my rationalizations, as well. I nearly died. I was reborn on a world teeming with life. I learned that it was wonderful and needed care even before I remembered that I was a Go'el. Even the Shapers are precious.''

Rita forced a smile. "Is that so bad?"

Hickock took a deep, shuddering breath. ''Yes. There used to be a solution. Horrible, perhaps, but a solution. Now there is just a dilemma. The Shapers are even more dangerous than we believed. We thought they were just an advanced civilization. They find the very concept of civilization incomprehensible. Instead, we are faced with twenty thousand geniuses, each one so much more intelligent than anything the human race has produced that we don't even have a scale for comparison. How can we threaten or negotiate with twenty thousand individuals? Hell, it would be impossible even to work out a surrender.''

Rita moved closer and put her hand over his. "I think you are wrong," she said pensively. "At least you don't have all the truth. The Shapers could have destroyed Earth after they captured our ancestors. They did not. I am not trying to minimize the devastation Earth endured; I'm just pointing out that it could have been worse. Maybe it would be important if you understood why they restrained themselves.''

She thought for a few moments. "You may have to be in security to have any clear understanding of history. You need a pretty high clearance to see most of the relevant documents. For good reason. Living conditions for first humans were—horrible. It's a wonder any survived. But we did survive because the Shapers made things better. Not out of kindness. That concept probably has even less meaning to them than civilization. But for whatever reason, most Patriarchs have decreased the amount of genetic experimentation on humans and allowed freedoms unthinkable a generation ago. At the same time, humans have become even more important to Shapers. We have completely displaced certain spawn varieties. What I'm thinking is that if we could understand why Shapers have become increasingly dependent on humans, you might find a way to use that to insure Earth's safety.

"When I was head of my familial society in the crèche, I used to hear rumors of a Council of Cooperation. It was supposed to be made up of leaders of various herds, even those belonging to Shapers in totally different lineage groups. The members were supposed to exchange mutually useful information. It was even said that sometimes they established common herd policies. Obviously if such a council did exist, its activities would have been treasonous by definition. All I could learn as security director was that some such group had been repressed twenty years before.

"The rumors still persist. If such a group exists, Garrison may be able to get in contact with it. Your people might well want to negotiate with its leaders. If it exists, the Council must have the greatest corporate knowledge of Shapers of any group of humans in the universe.

"We can look into that. Tomorrow."

The stars were brilliant in their strange patterns. A wind turned suddenly cold as it came off the waves. Rita's warmth radiated through the darkness. The subtle scent of her hair was carried on the wind.

"Yes," he agreed, drawing her, unresisting, to him. "That can wait until morning."

In his room, two hours later, he surrendered to exhaustion. So he did not hear the muffled click of the autolocks in his door or the hissing from the ventilation grill. He did not stir as hulks, made anonymous by breathing masks, entered his room. He did not resist as the hood slid over his head and the bonds tightened wrist to wrist and ankle to ankle.

Even being carried to the transport capsule made no impression on his dark, dreamless sleep. The lid sealed shut. The capsule accelerated down the nearly airless magna-tube toward the depths of the ocean.

XXVI

THE HAND SLAPPED HIS FACE SIDE TO SIDE, THE MOVEMENT as rhythmical and passionless as a metronome. It stopped just as it was beginning to sting.

Brilliance flooded his retinas. Images of blood vessels, blue against red, played across his vision.

"Two more ccs. Be careful. We don't want to overstimulate him."

A hydraulic injector spat painfully into the base of his neck. The dull roaring in his ears resolved into discrete sounds: the breathing of his examiner, the clink of metal instruments being moved on a tray, shoes gently scuffing across a tile floor. Eyes, a nose, a mouth came into focus; became a face.

It gave him an appraising stare.

"State your name."

"Patrick M. Hickock." He spoke overdistinctly to compensate for a residual numbness in lips and tongue.

"You have a circle with a ten-meter diameter. Give me the circumference."

"A little more than thirty-one meters."

"The area?"

"About eighty square meters."

"What is the cube root of nine hundred?"

"Between nine and ten. Closer to ten. You could speed this up with a hand calculator."

Gray eyes regarded him dispassionately. "This is a check of your mental alertness. Innovator wishes to question you. You would surely regret an incorrect or merely incomplete answer caused by drug-induced inattention."

An older man, graying fringe beard perched atop a white lab coat, looked in from the door. "Are we ready with that one? The Speakers have queried. Again."

"Yes, sir. Just finishing up."

Two technicians strapped a metal framework to Hickock's left arm, a high-tech exoskeleton in silver and black, with primary-colored wires connecting microprocessors. It was Explorer's response monitor, miniaturized and looking considerably more sophisticated than the version he had been screened with at the Trade Talks. One of the technicians adjusted a sensor cluster under his armpit.

Breathing mask and wet suit went on next. After a quick air check, Hickock was led down the corridor to an air lock. A circular pool dominated the small room beyond. The walls were a translucent white, unevenly rippled and dimpled: morphion made.

Webbed hands grabbed him as he jumped in.

Mers flanked him, guiding him to the metal framework of the watersled. The propellers kicked on with a high-pitched whirring. The sled pulled him out from under the shadow of the Nares. The surface was a silvery chaos, impossibly far above.

The mers dropped him off, steering the watersled back to the Nares. Unrecognizable figures floated to either side, approximately ten meters away. And above. And below.

A stomach twice his size floated below and in front of him. Its upper portion was open, all three fronded lips swaying in the current. Mottled redness pulsed deep within.

Farther below, a mountainous mass loomed out of the

shadows. Small blisters covered it. As he watched, several detached themselves and swam languidly away. One passed close enough for Hickock to identify it as a stomach even larger than the one stationed below him.

A pulse of sound complexly textured into a sonic tissue washed over him.

"Experiments fail." The Speaker's voice was soft, almost fuzzy, in Hickock's earphones. "I remember only imperfectly why you were taken from the planet you call Earth to World. I have no accessible memory of why you were created.

"It must have been to explore a logical paradox. Could evanescent, quickly reproducing creatures of limited intelligence be more efficient tools than specifically imprinted spawn? Could the freedom to try multiple approaches simultaneously produce better results than coordinated planning controlled by a Shaper? The answer should obviously be in the negative. Yet now only those Patriarchs with extensive human herds survive. Those Patriarchs who have permitted the greatest amount of purposeless and unplanned activity—" The Speaker paused, as if wrestling with some particularly difficult concept. "—who have allowed the greatest amount of freedom in their herds, have received the greatest productivity, have received products, insights, and strategies never contemplated, much less commanded.

"This was the short-term result. Explorer, budded by Starswallower to be my counterpart, to be superior to me in what had been my unique strengths, perceived long-term detriments. There is precedent. Certain marine parasites can cripple a Shaper with their painful infestation. A simple and obvious genetic modification can be made to the main group of Shaper antibodies. The immediate result is the elimination of the parasites. The secondary result is that the modified antibodies attack the Shaper itself. Unless they are quickly destroyed, the Shaper will die.

"Explorer saw a similar case with humans. They had enabled it to escape Starswallower's domination, but only by replacing it with their own. It planned on disposing of its controllers. In the long term, it contemplated complete elimination of its human herds. When safely restrained/programmed/imprinted, they are only marginally more effective than Shaperspawn. If allowed freedom to develop on their own, they become unpredictably dangerous. Within the last two days, my own herd has utilized tactics to nullify a Patriarch's control over its spawn. In so doing, it has jeopardized not only my dominion but my very existence—"

"We acted to destroy your greatest rival!" Mackern said, distressed enough to interrupt the Patriarch. "How was that disloyal? You may now be the most powerful Shaper on the planet. How can that jeopardize either your dominion or your existence?"

Sleek, sharp-edged shapes moved quickly at the limit of visibility in the blue murk. Warrior spawn. Hickock held his breath, wondering if Mackern and perhaps the rest of them were about to be punished for that insolence.

"Again, a confusion of short- and long-term effects." As much as one could tell with Innovator's thoughts being channeled through a Speaker, the Shaper was, if anything, more frustrated than angry with the question. "There is little gain to me in becoming dominant today if tomorrow every Shaper under my control may rebel against me. Explorer's herd discovered the chemical means to allow that. You have devised tactics which in certain situations make even that pheromone blockage unnecessary. Today, only those of you floating about me know how to effect either severance. If all of you are eliminated, only I will know.

"Yet even that is insufficient. What has been discovered once will surely be discovered again. As the intelligence services of other Patriarchs investigate/meditate on the abrupt demise of Explorer—already I have indications that several of them have begun to suspect Explorer's imposture—many will come to generally correct conclusions. They will test their conclusions by seeking to reproduce artifcial phero- mone commands and pheromone blocks. I extrapolate that they will succeed before a full year passes.

"It may occur much sooner. Rita Lieder already intends to form forbidden contacts with other herds. Part of her rea- son for doing so is to formulate a position for dealing with Terrestrial humans. She confirms Explorer's diagnosis: only the complete extermination of all human herds can control the menace of uncontrolled humans."

There was more quick movement at the edge of sight. Warrior spawn had englobed the humans. Hickock looked hard at the figure to his left, thinking he could recognize Reeve. He wished she would make some optimistic predic- tion, even though he would disbelieve it.

He fought down his fear. "That cannot be the whole story," he said, thinking aloud. "If it were, we would al- ready be dead. There is either some other problem—or you doubt your own analysis."

The Speaker was silent. Innovator's dark bulk remained motionless. Hickock tried to control the roaring of his own breath.

"Here's one problem," he continued. "If you are right, all Shapers must eliminate all humans simultaneously. Be- cause if some Shapers retain their herds, they gain a crucial advantage. This scenario was played out when humans first came to this planet. That's why all remaining lineage groups have human herds. The same thing would happen again.

"My race once faced a similar dilemma. Every nation *knew* nuclear weapons were too dangerous to use, but none dared get rid of them. As long as the nations had basically irreconcilable interests, there was no solution.

"Your situation is worse. Shapers, I'm told, don't even consider each other members of the same species. It has taken more than three hundred years to allow something as harmless and mutually beneficial as the Trade Talks. You could never unanimously agree to do anything this radical.

"So your long-term analysis is irrelevant. You would never survive the short-term effects of eradicating your humans."

It was not enough, he thought, licking his lips. All he had done was offer Innovator a choice of deaths. There was no reason for the Shaper not to choose the one that would entail the destruction of the humans. But that was the least of what was wrong.

"You don't need me to tell you these things. There must be something more—something you already know that would convince you to spare your humans *if* we are smart enough to realize what it is ourselves."

"Innovator." Garrison's discipline all but concealed the tremor in his voice. "Dalkan and the Committee of Leaders made the decision to attack Explorer within hours of learning of its imposture. My own urging was probably crucial. Breaking up Starswallower's lineage group, by disclosing its death, seemed the most efficient route to victory. If that decision was made overhastily, to your detriment, I—am willing to accept whatever penalty you may deem necessary.

"But that penalty should not fall on your herds generally. They have repeatedly proved their loyalty. Reeve gave you advance warning of Hickock's importance, and where he would be found. Yader got word to you that Starswallower was dead and that Explorer had taken his place. Mackern has been crucial in developing both Reeve's and Yader's abilities for you. All have substantially advanced your interests. Nothing has changed."

"I have changed it," Hickock said. "Just the fact that unherded humans exist, that we can prove that the Shapers nearly destroyed the human race rather than saving it, makes me a magnet—"

"A catalyst," the Speaker interrupted. "A—a firing cap."

"—for the Church of the Babylonian Captivity and every other group of malcontents and revolutionaries on the planet. Malcontents the Noram Defense Forces would certainly exploit—" Hickock paused, overwhelmingly aware of how close to death he was taking them all. Not that there was any alternative. His body would betray any lie. His only chance was to find an honest way out of the dilemma for all of them. If one existed.

"Certainly exploit in the event of war," he said slowly. "However, Earth simply does not have the resources to sustain that sort of war. We have only just rebuilt our own ecology. We have strength enough for one blow. If you were not immediately defeated, you and other Shapers might launch a counterattack. Earth would not be likely to recover this time."

"Therefore," the Speaker said, "as soon as your fleet commander overcomes his emotionalistic fixation with the human herds, he will follow his original directive. He has no alternative. He will detonate the chromosphere of this sun."

Behind the Speaker's deceptively soft voice, Hickock felt all the weight of Innovator's intellect, forcing him inexorably to a disastrous conclusion.

"If we do that, we destroy everything my race has come to believe in during the past three hundred years. And to no purpose. There are new Shaper colonies in other star systems. If we did not eliminate them all simultaneously, Earth would still be vulnerable to a counterattack.

"However, you face the same dilemma." Another door had opened in his mind, a memory now accessible that he had not had occasion to call on since the mind block had been removed. The fact that what he intended to disclose was top secret even on Earth, and might well be grounds for his execution, gave him pause for less than a second.

He might be able to prevent genocide.

"As soon as we had stardrive, the first priority was to

construct a fleet which could protect the inner solar system. Launching an attack fleet was only third on the list. The second effort was to construct arks—I don't know how many—that set out to found interstellar colonies, so that the human race would never again come so close to extinction, no matter what happened to the solar system.''

A sound pulse vibrated Hickock's chest cavity, as if Innovator were verifying for himself the reading of his instruments. If so, the Shaper should now be convinced of the truth of the man's statements.

''You present me with a less than zero-sum game,'' the Speaker said. ''If you are correct, we must fight a war that will cripple both sides and that neither of us can win.''

Perspiration had condensed on the inside surface of Hickock's breathing mask's transparent plastic. In an odd way, the blurring of his sight aided his concentration.

''What I have said necessarily follows from the facts I have recited. If you could find a flaw in the logic, I am sure you would point it out to me. So let's change the facts.''

''You evidence the true nature of mental inferiority.'' The Speaker's voice seemed to carry real regret. ''Facts do not change to suit our desires.''

An odd thing for a Shaper to say, Hickock thought, surprised. Perhaps it isn't insane after all.

''Among humans, comprehension of facts is sometimes faulty,'' he said. ''Given two diagnoses, one of a disease that is always fatal, a doctor will always treat the second disease. It is always sound strategy to suppose that the situation is not hopeless, even if that seems most likely the case.

''You consider it logical to destroy your herds and attack Earth because a human fleet has entered your star system intending to destroy your race. That fleet exists because Terrestrial humanity is scared to death of Shapers.

''I am the only human who can tell that fleet commander and his superiors back on Earth that that fear is unnecessary.

I can explain that Shapers are callous and immoral, but not malicious. I can give them insight into the evolutionary conditioning of Shapers, which ensured that Earth would intentionally be allowed to recover. I can set before them the advantages of trading for technology with the minds that invented the stardrive. I can make them aware of how much you would like access to think tanks, corporations, and institutes to supplement your herds on special projects.

"More important than any of that, however, I can let them know that the race which nearly destroyed our planet no longer exists."

Hickock's breath rasped harshly in his breathing mask. Something flicked quickly overhead. He mastered an almost overpowering urge to look behind him.

"You seem to believe what you are saying." Was there irony in the Speaker's voice? "How will you convincingly convey such a baseless fallacy?"

Hickock took a deep breath, carefully considering the pieces of his argument. "The Shaper ability to determine the genetic makeup of its offspring is so important that it's easy to lose sight of basic constraints. Shapers who consider the universe as a whole to be a budding of forgotten purpose carry this delusion to its extreme. But even humans are so overwhelmed that, without thinking about it, we consider Shapers to be immune to natural selection."

"I control absolutely the genetic makeup of any budlings. My own genetic design was determined by the Patriarch before me." The tone had become sharp, impatient. "By definition, that is the antithesis of natural selection."

"Not so!" Hickock said firmly, feeling more certain of himself. "*Every* Shaper, including you, always buds off a series of generalized offspring, no matter what specialties— warriors, hunters, fabricators—it may also beget."

"To command a lineage group extends my power and

my—honor/prestige.'' The Speaker sounded strained, as if having trouble with the translation.

''It also competes with you directly for the same food resources and greatly multiplies the number of times you must battle other Shapers. Can you prove the benefits outweigh the burdens? Or is—honor/prestige—the main motivation? Whatever you think the answer is, I'll tell you the real reason: Any Shaper that did not bud generalized, reproducing Shapers bred itself out of existence within a generation. In the past million years your genes have been set so that whether you call it honor/prestige or rationalized self-interest, you will always follow the same reproductive strategy.

''There are other constraints on you. Until about a hundred thousand years ago, Shaper populations followed a feast-famine sine wave, expanding exponentially until they outstripped the food supply, then collapsing in periods of catastrophic famine. Then there was a change. Lineage groups became more mobile. Population growth slowed. Neutral zones were established—''

''So that war would be a matter of deliberate policy, not of momentary friction,'' the Speaker interrupted.

''A good secondary purpose and an excellent rationalization,'' Hickock retorted. ''The primary reason was to provide fallow areas where the food chain could rebuild itself.''

It was a lot to build on a casual conversation between Howard Yader and the Eggman. Hickock plunged on, conscious that he had nothing to lose. If he was wrong, they were all dead.

''That brings us up to about three hundred and fifty years ago. A group of Shapers more willing to experiment, perhaps because more desperate than their peers, raided Earth to add humans to their herds. The effort was so successful that within three Shaper generations, Shapers with human herds had eliminated all rivals without humans. During the same time period, Shapers learned that there were crucial differences between humans and their other budlings. Genetic manipulation of humans by and large does not pay off. The usefulness of humans lies in the flexibility of their generalized natures. And the more freedom that is given to humans, the more effectively they can exploit this flexibility."

Hickock realized with dismay that he had run out of words. Doubts, qualifications, second thoughts clamored in his mind. He shook his head. He had stated the case as clearly as he could. He could only hope that it was correct, and that Innovator could think clearly enough to recognize its correctness.

"That's it," he finished lamely. "You are not the same creatures that raided my planet. Natural selection has bred you into creatures who function best in conjunction with human beings. You will not enter into a war that would deprive you of your most important resource.

"This is the message I will bring to Fleet Command. And beyond that, to Earth."

Epilogue

i

THE STARS TUMBLED OVER HIS HEAD. HICKOCK TIMED THEM with his breath, imagining them swinging behind his back, red- and blue-tinged points of light, piercing the blackness like steel pins. Three, four, five . . . The three blue-white stars he had christened the Sword reappeared beneath his feet.

His period was slowing. The Sword came up his torso and paused for a breathless moment even with his eyes. Then the tension in their knotted safety lines overcame inertia, and the Sword accelerated slowly back toward his feet.

Hickock tried to summon sufficient energy to curse the amateurishness of their launching. It would have taken only a little less haste to launch them into the void devoid of angular momentum.

Not that that made much difference now. The warning light at the base of his helmet had long before gone from yellow to red. His lips were cracked. Each breath required more conscious effort, and when he made it, he felt as if he had filled his aching lungs with emptiness.

Why? The message, brief as it had been, had seemed clear enough. Caution he could understand. Much more caution, and Fleet Command would have to content itself with corpses.

Something struck him along his right side. The stars slewed sideways. He hit Rita's pressure suit and bounced—but only a few centimeters. They were pressed together in a tangle of plastic arms and legs.

Netting stretched itself along one side of his helmet. Craning his neck, Hickock tried to follow the direction of the cords to their convergence point. For a minute there was nothing. Then a star slid into existence from nothingness, for less than a second defining the edge of a darkened hull. He squinted, trying to discern outlines. Flanges, lifting surfaces, repulsion pods . . . Abruptly he realized how quickly they were hurtling toward it. A horizontal slit opened like a mouth to engulf them.

Walls flashed past to either side. He stopped *very* quickly. His breath had been knocked out of him. One arm felt as if it had nearly been dislocated.

Expert hands grabbed them and cut away the deceleration nets. As the cargo hold pressurized, Hickock could hear the painfully high whine of the vibroblades slicing through the elastic cords. Shreds of plastic floated about them like confetti.

There was barely a pause for lights on either side of the interior air lock to turn green. Hickock's handler immobilized him while the vibroblade sliced through shoulder and leg joints, down above his sternum, and around his neck in six quick, delicate movements. The pieces of his pressure suit fell away. They were grabbed by a figure in space armor who ran a sensor wand carefully over each piece. A second soldier made quick brushstrokes over Hickock's body with a similar wand.

Hickock pulled in a deep lungful of air. "I never thought chloro-carbed air could taste so good!"

Laughter came from a large, fringe-bearded man anchored

to the railing of an elevated walkway. Raised lettering on his pressure suit read DAVIES.

"Seems clean," the soldier holding Hickock said, releasing him. "Body scan confirms identity. No bugs or other surprises."

"Jettison it all, just to make sure," Davies ordered. He regarded Hickock with dark humor. "Doesn't sound like they've messed with your mind much, either. You always were bitchin' about air recycling."

The man's eyes widened appreciatively as another crewman finished cutting Lieder out of her pressure suit. Utilitarian was definitely an inadequate description of the form-fitting single-piece undergarment.

"I should have known you would make the best of captivity," Davies said. "Is this a prisoner you've brought us?"

"Only an unredeemable cynic like yourself would so characterize the relationship." The next words stuck in his throat. He thought of how long he had known Davies, of the classes at the Institute, the chess games, and the debates that, fueled by uncounted pitchers of beer, had only paused when the bars closed. It hurt that, after the next few words, Davies would never fully trust him again.

He bowed with all the formal grace he was able to muster in zero gee. "May I present to you Rita Lieder, former security director for the Shaper Explorer, now ambassador to Earth from Patriarch Innovator." He met Davies's consternation with an ironic smile. "My wife."

ii

MOST OF THE CEILING OF MACKERN'S BEDROOM WAS A HUGE transparent skylight. The architect of these quarters, having lived all her life undersea, had been fascinated by windows. Having here no access to an exterior wall, she had carved the ceiling into an octagon of raised glass.

Mackern lay on his bed in the darkened room, regarding the stars. It took no effort to project on that sky the holograms Hollings had displayed at the noon briefing: spiked spheres of light, layer within layer, crimson, orange, yellow, green, blue, as matrix stressor drives pooled and froze the wormholes simultaneously forming at the quantum level until they were big enough to suck through the length of a starship.

"Analysis indicates approximately twenty-five to thirty-five wakes," Hollings had said to Dalkan. "Rather more than intelligence had previously estimated to be in-system. Of course we have no means of being sure that all craft have left this stellar system, or how far those that have left have gone.

"However, all data received thus far indicate that the entire Terrestrial fleet has departed. Presumably for Earth."

It was the best they could hope for. With Innovator about to launch strikes against all other Patriarchs simultaneously, a Terrestrial warfleet would be one variable too many.

They had been stunned by Innovator's announcement the week before. "You must begin immediate preparations for war against all Patriarchs. Hostilities will commence within seven days."

"*All* Patriarchs?" It was the first time in Mackern's experience that Dalkan had questioned Innovator.

"Of course. The analysis I revealed to Garrison remains valid. Every Patriarch on this planet is now attempting to uncover the means by which Explorer defeated and impersonated Starswallower. Several have unquestionably already surmised the outline. Within four weeks, at least one will have deduced the details. Whichever achieves that first will be able to disintegrate the lineage group of every other Patriarch, including my own. I do not choose to await that eventuality. It is my command that before four weeks, every Patriarch will respond to me as if part of my own lineage group. In that manner, lineage groups will not dissolve into mindless civil wars. My own group will be preserved.

"And your cousins will have a race leader to parley with, since they seem to need that."

Since then, most of them had been working twenty-hour days trying to meet Innovator's absurd deadline. Now the halls of Freair were silent and empty. Assault teams were on their way to all Patriarchs whose territories adjoined Innovator's. With luck, at least one team would be able to blast its way through to each Patriarch. With a bit more luck, the synthesized pheromones each team carried would actually work, enslaving the Patriarchs to Innovator.

So much was uncertain! Mackern had personally debriefed Reeve. Even after he had completed the list of questions prepared by Garrison, he kept probing, pushing for more complete and definite answers. Reeve finally rebelled.

"What do you *want*? I've told you as much as I know! It's fuzzy, it's frustrating, but *that's all there is*!"

"You knew when and where we could pick up Hickock," he blustered. "You knew how important he would turn out to be!"

Reeve looked up at him with an air of impatient long-suffering. "Sometimes I hit it right. Like when I talked to Innovator the first time. Like when I saw Hickock. But I can't control it. You *know* that.

"This—thing." She held her hands to either side of her head with fingers outstretched, frustrated at the imprecision of mere words. "It's like—like some Precambrian floater with a light-sensitive spot. Knows light, knows dark. Knows, maybe, that dark is a safer time to feed. So all of a sudden it's dark and it thinks whoop-tee-do, it's safe. Only maybe the dark is the shadow of the next step up the food chain, all teeth, just about to swallow it whole. Or maybe it's a cloud or an eclipse—heh, try explaining that to some poor floater who can't focus, can't look left or right, just knows light and dark.

"That's all I can see. Or maybe sometimes something is just at the right distance and is just simple enough for me to understand the outline from things I've eaten, or empty shells I've crawled over on the sand. But that's all. You've seen all my test reports. You even decreed my gene mix. So if you want anything more exact, you know you have to come back in ten generations. So what more do you want from me now?"

"I want—" Mackern stopped, feeling suddenly lost and helpless. He sat down and looked away from her. "I want to know that it isn't all going to end here. That Innovator isn't going to decide we're failed experiments and flood our rooms with nerve gas. That our long-lost cousins don't explode our sun for the good of all humanity. That it is going to go on. That it's going to mean something!"

Reeve smiled at him sadly. "Well, why didn't you say so? When I 'see,' it's glimpses of hundreds of things, stretching out to the horizon like in some painting by Bosch or Brueghel."

You could have picked more comforting painters, Mackern thought sullenly.

"Here there's a wedding and people are dancing. There soldiers are killing children. Further on, a farmer is plowing a field by the sea. In the corner, corpses litter a barren field.

"It just goes on without end, to the horizon, where everything just becomes so small that I can't distinguish anything but splashes of color and a distant roaring.

"On and on. Beauty and horror. But it doesn't end."

Which, Mackern thought, rousing himself, would have to be enough. He swung his legs over the side of the bed, touched the plate on the wall, which brought up the room lights. Opening a drawer in his nightstand, he lifted out a reading plate. Slowly he went through the call-up sequence, his breathing settling into a slow deep rhythm. Invisible sensors on the keys had been adjusted to his own signs: oil, sweat, acidity. Should anyone other than him ever try to access this file, or should he himself try to do so when under stress, it would be silently erased, leaving no trace that it had ever existed.

Words flickered across the display, line on line, paragraph on paragraph, deceptively neat and orderly. He had to remind himself of the commentary Chen had written three generations before.

"THE NOTES IS NOT THE PRODUCT OF ONE MIND, NOR IS IT THE CONSIDERED COLLABORATION OF A GROUP, CAREFULLY EDITED AND REVISED. INSTEAD, AS ITS TITLE INDICATES, IT IS A COLLATION OF WRITINGS THAT COME DOWN TO US FROM THE OLDEST TIMES OF HUMANITY ON THIS PLANET, SOME EVEN FROM OLD EARTH ITSELF DURING THE TIME OF THE BURNING. CONSIDERABLE CARE HAS BEEN TAKEN TO RENDER THE TEXTS EXACTLY AS ORIGINALLY WRITTEN AND TO EXPLAIN THE NUMEROUS OBSCURE ALLUSIONS, BUT THE READER SHOULD BE AWARE THAT THIS HAS NOT ALWAYS BEEN POSSIBLE. ALTHOUGH MOST OF THE WRITINGS WHICH COME DOWN TO US WERE WRITTEN IN ENGLISH, CHINESE, OR SPANISH, THERE ARE NO LESS THAN TWENTY-SIX LANGUAGES REPRESENTED. (IN THE CASE OF THE SILENT WRITINGS, NO SPEAKER OF THE LANGUAGES IN WHICH THEY WERE WRITTEN HAS

BEEN FOUND TO PROVIDE A TRANSLATION. THEY ARE AP-
PENDED IN THE HOPE THAT INFORMATION WILL ONE DAY
BE DISCOVERED TO MAKE A TRANSLATION POSSIBLE.) DUR-
ING THE EARLIEST TIMES, WRITING MATERIALS WERE
OFTEN SCARCE OR NONEXISTENT. ETCHED STEEL, CARD-
BOARD, CLOTH, URINE, AND BLOOD WERE ALL EMPLOYED
AT ONE TIME OR ANOTHER. LATER, WHEN VARIOUS SHAP-
ERS BEGAN TO REALIZE THE IMPORTANCE WRITINGS COULD
HAVE IN RESISTANCE MOVEMENTS, MANY WRITINGS WERE
CONFISCATED AND DESTROYED. ONLY FRAGMENTS OF
FRAGMENTS ARE LEFT.

THIS IS OUR HERITAGE.

Mackern scrolled up the screen, searching. Most of the
material there he had memorized years ago. Assembling and
preserving the *Notes* had been the first mission of the societies that eventually became the Council of Cooperation.
Whenever herds of other Patriarchs were conquered or assimilated, agents of the council were inserted into the occu-
pation troops with orders to find any local editions of the
Notes, possibly with new or more complete writings, and to
make contact with any surviving members of the local council. They had picked up Vaheri that way.

Or trade delegations could bargain for them almost openly,
as ''historical materials.'' Regala had made one of their most
important acquisitions that way, from a herd that had no idea
of the value of nearly illegible browned and tattered scraps
found stuffed behind a drawer.

Ah, there it was! Not a moment too soon, either. Soon he
would have to make his way to Leaders' Hall for the midnight
briefing, there to learn the status of Innovator's war to be
Patriarch of Patriarchs.

It was from the journal of Toshiro Hamakawa, one of the
first generation of humans taken from Earth by the Shaper
Farfarer. In the previous pages, he had written in sparse,

unemotional phrases of the suicide of his sister and the death
of his children from a bizarre surgical procedure, the exact
purpose of which was never understood.

TODAY WAS A VERY IMPORTANT DAY, I ONCE AGAIN AP-
PROACHED OUR CAPTORS, TRYING TO MAKE KNOWN TO
THEM THAT LACK OF PROPER TRACE ELEMENTS IN OUR
DIETS WAS THE CAUSE OF THE WIDESPREAD SICKNESS
AMONG US. I WAS MET BY A NEW TRANSLATOR. THIS ONE
APPEARS TO BE COMFORTABLE IN THE AIR FOR INDEFINITE
PERIODS OF TIME. IT IS SMALLER THAN ITS PREDECESSOR
AND LESS ENCUMBERED BY BONY ARMOR. MORE IMPOR-
TANT, IT SPEAKS BY WAY OF A SCREEN, INSTEAD OF BY
REASSEMBLED WORDS FROM BROADCASTS. THIS PROVED ITS
WORTH WHEN I STATED OUR PROBLEM. CHEMICAL SYM-
BOLS FLASHED ACROSS THE SCREEN, TOO QUICKLY FOR ME
TO FOLLOW. (WHERE DID IT LEARN STANDARD CHEMICAL
NOTATION? FROM EDUCATIONAL TELEVISION? WAS THERE
THAT MUCH EDUCATIONAL TELEVISION ON JUST BEFORE
THE BURNING?) I *THINK* IT UNDERSTOOD ENOUGH TO GET
US SOME DIETARY SUPPLEMENTS.

IT WANTED TO KNOW ABOUT ANIMAL GROUPINGS. I
THINK THAT ITS OWN BIOLOGY MUST BE SO DIFFERENT
FROM OURS THAT IT NEEDS THIS SORT OF BASIC INFOR-
MATION JUST TO GET ENOUGH ANALOGIES FOR ORDINARY
SPEECH. I EXPLAINED AS MUCH AS I COULD ABOUT
SCHOOLS OF FISH, COLONIES OF ANTS, HIVES OF BEES. I
TOLD HIM OF BARNACLES CLUSTERING ON ROCKS, ABOUT
SOLITARY HUNTERS AND WHY THEIR ENERGY CONSUMP-
TION NEEDS KEPT THEM SOLITARIES.

HERE THE TRANSLATOR SHOWED SIGNS OF GREAT IN-
TEREST. HUMANS ARE CLEARLY SOCIAL ANIMALS, IT SAID,
SEEMING TO FIND AWKWARD THE IDEA OF SOCIETY. WHAT
SORT OF SOCIAL ANIMALS ARE WE?

WITHOUT A THOUGHT I SAID THAT WE WERE HERD AN-

IMALS, PASSIVE, PROTECTIVE AGRICULTURALISTS, ALWAYS READY TO RUN.

WE MUST NEVER LET THESE CREATURES LEARN THAT THE CORRECT TERM IS *PACK*.

iii

ALL ALONG ITS UPPER SURFACE IS A CONSTANT PRICKLING AS the stomachs come and go, bringing digested food to the food pores and disposing of wastes down-current. Within, master and slave hearts beat out a subtle syncopation, timed to reinforce a steady flow of life fluid through thousands of kilometers of veins and arteries. In its eggsac, [sweetness] and {heat} and < pitch > press on the eggs until the chromosome-analogues kink and clip just so to begin division into morphions. In five years, starships shall fill the skies.

All of this is background. Images and less definable abstractions run in parallel through the seven lobes of highly specialized nervous tissue that correspond to a brain.

—Reports from the six fronts of its war, as frenzied and undisturbing as storm winds lashing the wave tops. Their assault forces report 80 percent casualties. Some attacks have been completely repulsed. No matter. One Patriarch, Skybreaker, has fallen under Innovator's control. With command of the most powerful lineage group on the planet added to its own, it is merely a matter of weeks until total victory.

Other thought patterns.

—A four-footed Terrestrial carnivore, almost indistinguishable from the dappled shadow of the bush beneath which it crouches, watches a herd of herbivores. Grazers on the perimeter gaze about placidly, dipping their heads from time to time to nibble the stringy ground cover. Suddenly the carnivore is a blur of motion. The grazers startle and wheel.

Again. And again.

Their forms flow with the generations. The herbivores become stronger, quicker, their sight and sense of smell keener. The herd develops a structure: fawns and does to the center, bucks on the periphery.

The carnivore improves his speed for short bursts. In the beginning, it was happenstance that he brought down a disproportionate number of the old and infirm. Now he actively searches for them from his hiding place—which now is always downwind from the herd. His success makes the herd stronger. Which means he himself must be faster and more clever to survive.

—Simultaneously, Innovator considers a similar scenario involving sharphin and Shapers. The contrasts and similarities are as pleasing to it as contrapuntal music is to humans. The Terrestrial carnivore's success rate stays close to one in ten throughout. Shapers hunt sharphin—and other food sources—to near extinction before famine decimates their own numbers, but the result is similar: sharphin become faster, more alert, and more intelligent.

It amuses Innovator to consider each pair a single organism. Across time and space, each component signals adjustments to the other: hormones feeding into bloodstreams, nerve impulses traversing axons and dendrites . . . Sense data up, commands down . . . Predator, prey . . . Image of a human strengthening himself with isometric exercises.

Sharphin. Innovator reviews the reports of their attacks on Explorer's crushers. It had not consciously appreciated just how intelligent they had become. Had their marine environment not sacrificed their limbs to streamlining, they might have developed into creatures almost as useful as humans.

At the recurrent thought of humans, both thought chains collapse together. Humans! Innovator does not have the respiratory apparatus for a sigh, but a human telempath tuned to this portion of its mind would find the emotion instantly recognizable.

Humans are so slow! They assemble facts like communal sectoids, grain by laborious grain. Only a few are capable of the five-dimensional gestalt of reality that constitutes real intelligence, and those few attain it only intermittently.

Instance: The knowledge that control and blocking pheromones could be synthesized made necessary an immediate war for hegemony. The only alternative was enslavement. Any Shaper would comprehend it immediately. Explaining it to humans, even those especially intelligent and flexible humans Innovator had bred, warred, and traded for, had been a feat akin to explaining in detail the actions of each individual muscle involved in swimming.

Instance: Presence of an in-system Terrestrial fleet capable of detonating the outer layers of the sun requires—accommodation. Not peace. Innovator has examined that human concept many times and has relegated it to untranslatable status, probably a remnant of primate emotionalism. What it has in mind is much more concrete. Since it cannot yet adequately defend itself, there must be a cessation of active hostilities, a formation of buffer zones—as there are between rival and approximately equipotent Shapers.

How many infinitesimally small steps Hickock had taken to understand this. Humans seem unable to see Shapers as things-as-they-are. Fears and hopes pour into images of gods and monsters. Innovator contemplates the insanity that would motivate Earth humans to build a star fleet for the sole purpose of exterminating Shapers. It had been crucial that Hickock reason the flaws for himself if he was to convince his superiors. If the extinction of humanity had been the Shapers' goal, it could have been accomplished by less than a hundred extra carbon-carbon catalyst fusors beneath the Sun's chromosphere.

But . . .

Humans are unpredictable. It is their value. Sectoids scuttling across the ground, never able to see from above the direct path to food or away from danger, sometimes discover the unexpected beneath the dust. Only the most rudimentary intelligence is required to perceive that Shapers have nothing to gain from a genocidal war with humanity. However, there had been no way to foresee that Hickock would reach that conclusion by way of a hypothesis of meta-genes beyond conscious Shaper control, meta-genes that had evolved to keep Shapers from destroying their food sources.

I feel no constraint prohibiting me from destroying the human race. Innovator recognizes. I simply choose not to. Still, Innovator is sophisticated enough to recognize that his constraints may be his desires.

Two more scenarios play out in his mind. The first occurred in substantially similar ways both on Earth and in the World. Single-celled organisms evolve a metabolism yielding oxygen as a waste product. Except to these new aerobes, oxygen pollution is deadly. In a geological heartbeat, all anaerobes not protected by silt and stagnant water are extinct.

The pattern repeats itself, maintaining integrity through an almost infinite number of variations. Last in this series, Innovator reviews the fate of those Shapers that could not obtain, or could not effectively utilize, human herds.

There is one more scenario, this one unique to Earth. During the same geological age in which oxygen bubbles into the atmosphere, the older cells, prokaryotes, somehow combine with the newer, more complex eukaryotes. With time, the symbiosis becomes so complete that the remnant prokaryotes appear to be mere organelles of their evolutionary successors. Only the separate strands of DNA that encode their reproduction remain as clues that they were not always totally interdependent.

The lesson, if any, is ambiguous. Innovator is nonetheless confident of its innate superiority.

We will see who engulfs whom.

Above all of these mental operations—reviewing, coordinating, evaluating—is something which, if there were a human analogue, would be both sub- and supra-consciousness. *Unexpected*. The concept echoes and reechoes, drawing forth a host of associations. That a Patriarch's conditioning can be broken. That there are inheritable traits no Shaper can influence.

That humans make accessible a totally new aspect of reality. Communication not as irresistible imprinting of will, but as provisional offering that may be accepted, rejected, modified . . . Nonaggressive interaction, exchange of data

resources

herds

services

which is nonzero sum,

leaving both participants better off than before.

Sexual reproduction itself. A mystery, for Innovator can demonstrate mathematically that such an unlikely mutation must inevitably be outbred and displaced by the unisexual organisms that preceded humans. Yet this continually shifting chance generator moved nonrandomly ever closer to conformance with an unknown underlying reality.

I could never have imagined any of this, Innovator realizes. If that is true, its greatest fear must be baseless. The universe must be more than merely the projection of its own hopes and guilts and fears. There must be nourishment other than its own flesh or endlessly recycled excrement.

Without changing at all, the universe has become an infinite treasure trove of potential discoveries.

The complex of (pressure), {heat}, and [sweetness] assumes a new configuration around one egg. It will grow into a generalized Shaper. Its name will be Discoverer.

But if I did not dream the universe, what did? Innovator

wonders. How is it that it is trapped with so many dangers and delights?

An emotion surges through it, like that it experienced when it found itself freed of the constraints of its just-deceased Patriarch, but this is stronger, purer. In all the multiple layers of the Shapers' language, no concept quite fits.

In something like desperation it turns to the human languages. They are so imprecise, so redundant. . . . Yet all of them share a term that Innovator does not fully comprehend but keeps examining from every conceivable angle, for the feeling this term represents is more than a simple emotion, and may even be more important than life.

Perhaps it is joy.

ABOUT THE AUTHOR

Born in Massachusetts in 1948, Robert Chase was educated at Phillips Exeter Academy, Dartmouth College, and the Duke School of Law. He presently lives in Maryland, working as an attorney for the U.S. Army, with his wife, two children, dog, and cat.

HAL CLEMENT
THE
FATHER
OF
HARD
SCIENCE
FICTION
PRESENTS